THE RED FIELD

Book One
The Redemption Mountain Collection

A Novel

Jason Taylor Morgan

9 Swans Literary

ISBN-13: 978-1546566410
ISBN-10: 1546566414
BISAC: Fiction / Visionary & Metaphysical

Edited, formatted, and book design by Kristen Corrects, Inc.
Cover art design by Jessica Bell

www.jasontaylormorgan-novelist.com

First edition published 2017

NOVELS BY JASON TAYLOR MORGAN

The Redemption Mountain Collection
The Red Field (Book 1)
Still River (Book 2)
Black Angels (Book 3)
Appalachian Dusk (Book 4) Coming in 2022

O'Rourke The Medicine Man
Magnificent Among the Angelfish

www.jasontaylormorgan-novelist.com

For my sweet Southern mother, Josie, who passed on her love of equality, self-empowerment (female and male), education, art, music and literature. And for my magnificent Northern daughters, Julia and Caroline, who carry on the tradition.

Dedicated to my precious sister, Joan, who is the tradition.

Extraordinary women all.

Naked come to Thee for dress,
Helpless look to Thee for grace.

Rock of Ages

AUTHOR'S NOTE

The Redemption Mountain novels are literary works that focus on generations of Johnson women. Magical women who are healers, enchanters, and spell-casters from the American South. I did not write these novels as genre fiction. Rather, as literary fiction about a family of women who are magical. The emphasis of the stories is the life journeys of these women—their strengths, their vulnerabilities, their struggles, their intelligence, their losses, and their victories as they navigate the rigors and challenges of a sexist, racist, superstitious, impoverished, and often violent world in the South from the Civil War to present-day.

As a male writer—THE RED FIELD, Book One of the Series, and my debut novel—it gratifies me to have written what I hope is a good, solid story about one young woman's journey to stay true to herself and fulfill in that truth what needed to be fulfilled. Ruby, in her strong and gracious way, not only takes on the harsh, sexist, white male world in the 1920s American South. She takes on the U.S. government. She takes on the conservative, superstitious, judgmental "moral values" of her whole Southern Christian world. She is a healer-enchanter from an infamous "witch-enchanter" family and is of mixed blood—black, Cherokee, and white.

Their Johnson kinswomen's magical lineage delights me and gives me endless ideas and possibilities for both the character's gifts and talents and the novels' often harsh and often magical story lines.

One more thing. It pains me greatly to use racial slang terms and outdated forms of description for African Americans and Native Americans. *The Red Field* is a period piece and those words were the realities of the day. However, neither Ruby, in her day, nor I in mine abide those sentiments. "Folks are just folks," as Ruby says. I look forward to publishing the next Redemption Mountain novel. Stay tuned!

~JTM/ June 2017

PROLOGUE

Redemption Mountain, North Carolina – 1864

For most of the fall of 1864, twenty-five magical Johnson kinswomen and their daughters lived in white silk tents among the graves of the family's high mountain cemetery field. Living off the land, teaching the young ones the secrets of conjuring, witchcraft, and healing, the women hid from Sherman's Union Army as it rolled through the valley like wildfire.

Almost translucent under moonlight, Yankee soldiers had stolen bolts of the dazzling silk from the South's fine millenary shops. Then, along with other fine pilfered treasures of the South, they left it behind on deer trails and dusty red dirt back roads as the Union Army marched deeper into the Confederacy.

The Johnson Cemetery Field was well concealed on an untraveled, steep-pitched side of Redemption Mountain. Though everyone in Redemption County knew it was there, no one in their right mind would creep up on a live Johnson, let alone a dead one.

One night, after their evening meal, and as darkness fell, the women sat in campfire light listening to the sounds of rifles cracking and cannon fire booming. The lethal maelstrom had clawed and raged through the valley all day. Now, smoke, death, and ugly flashes of yellow light rose like eternal damnation up the mountainside.

To ease the tension, three young green-eyed singing Johnson sisters scooted up on a flat aboveground grave of a Johnson kinswoman, hanged for being a witch by the town fathers down in Redemption in 1692.

With lovely self-taught harmonies, the young sisters sang a love song tragic and cruel about the kin girl named Evangeline Johnson, who loved an ordinary town boy named Harlan Lee, and how the townspeople's fear of mixing blood with a heathen Johnson female doomed the young lovers.

Their sweet voices spreading out over the graveyard, they sang:

He's so handsome.
So pure and sublime.
A town boy cain't never loves a Johnson gal.
His heart never to be mine…

With those words hanging delicately in the night air, Yankee soldiers broke out of the dark woods and washed over the cemetery field like a violent black wave. Without regard for age or innocence, some they raped before they shot them all.

When they finished, the soldiers tore down the tents, sliced the glimmering silk into twenty-five long beautiful shrouds, and lay them on the ground. They rolled the dead or dying Johnson women into them hurriedly, some tidy, some barely covered.

As the soldiers carried the blood-soaked shrouds to a hastily dug trench, the shrouds began to glow. As the mixed and magical white, black, and Indian Johnson blood poured out of the sides—the whole field lit up like glittering red glass.

CHAPTER ONE

Redemption Mountain, 1928

A story like ours never begins anywhere. It just always was and picks up somewhere in a place worth talking about.

Tuesday up to Raleigh, the State of North Carolina dropped the noose on Lonny Dale Jessup's neck and tore his feet right out'a his shoes. This morning he's lyin' naked and lean as the Sunday meal on his ma's kitchen table—barefoot, no soul, no beating heart, one of our own, blood drained and stiff as Jesus.

Hardy Jessup, Lonny Dale's twin, came banging on the door in the middle of the night to tell us, somehow finding his way up our two miles of driveway road under no moon and carrying no flaming torch. Hardy's banging woke Granddaddy up enough for him to shoot his grizzly old head out his second floor bedroom window, a-squintin' in the dark.

"Hardy Jessup…that you?" Granddaddy called down to him.

"They done it, Mister Jeb."

Hardy was so drunk he was leaning with his cheek mashed up against the door, mumbling into the wood. "Lonny Dale's home dead as dirt. They come in a truck and just drop him in the grass in the front yard next to the porch slider. His head near tore off. Ma won't stop a-prayin' and a-rockin' him."

Then Hardy vomited into the white azaleas.

Later, after sunrise, I found Hardy sleeping between the graves in our old family graveyard, the one we call the spirit field. He was buck-naked and clutching a dead lamb to him like it was his last possession on this earth. Granddaddy said later on, "If Hardy Jessup needs to squeeze one of'm lambs to death because his heart is broke over his dead twin brother…it ain't nothin' we cain't spare. Ruby, wake him up and let's feed him something to fill up where his sad heart just slipped right on out."

But Hardy wasn't ready to wake up, drunk or sober. He just lay there all day between the graves, clutching the dead baby lamb.

Seeing Hardy all tore up like that, I tried to imagine it was charming, handsome, dead Lonny Dale out there naked and drunk in the spirit field. Late afternoon sun crashing down on him, Lonny Dale the one so hurt and angry because his twin Hardy was dead.

But Lonny Dale Jessup, alive or hanged, didn't love but one thing serious on this earth: me, Ruby Johnson, age nineteen. Daughter of the famous healer witch Dalilah Faircloth Johnson. And oldest sister to all what's left of near two hundred and fifty years of our magical kin.

The next day, a Sunday, my new husband Silas wouldn't go to Lonny Dale's viewing or his funeral. For a while, he didn't want me going. "Shoot, Ruby, those Jessups don't abide the Lord's way. I ain't like all them others who can forget what he done to git himself hanged in capital punishment. Blood ain't thicker than water for me, girl," Silas said.

But I went.

I married Silas over Lonny Dale not just because Lonny Dale went to prison. Lonny Dale couldn't offer me a thing except his ferocious love of life and his ferocious love of me. Not that Silas was much of a prize. With Mama dead and Daddy run off, I needed more than Lonny Dale's cocky, sexy grin and all'a his tore apart truck engines (that have never been put back in any truck) to take care of me.

If I had to judge my whole life on my decision to marry Silas after only a few months of him talking a good game but turning out to be about as dead wrong a choice as it can be, then this story would be pitiful—and should end right here. Silas had gone through seventh grade and claimed he read some "smart folks" books: Mark Twain, who I had heard of, and Charles Dickens over in England, who I had not. Him knowing something about something gave me hope that a man with brains could be a man with a heart. I thought I could change his crude ways by simply loving him proper and tender. Lord knows I was smarter than he was, book reading or no book reading. I could see his crude actions and crude ideas coming from a mile away.

Still, I thought I could change him to be less a Bible Belter when it suited him or when he couldn't find any other explanation for something, and more a free spirit, even though folks here in Redemption all say men from Bulls County are as ignorant as they are hateful, and plumb untrainable. Handsome as he was, I was willing to take a gamble with Silas for another reason besides him having half a brain and sweet to look at. Most folks over in Bulls County did not know much about the Johnsons over here in Redemption. They did not know our full history. Before he moved over here to live with us, he never heard of us. I was hoping to win him deep and true before he did.

But you know what? Sometimes it takes grievous errors in believing how things should be and how you want them to be and then them turning out sour, maybe even dangerous, so a woman can get a little harder in the heart and learn something about how to survive all the heartbreak and struggle in this world.

I was thinking about that as I was walking into the Jessup front yard, with its broken-down stuff lying around the property. An old roofless Studebaker filled with chestnuts was parked under a huge ole lightening-struck chestnut tree. Out in an overgrown field, three rusty tractors with no tires were all in a line and following one another nowhere. And tore apart truck engines were squatting all over on woodpiles and tree stumps, right where Lonny Dale left them.

And those crazy old Jessup aunts and their twenty rickety old front porch sliders all colors and models and all rusted up rigamortis solid, arranged all over the property. Some under whispering white willow trees. A few alongside a little brook. A bunch looking out over a daisy and black-eyed-Susan hillside. Two beet red sliders looking at the yellow outhouse's purple front door. And a sky blue one was even setting all stately up in the barn hayloft, door open, facing the old Studebaker like ghosts were sitting up there watching the wrecked old vehicle racing all around.

Most everyone in town was lined up at the Jessups' open front door. And every one of'm was looking at me stone cold. I had half a mind to think most of'm come just to git a good look at me close up, to see what the air around a Johnson witch feels like when they're standing right next to one. One old Presbyterian lady, wearing her Sunday hat with a big yellow feather stuck out'a it, came straggling up to me. With her hateful eyes shooting sparks, she puffed up her cheeks like her mouth was full of sharp rocks and blew her musty old air all over my face.

As I was trying to look around her into the Jessup house, pretending she wasn't there, I could see Lonny Dale's bare feet on the kitchen table. It hit me then. My childhood sweetheart, the boy I loved since I was twelve years old, was lying inside the Jessup house, dead.

As the shock of seeing those bare feet was taking hold, and I was holding back a wave of overwhelming grief and sadness that waited to hit me until just that moment, that old Presbyterian cow whispered to me low and wicked. "Y'all be joinin' that one there soon enough. I ain't gonna sleep sound 'til all you Johnson witches are stone dead." But she was pretending she was saying something nice and smiling big and respectful for everybody to see.

Y'all would think it would have died down after Mama left us, but we were still the family so feared and scorned in this county. Folks far and wide told tales of terror and witchcraft and murder done by us. Some of it's true. But a good size of it was nothing but made up ghost stories and drunk talk.

Still, folks got mobs together every couple of years to come up to burn us out. But they always got so drunk and scared they realized they sure as hell didn't want to be anywhere near us. Not a half a mile up our driveway road they ended up stumbling over rocks and knocking themselves out, falling into briar patches, and shooting at each other thinking they were seeing ghosts. Then they were running back down the mountain as fast they could with their lives still their own.

All these years, none never did make it all the way up here 'cept that one time when Mama was still a living soul. Six or seven of'm, all Klan brothers, came storming up the mountain looking fierce and dangerous, trying to bully Ma, demanding she give them "one good goddamn why they shouldn't light our raspberry acres an' all'a the fields on fire an' burn us Johnson female devils right to Hell."

Up mountain wind swayed pines older than Granddaddy. Cloud shadows scooted over bushes of wild roses and honeysuckle, petals like lost souls floating away on breezes all lilac smell and yellow pollen. And all pretty and young, her clear blue eyes, the wind whipping her long black raven hair, her blood-red shawl flapping wild like she was about to reveal secret wings, Mama stood there smiling at those dirty men. Never saying nothing. They went on sputtering about burning us clean off our side of the mountain.

Then Mama's smile faded as the men, especially one, started screaming, "Give us one good goddamn for not taking care of you Johnson wicked bitches once and for all! Just one good goddamn for not killing you right here!"

Slow and thoughtful, Mama picked the biggest, ugliest man out'a the group, the one screaming loudest, Mr. Tolbert Greaves. The blood had always been bad between the Greaves and the Johnsons, and none of us, not even Granddaddy, knew why. Shutting him up right quick, she gently held out her right palm and pointed it at him all delicate like she was about to bring life back to a dead child.

As something cloudy and sinister descended on Tolbert Greaves, his eyes bugged big as cannonballs from being the one singled out by an angry Dalilah Johnson, known in counties throughout the South as an honest-to-God purveyor of real and powerful witchcraft. Mama, twenty feet away with her palm still outstretched...the crotch of Greaves' overalls burst into flames.

Mama smiled sweet as spring rain and, answering his mean question, said, "There's one."

Big old scary Greaves yelping like a beat dog, the other men started whacking the bastard's fiery privates with their palms and rifle butts trying to put him out.

Murderous and angry, that man swore right there with his nuts still smoking that he was gonna kill every last one of us. "Ever' last one!" he kept screaming as he got carried down the mountain, leaving a little smoke trail rising up behind him.

That was only one reason why folks hated us—for lighting a redneck on fire. They hated our whole family, Johnson womenfolk especially. Over the decades, Johnson women cast a hell of a lot of spells on folks. Spells more miraculous or dangerous than lighting a cracker's nuts on fire. Most all'a our women kin from all the way back were witches. Near ever' single one an enchanter. Since

Colonial days full up with magic, all kinds of magic. Healing magic. Putting the spell on magic. Whispering babies inside 'a women who ain't been able to conceive. Breathing life into stillborns. Curing cancer. Let 'em talk to their dead kin. Change futures. Kill off rivals. And casting spells for every reason under the sun.

One even made a Kluxer's guts just fall right out on the road, no reason, while the jasper was telling somebody how he drove a knife through a colored man's hand.

Even evil magic, necessary for some good reason, to a Johnson woman inaway.

One of'm old, old ones, Effie Trueblood Johnson, the one hanged for being a witch in 1692, could turn folks into animals. Many a dumb ole white farm wife woke up screaming with a pig's snout rooting around in her privates, wondering where the hell her mean old colored people-beating husband went.

And, stars, they hated us for being magical, godless, non-Christian heathens. But without us, the population around here would've been even worse off. None of these folks could skip right over ordinary human life and its lack of magical imagination and git themselves miracles or healing or a spell to bring money to help make their lives livable without us. And imagine this: upright Christian folks still pitched salt on our tracks after we walked by. Some'd even go so far as finding themselves a big old blacksnake, slice its head off, and creep along behind us, spilling snake blood to ward off Johnson evil. But none had call to want to kill us. Not the kids and me, inaway. But if I weren't a Johnson, I'd probably hate us, too; if you consider being different, so-called godless, unapologetically free of mind and magical is an evil to fear and hate in Redemption.

Miz Jessup had Lonny Dale laid out on the eating table in the kitchen, wearing a set of somebody's new clean clothes, his good twin brother Hardy's, I suspect. He was dressed awkward on account they didn't fit and he was stiff when they readied him up for his own burying. Spose because there wasn't nowhere else to put it, she had the food on the same long table as her neck-stretched son. The lamb chops were on a dent-up silver tray right at Lonny Dale's bare feet. Finally, one of the crazy old Jessup aunts was kind enough to drape a pink pillowcase over them for the mealtime.

The Jessups didn't have money for a proper funeral. And were never churchgoers, so the event would not include a proper minister. After the meal was done and most town folks went home, Miz Jessup cleared the table. The Jessup men picked Lonny Dale up and laid him on the parlor rug, waiting to see what Miz Jessup wanted to do next. Surprising them, she said, "Wrap him up in it."

The Jessup family, led by those crazy old aunts dressed in what looked like rotten old black theater curtains, with me and my brother Bobby Lee (the only family outsiders on account I suspect that Lonny Dale was a murderer and no one else would be seen with the Jessups in public), walked in a scraggly procession down Beauregard Street. The old oaks swaying. The ruts in the road still full of water from the week of rain that just finally let off. Lonny Dale wrapped in the Jessups' parlor rug carried on the men's shoulders.

They buried him that way, inside a big old dirty carpet that hadn't even been cleaned. The hole they dug at the Redemption Town Cemetery was full of rocks and roots jutting out from the sides. When the family men lowered Lonny Dale in the carpet down with ropes, Lonny Dale beginning to come unrolled, the carpet snagged on a big underground root and Lonny Dale, half uncovered, toppled right in. The men all shrugged and just dumped the dirt on him inaway.

Right before they filled it in with red dirt that had a fiery look almost like it was smoldering on account of Lonny Dales' grievous crime, Miz Jessup did something I ain't never seen before. Late afternoon sunlight dappling the ground below those big oaks, she leant over Lonny Dale's grave hole. Gracefully, she dropped a big bunch of blue irises and white rockroses in one at a time. Then she closed her eyes and sent a load of spit in right after. None of us was sure why she did that—spit on her hanged son—not even Hardy. For Miz Jessup loved that boy Lonny Dale no matter what he ever done.

Or who he kilt.

After the burying, and not even looking at each other, both of us feeling hurt and hollow as a couple of dying willows about to crumble to the ground, Hardy and me walked away from everybody. I took his hand, and we walked out the graveyard and up the length of Beauregard Street, past the Redemption Baptist Church of the Second Coming whose steeple was lying on the ground in the side yard after blowing off during a violent thunderstorm from nearly a year previous. The one-room town library, where the town drunk, an ancient white-haired man named Old John Blue, supposedly a general during the Civil War, slept on the floor all day. If you wanted to read or take out a book, you had to step over him. And the old soldier's home where six or seven real old men that had served with Lee and Stonewall Jackson played checkers on the veranda, pulling indiscreetly on small jugs of still whiskey donated every week by the Grimer Brothers, biggest still operation for a hundred miles in any direction.

We walked right off Beauregard and up a deer trail that led to a high field that no one seemed to know who the owner was. In the middle of the field, there was a little pond with a family of black swans living in it, year after year. It was a beautiful afternoon, even if it was Lonny Dale's funeral day.

We came out from under a stand of tall white birch trees and walked into the field. The heat bugs were going at it up in the cottonwoods that circled the perimeter. A family of cardinals kept whizzing past this way and that, like little pieces of red lightning.

"Ruby," Hardy said as we sat in the grass beside the pond, "why do you spose twin brothers like me and Lonny Dale can be so night and day different?"

I couldn't git the image of Lonny Dale's lifeless cold bare feet out'a my mind. Me never leaving the Jessups' front room and him in the kitchen. I never once looked at inathing else. Not his face. Not his stretched neck. Just those cold, bare feet that I knew would haunt me until the end of my days. 'Cause Lonny Dale had been barefoot the night of the murder. His footprints, made bloody from stepping on the broken leaded crystal flower vase they say was the murder weapon, led the authorities right to the Jessup front door.

Then Hardy was suddenly kissing me. Running his hands and fingertips all over my body and I let him. It felt good to feel a man with heat touching me everywhere and not just scooting me around and making me bend over like my new husband Silas did.

As we pulled off each other's clothes, Hardy kept moaning, "Ruby…"

Because of his brother's funeral, I spose, Hardy took a bath with Ivory soap that morning. I could taste Ivory soap on every part of his body. Why were we doing this? Because the boy I loved was in the ground? My husband, Silas was home drinking something that would surely put him out or make him mean? Because, with Mama dead and daddy gone away on a lifetime drunk, the kids all needing me now made me their ma?

And me being only nineteen?

Maybe.

But mostly, both Hardy and me didn't know what to do or how to live happy in this world. Sometimes I think me and Hardy were made for each other more than me and Lonny Dale because Hardy and me were so lost.

After I pulled my dress back down and Hardy pulled up his pants, we lay in the tall grass listening to the birds sing, feeling cool breezes wash down from up top the mountain.

"Ruby," Hardy said, "you gonna try to wash that seed out'a ya?"

I held him close and felt his wetness up in me. It felt different from Silas'. Not as coal foul and gritty. Not full of his hate and ignorance. It wasn't like Lonny Dale's, all boyish and rough. Hardy's felt warm and sweet. I put my finger in my mouth and made it wet. Then, I put my finger into Hardy's mouth, and he sucked on it.

I said to him, "It don't matter, Hardy. What's done is done. Washing it out after doesn't do nothin' but make ya feel hopeful 'til they tell you you're with child inaway."

But secretly, just a couple of days before Lonny Dale was hanged, I got the feeling I was pregnant - by Silas. He had come home unexpected from his monthly three-week stint coalmining in Foster, a dirty, ugly town over the west side of the mountain. Walking out'a the woods, saying nothing to nobody, he walked right past my brothers Bobby Lee and Tom Sawyer cutting down a dead catalpa tree right next to where the trail comes out. He walked past my little ole sister Dahlia Rose floating daisy heads in a big puddle about halfway from the trail opening and the house. And he walked right past Granddaddy slumped over and snoring on his yellow rusty wheezy old slider on the front porch.

Silas Silatoe, a man nearly thirty years old, stormed into the house. Finding me in the kitchen peeling peas with my sister Macy, still saying nothing, he grabbed me by the hand and roughly led me upstairs. Once in our bedroom, he swung me around, bent me over, tore down my underwear. Gripping my breasts hard, he took me from behind. My new husband Silas, not even bathing first, doing it rough and pushing his coal dust right straight up into me.

"You want to do it lying down?" I asked him tender. But I didn't want to do nothing sexual with him no more…lying down, standing up, half-dead. Nothin'.

I straightened up to unbutton my shirt. I guess he didn't like me asking him that 'cause he pushed me over and poked it hard up me again. Silas did it that way until he had no more stiffness, and all his seed was either up inside or dripping down my legs.

When he yanked out, Silas looked all set to embarrass me and say something mean about the mess he made. Like he had done all those other times when he stepped away to look me over 'cause I was still all sweaty and quivering. He took hold of his dick and grinned evil.

"You like taking it hard, don't ya Ruby Lee?" he said wicked, looking my body over good, making me feel dirty. "Yer one fine-looking female, damn it. More'n beautiful. Hollywood beautiful, just like folks say."

He seemed real impressed with himself. "Magine me married to somethin' Hollywood beautiful. Maybe sometahm later this evenin' I'll give ya some more."

I always wondered, is this what Daddy did to Mama? Bend her over and rut her so hard from behind that she had to grab hold to the footboard of the bed that's all a-shaking and squeaking? And the sex is making her crazy with the heat but she's crying too. Because her man's loving her heart and soul no better'n a bull taking a piss all over a sweet-smelling thicket of high mountain daisies.

After Silas let go of my hips and scraggled off to find his supper, time would start moving again.

That I let Hardy let go his seed inside me was no accident. I spose I needed to make clear to myself that in the months down the road there'd be a good chance my baby'd, if I were to have one, come from somewhere other than just the darkness inside 'a Silas Silatoe.

When me and Hardy came back down to town, nobody, not even Silas, suspected inathing had gone on between the grieving twin brother of the dead twenty-one-year-old boy, and that dead boy's teenage black magic girlfriend. Even though I didn't do white magic, let alone black.

I didn't see Hardy again for a while after that. And until he was back to coal mining, Silas was always hungry, drinking rotgut and a-leading me upstairs.

Every single time as he did me from behind, I looked out the bedroom window to see as many things as I could about my life that was graced. There was Granddaddy a-pokin' around looking useful but not really doing inathing. The kids were always eating the raspberry profits before I could git all the baskets loaded into the truck to take 'em down to Mr. Jesse's Produce Warehouse. Boolie was usually sleeping under his old cottonwood with his nose tucked under his tail.

I would see the steeple spikes way down the valley and away in the distance, pointing up to something mysterious and holy that none of us humans has figured out yet. I would see the logging project across the valley that left the mountainside looking like it died of a horrible disease.

I would see the top of our two-mile driveway road leading up to our big house.

And I would look to see if we had any visitors driving up, so maybe Silas would git out from behind me.

But no one ever did come up in the nick of time…just before Silas would start to wheeze and grunt and sometimes pull out some of my hair as he bunched up his face and released himself into me. Him wheezing and throwing me around, I would see my old pickup a-teetering on half-flat tires in the side yard, looking like it also wanted to go somewhere, anywhere, other than here. I would be wondering what it looks like over the mountains in the valley on the other side. Places I hadn't never been.

This new husband of mine wasn't much better than that run off husband of Mama's, who we hadn't seen around those parts since a few months before they brought Lonny Dale's body back to his ma. And when Silas began pumping his dirty coal dust up into me.

***

For a time, folks all over these parts were passing more judgment on the Jessups and their hanged son than they were on us Johnsons, as they had been doing for over two hundred years. It's a distressing time when everybody you know wants you dead unless they need healing or some conjuring.

I wasn't a true healer like Mama was.

I wasn't interested in doing any healings; I just wanted the world to let me be. And I wasn't planning on doing any magic, ever, that required more than me doing nothing more magical than walking. Leading the one needing healing into our spirit field. All I do is bring people in. The spirits of twenty-five of our women kin kilt, massacred really, by Yankee soldiers in the Civil War a-flying and a-sailing all around above the gravestones in beautiful, sparkling red light do all the rest.

Struck me strange sometimes, a person from down the mountain who couldn't decide whether they hated us more than they feared us or the other way around was getting them a miracle performed to set their lives right. And I, looking like the last Johnson healer witch—but who wasn't interested in being one—I was feeling sad and lost and alone as can be.

Even with Mama dead those last four years, folks still walked all the way up here. Maybe expecting her ghost to be waiting for them. Since being ghosts is what we Johnson women were best at.

But all they found was me.

This one time a fella got his whole family to push him the two miles up the driveway road in a wheelbarrow 'cause he lost a leg logging on the other side of the valley. They whomped him all the way up and near kilt ten men and a bunch of kids from the effort. Fella was lying in the wheelbarrow like parts of a scarecrow, all busted up. In another wheelbarrow, they had his cut-off leg wrapped up in burlap packed with ice.

"Miz Johnson," one of the kids said when I heard 'em out front and came out'a the house. "Ruby, mam, my pa's leg got sawed clean off. We's here asking if you'll stick it back on. We got four dollars and three new-carved fiddle bows 'cause we know how fine your fiddlin' is."

An hour later, his pa was reattached to his leg, and the lady kin ghosts were quieting down some after doing what they do. I took one fiddle bow and one dollar and let 'em keep the rest.

As I was thinking maybe finally somebody would leave our company peaceful and kind, and as they pulled the fella out'a the spirit field all passed out and bloody in his wheelbarrow, but he'd walk again, one of his brothers turned to me. Saying all ugly and hurtful, "Y'all may've saved this one here. But you still ain't nothin' but a Johnson witch with a black soul. Don't you never come near none of us agin." He chunked a big rock at me.

But this ain't even close to the most peculiar healing that'd happened since Mama left this earth and I had to become Ma, and Pa, to the kids, since he ran off. One morning, me and the kids woke to church gospel singing floating up and down the mountain paths. Christian hymns and Negro spirituals drifting on the morning breeze like "We All Gather at the River" and "We All Walk De Heavenly Road." Those old Baptist hymns came singing out'a the woods and float right up into our bedroom windows.

"Jeez almighty, Ruby," Macy, fifteen that spring, came screaming out'a her bedroom with her white lacy nightgown all bunched up high and twisted around her waist. "I ain't ready to be took nowhere by Jesus' angels."

With two or three different expressions crawling around his handsome face, Tom Sawyer, sixteen then, trying not to look at Macy's privates, but also having a hell of a time looking away, clunked out into the hall. Followed close by Granddaddy, who must have got lost trying to go to bed last night and ended up in Tom Sawyer's room. By Granddaddy's bewildered eyes shooting around, I expect he thought he had died of natural causes during the night, and this was the heavenly host streaming down to carry him up on the sweet chariot. You should've seen him tear out a back window, hop down to the roof of the shed, fall down heavily to the ground, and limp fast to the barn like a crippled man trying to outrun Noah's flood.

Dahlia Rose came a-running out'a her pink bedroom, barefoot like all'a us. Her little feet were tapping like a chipmunk across the hall floor, and she came a-sailing right into my arms. Dahlia Rose took the hair on both sides of my head in her fists and pulled my face directly into hers. It hurt.

"Ruby Lee," the six-year-old demanded, "Does this racket mean Mama's finally comin' home?"

And Bobby Lee, a year younger than me...he was there, I spose. But I didn't remember him waking up with us out'a sound sleep hearing God Almighty singing in the morning air.

We all streamed outside. All around the spirit field, with Squirrel Martin (some said retarded, we said smart as all git out except for speaking his gibberish) already there and standing among them with his mouth hung wide open. Like he was thinking they were a whole hell of a lot crazier than he was. About twenty-odd old colored people from all over the valley were standing like rickety church statues, singing hymns.

Laid out on the little path leading into the spirit field, five children and two adult-size bodies were all wrapped up in new dazzling white bed sheets. Still with their neat store-bought creases cutting across up and down like bold roads on maps that didn't lead anywhere. None of us had ever seen any of these people before, dead *or* alive.

Seeing me and the kids come running over the hill from the house and walk right into the crowd of'm, these folks all stopped singing, with a few stragglers not noticing they were singing alone for a while.

Tom Sawyer whispered to me, "Man alive, girl, these here don't want us to bury these folks up here, do they?" Then, he smiled a soft thing, trying not to show how nervous he was. But I knew. "If they do, Ruby Lee, I'm a-gonna git the fencepost hole diggin' tool and dig fence pole holes that go down about seven feet and jus' slide them right in nice and tight standin' up." That would have been funny at any other time.

An old colored man wobbled over and sort 'a croaked at me, "We's ready now, Miz Johnson."

I stared at the man. He was tall as a mature oak sapling and just as skinny. He said it again. This time he reached out his old, withered hand and gently touched my shoulder. "We's ready," he repeated soft, looking right into my eyes.

That old colored man's gaze was like looking into a bright, soft, smoldering setting sun. It made me squint a little. I felt like my soul was all smooth, melting and dripping out.

But I didn't know what on earth he was talking about or what he was ready for. Then, before I could guess what I was supposed to do, the spirit field just plain leaped into life. All was a-swirling and flashing a beautiful color red, and we all saw the see-through Civil War-kilt Johnson women all ages all a-standing in the air looking back at us. Smiling. Lovely. Holding out their arms. The red light was blinding, but so beautiful.

Squirrel Martin was enjoying himself immensely. He was lying in the grass, splashing in the red light, his arms and legs swimming him all around. When we Johnsons had gathered back some of our wits, the colored folks were all leaving and heading toward the top of the driveway road for the long walk down.

The deceased family was plumb gone.

I didn't know why our Johnson spirit field took the dead colored family as one of its own. Or why they all came up *here*? I was muddled. Us Johnsons had almost as much black blood as we do Cherokee and white. These old saintly people never done such a peculiar thing before. Why didn't I know nothing about any of this?

***

Being a healer means nothing to me, but most every day since Mama died, I'd been going up to the spirit field at night. Sometimes, I'd just stand on the rise, look up at the stars, and feel my heart and soul burn.

Sometimes I sit on a grave an' play slow fiddle for Mama and the ghost kin ladies. Sometimes, I strolled right on in, jumped up on the aboveground grave of Effie Trueblood Johnson, died 1692 from hanging by a mob for being a witch, and called out, "Y'all home, ladies? Y'all ready to see me as one of your own?"

First time I did that, it wasn't a month after Mama died, I reckon. I was fifteen. Pa was still coming around, so I wasn't in full charge of the kids and the place yet. And back then, Granddaddy was soft in the head, but it was his natural softness he had all his life. Not the dementia he had now.

I reckon those first times I went up there I was looking for Mama. I was hoping somehow the lady kin ghosts would convince her to come back to us. And out she'd walk beautiful and lovely from out behind a chipped old gravestone. Right back into our lives.

It took almost a year for the kin ghosts to hear me. Or else it took that long for them to decide they wanted to show themselves to a little old teenage gal, not Mama. Mama had more magic than all'a them combined. Or so it always seemed to me by the way they would crowd all around her when she was living. They'd pass their sparkly red arms through her body as if they were washing their hands in a sacred and miraculous spring.

When one finally did show up, she was illuminated in red light that was soft and pale, almost shy. She was young, about twelve, and had long, long red hair down to the back of her thighs, like me. Hovering there in the air, looking lovely and terrifying at the same time; she wouldn't talk to me. All she'd do is wait until I finished playing a fiddle tune. Then she would sing a bittersweet mountain love song about centuries of Johnson girls trying and failing to git men down mountain to not fear them so and love them kind and tender.

Or love them at all.

***

On part of our land, we had five hundred acres of wild berries, mostly raspberries, down the mountain about a half mile from our house. What we call *the Raspberry Acres* and all'a it grows wild and free. Johnsons have owned most of Redemption Mountain since before Colonial days when one of our kin won it playing a game of horseshoes. For all this time, we Johnsons have supplied most of Redemption County's raspberries. Our name right there on the basket. Folks have no problem eating our high mountain-grown fruit but would surely take a shot at one of us if they caught us alone.

CHAPTER TWO

With hardly any brakes and the kids screaming, once a week we'd go flying down the driveway road in my cranky old Dodge pickup on two wheels at almost every turn, the raspberry crates in the back teetering and rocking. Macy, Dahlia Rose, and Tom Sawyer rode up front with me. Squirrel Martin and Bobby Lee rode back in the truck bed, holding on for dear life among waves of falling raspberries. We rarely lost too many berries out'a the truck. When we'd finally git to the produce broker, Mr. Jesse J. Brown, Squirrel and Bobby Lee'd usually have them all basketed back up.

Those brakes needed to be stripped off and better ones put back on before I kilt us all. Problem is, with me down in town, the truck hoisted up, and not drivable for a few hours at Coates Fill Up & Repair, word would git out in jig time. All kinds of people who don't care for us Johnsons will come by to say mean things to me. Threaten me. Or just to ogle, thinking with my green eyes and my red hair the color of wildfire, I am the most Hollywood beautiful ugly old mountain witch they ever did see.

One time we ran out'a gas near the big old sycamore that serves as the Redemption Bus Stop for the Greyhound Cruiseliner, just outside downtown Redemption. While my brother Bobby Lee went to fetch a can of gas from Coates, I sat on the running board tallying some figures on the bushels of raspberries we just sold. I was wearing men's work pants that were tight on me and one of Bobby Lee's white undershirts that was even tighter 'cause it was hot as blazes that day and it was clinging to me. It was so hot apples were boiling on the branches and exploding the air full of applesauce.

I ignored them all, the townspeople, who started showing up to stare at the fire-haired magical daughter of famous healer witch Dalilah Johnson, probably for a good ten minutes. Soon the sidewalk and some of the road were filled up with folks, men mostly. A few women stood there too, with rubbed-in splotches of red clay on their cheeks they scooped right off the side of a dirt road 'cause they couldn't afford store-bought makeup, their scandalized eyes hammering right into me wide open and round as trash barrel lids.

Aside'a some ladies yelling for me to go burn myself to death or something stupid like that, nothing much happened until a teenage boy on a dare from his friends came flying out'a the crowd like a boy on fire and bumped me hard on the forehead with his head, trying to kiss me on the cheek. That ain't got makeup on it, dirt or store-bought.

The crowd was laughing at the clumsy but gutsy young fella. And me sitting there rubbing my head trying not to look up at 'em. But then, with looks of concern skittering around on their sunburnt faces like the hornet's war dance, recalling every Johnson witch story they ever heard, they were all wondering if I were about to turn the boy into a rotted tree stump or something. Or worse…a Catholic.

Striding through the crowd like Appalachian Jesus, and the crowd parting for him, I'll never forget when Lonny Dale Jessup walked up beside me and gave me a kiss. Then, like a rattlesnake, he whipped around and got up into the face of one of the women heckling me the most, with her husband standing right next to her, too dumb, or too smart, to move.

Lonny Dale said nothing. He did nothing. But his eyes were so close to that lady's; their eyelashes were passing through each other. His mission accomplished without uttering inathing offensive to nobody, in about twenty seconds, the little crowd of fifteen or twenty people dispersed.

"Seems you're good for something other than taking me up the mountain and lying me down in the sun, Lonny Dale," I said, pretend sarcastic and smiling. "Ain't you in the least bit intimidated by us terrifying Johnson females that eat Presbyterian babies whole?"

He smirked huge at me. "Girl, I got me the most Hollywood beautiful girlfriend in all North Carolina. Why'd I give a care about some witchiness here and there?"

Lonny Dale gave me another kiss, a long wet one. Playfully slapped my ass, smiled that crafty thing of his and walked away whistling.

He hadn't kilt anybody yet.

Back to tumbling down the driveway road in the truck that time, Squirrel Martin clunked his head on something but he wouldn't cry. Never would, no matter what.

Thank God all the kids were doing fine. Even Squirrel Martin. Sometimes he yelled and carried on throwing things at ghosts and such he saw all over the place. He still didn't talk. And he didn't sleep much. But he was letting me hold him, sing some, an' he'd tolerate me whispering into his ear the first half of Battle Hymn of the Republic before he twisted out'a my lap like a wet cat.

I played fiddle tunes for him sometimes after supper before I'd go up to the spirit field to look in on the women kin ghosts. Mostly I played the old sad laments every child on this mountain knows by heart by the time they're five years old. Sometimes Bobby Lee sat with us plonking on Granddaddy's old Civil War banjo, hitting the right note once in a while. Those gentle times and those beautiful sounds help ease Squirrel's hurt mind.

The others are all growing up and developing into people. Macy's hair was as long down to her behind as mine, but pure dark midnight like Mama, while I was pure red sunshine. She had breasts now, and the town boys were chasing and a teasing her whenever they can. She was a beauty. Fifteen and the prettiest of all the Johnson women.

Tom Sawyer, seventeen, spent most of his time writing words for songs no one had written yet. He wrote down the words in a book of high school marching band sheet music somebody who went to school gave him. He just wrote down words. Didn't give a hoot about the music. And he stuck like tar to Granddaddy. I couldn't tell if he was wanting to learn about life from Granddaddy, or if he thought he needed to make sure Granddaddy didn't go more senile than he was already and wander off a cliff.

Either way, Tom was with Granddaddy all the time, even sleeping. They shared that big room over the front door. Tom didn't even care about Granddaddy's snoring, or Granddaddy's midnight peeing out the window 'cause he said his old legs wouldn't git him out to his old peeing tree in the side yard in time anymore.

Dahlia Rose was six and just so lonely and sad sometimes. I did my best to mother her, but she missed Mama. Most days, when she wasn't helping with the raspberrin', she played in the spirit field and talked to her baby dolls right out loud. When you listen quiet an' close, you could tell she ain't talking to baby dolls.

One time, I heard her tell one of the lady kin ghosts: "A 'course I know them ailin' folks Ruby brings up here go back down a hell of a lot better off. Stop askin'."

And Bobby Lee? I didn't think he'd be living with us much longer. He was nearly eighteen and had it set in his mind that he wanted to up and join the military. He talked all the time about going away to find old Stonewall Jackson. Out further into the world than any of us Johnsons knew inathing about, to fight for the South. I told him all the time the USA was in no war with anybody right then. Not even ourselves. But he didn't care. He wanted to live in a uniform and shoot rifles at whoever he pleased.

After we got the raspberries back settled and the children's eyes back in their heads from the wild ride down, we drove the six miles to Jesse J. Brown's. This time, we unloaded the whole truck and stacked the raspberry crates up next to his barn-office door *before* we went looking for him.

Ten crates with fifty one-pound baskets each, with our name on it. More raspberries than the whole of Redemption County would ever need for one week. I have to be smart with Mr. Jesse. He's fair with his prices, but he ain't keen on buying more raspberries than he can broker in two or three days.

Even the raspberry buyers from stores a hundred miles around when they are there, doing their business with Mr. Jesse, they look right over my shoulders for signs of our lady kin ghosts following me into town. Which they ain't never done, at least I don't think so.

When we finally tracked him down, and before me or him could git out a word of hello or smile at each other or nothing, a big explosion up in the hills swept the budding smiles right off our faces. It was a huge, huge thing. About a mile up the hillside. It roared out'a the trees like it wanted to eat the whole world. It shot the birds right out'a those trees, and they went a-screaming off in all directions. Then, a few seconds later, another one came. Even bigger and louder. The ground was shaking.

Me and Mr. Jesse just stood there, looking at each other, each of us putting pieces together of what the hell just happened. Both of us knew the only thing capable in the valley of creating such massive violence was the government work camp, the U.S. Army Corps of Engineers and their massive logging project way up the mountain. The kids, they were hopping up and down, and looking all over for giants or something.

After the enormous sounds went away and we could hear birdsong again, Mr. Jesse turned to me, a real serious look in his eyes. "Ruby," he said to me, looking over the stacks of crates we made, "thank God all them wild raspberries grow all over your side of the mountain. You ever think about what would become of y'all if them berries didn't grow wild? Right there for y'all to pick right off the earth like coins that fall smack outta the clouds?"

I reckon he was right, and I didn't really say inathing to him in return, but *thank you for the money, Mr. Jesse.* But I'd been thinking about that very thing. What if somehow all our raspberry bushes did die? Or fire came and burned us out from lightning strikes like it did to all those people over in Red Hand some years back? What if folks suddenly took to hating raspberries? They didn't make us rich by no means. But they kept us alive with enough cash money so we ate good and paid the land taxes, doctor and truck payments.

Sometimes, with the extra earnings, we piled into the truck on Sundays and went tearing down the driveway road to go to the Time Square Movie House. An old cow barn painted blue, with all the windows painted-over green, down on the outskirts of downtown Redemption.

Squirrel Martin still couldn't understand how people and places can live flat on the big screen. He kept wandering out'a his seat to go up to walk into the movie and into some other world he thought looks like a black and white place he'd rather be than ours right here in Redemption that's in full alive color. I spose all'a us remaining Johnsons think that from time to time.

Sometimes on the way driving down that treacherous two miles, I imagined the truck was the rattly old palm of Jesus, and me and the kids and the raspberries just sat there waiting to see what was gonna happen.

Driving down the driveway road is much easier than driving back up, even if we just narrowly missed Tarnation every single time on the way down.

After doing business with Mr. Jesse, then going back up, the old truck wasn't never at'all happy. Second gear never worked for some reason. Didn't make any difference on a decline or on a flat road, though. I just got her rolling in first, then shifted to third when we were going fast enough. Going back up, second was what we needed the most. But we ain't got it. So it was first or third. And third sounds mighty painful to the truck. So, mostly we staggered up the mountain in first gear a-groaning and a-whirring high, like Pa always did in them days he still cared enough about us to try to stagger walk drunk up the two-mile driveway back home every once in a while. Not makin' it up here sometimes and passing out in a pine grove.

But we always made it okay. I was thankful every time we made it down alive. And I was thankful every time I made it back up and Silas wasn't there waiting for sex more than food. But hungry for that, too. And we found Granddaddy still alive and breathing, scooting around somewhere chopping wood that we didn't need and trying to git his overall straps fixed up the right way.

And when Boolie wasn't with us in the truck protecting the kids, I was thankful to see him sleeping under his big cottonwood, his feet running once in a while like dogs do when they dream of finding somewhere they want to be more than with us here.

And making me feel even a little lower sometimes, I wasn't even sure Pa or Granddaddy had full grasp on Johnson women's magic. Lonny Dale did, but he wouldn't say much to acknowledge or encourage that. Our husbands and lovers kind or cruel for hundreds of years, only a might precious few were willing to grant us full acceptance of our magical ways. And they didn't like admitting it, but town folks know our lady ghosts were as real as real can be. If they want a healing, they got to stumble right into the middle of'm.

***

But what was troubling me far worse than just Johnson women being scary to people…and what this story is really about.

We had crawling all over us men from the U.S. Army Corps of Engineers. Tromping the mountain, they were taking measurements and surveying acreage and property lines of what we owned and what of the mountain and valley we didn't.

These men were trying to figure out how they were gonna destroy thousands and thousands of mountain and valley acres of trees and animal life, a huge bit of'm ours. They wanted to build a hydroelectric dam, powered by the runoff from three different rivers and flood the valley up with seventy feet of water. *Seventy* feet. A couple of pine tops sticking up here and there. Everything else, at the bottom of a lake so huge it'll have over a hundred miles of shore wrapping around it.

A reservoir, they call it. A fancy French word for drowning dead a whole valley.

Those men weren't too clear on what they intended to do with all that water, besides us drinking it. We heard that word *hydroelectric* but none of us had a clue how they were fixin' to git electricity out'a that dam and this new lake. Granddaddy thought that's bullshit. *How ye git fire to travel through a wire that come from a lake full 'a water? Bastards are lyin' to us. Must be a mess 'a Yankees still vengeful for Abe Lincoln gettin' kilt. Gonna try to flood kill us all.*

Those government men knew everything about us. Our names. Our kin. Mama and all her charms magic and healings. The Johnson great-great-great grandma they say walked on water and flew through the air. Even the two old Johnson witches from 1720-something that got put in jail one night and next day there were two coon cats waiting there for breakfast.

They knew Granddaddy shot his own eye out drunk in the Civil War. They knew Squirrel Martin was brainless. Knew Tom Sawyer was proud 'cause he steamed up fast but held his tongue when they teased him about his name.

They knew how many raspberry acres we got. How many ponds. And damn, I bet these fellas even counted the trees.

One good thing come out'a it. No Johnson from the first one here on the mountain two hundred years ago knew how big our land was. Not a clue. Just damn huge is all we'd say. Our men were always fond of saying, "Just climb to the top of iny tree anywhere around here. Everything you see is ourn."

There were 3,957 acres of Redemption Mountain that we got one way or t'other. I reckon that's bigger than Heaven and Hell combined. And the U.S. Army Corps of Engineers were going to steal it right out from under us.

CHAPTER THREE

Since Mama died, our big old rambling house was pretty much the same. At the end of the two-mile near straight up "ride 'a doom" driveway road, as Hardy Jessup calls it, the old place is doing well considering the time passed since our ancestor won it playing horseshoes, while holding a loaded musket. And since progress in Redemption hadn't exactly been running rampant since then, we are the only Johnsons to have ever lived in a proper dwelling with window glass, real tarpaper on the roof, and store-bought door hinges.

The boys and me took down all the scraggily hemlocks out in front of the house. Now there was a big sloping green rise we sit out on almost every late afternoon to watch the red and violet setting sun smolder and drip the end of day all over Redemption Valley.

Up the far hill a piece, the barn was painted pink for no good reason than Bobby Lee and Tom Sawyer bought twenty gallons of it for $9 from Mr. Jesse. Some old man named Adolphus Clapper crept around the valley stealing things at night. He paid his produce bill with those gallons of paint. He snuck all twenty cans right out the shed of someone living on the far end of Redemption. Carried six at'a time on a long pole, three fore, three aft, balanced on his shoulder like a Chinaman. Telling Mr. Jesse it was *church-color white.* When Mr. Jesse found out it was pink and knowing it wouldn't take much for the owner to trace it back to him, you shoulda seen him smile when he saw me holding my left arm out the window of the truck and take the turn to his produce warehouse parking lot.

He knew no one in their right mind would challenge a Johnson over stolen goods.

Nothing ever lived in our pink barn but mice and black snakes that ate them, and a near domesticated rattler that didn't seem to know his job in this life was to try to bite and kill people. You could pet it; it was so disinterested. And, once in a while, Pa lived in there when he was still coming around.

We had a woodshed…with an old Model T Ford up on its roof, I swear. Was just there one day. Somebody said, "Hey y'all, there's a jalopy on the woodshed roof." Somebody else said, "An' I'm Andrew Jackson." It was never mentioned as inathing unusual again.

Squirrel Martin painted the woodshed with cans of paint he found in an old, abandoned hill family's shack lost up the mountain halfway to Red Hand, and that black Ford perched on it like a big rusted old crow as if they were one thing. He created his own special color that exists nowhere else on earth. Something he calls holy murple. Red and purple paint and red clay and red dirt, some orange soda pop and a few dead honeybees all mixed up. Looks fine. Imagine that.

He liked it so much; he moved himself right on in and lived in that woodshed most nights.

I loved going out to look at it on account'a Squirrel Martin being brainless and nobody expected him to do inathing but eat with his fingers and chase the squirrels. That's how he got his name. Six months old, lying in a cushioned washtub under Boolie's sleeping tree, his little crossed-eyes saw a puff of gray scampering by all herky jerky. My baby brother was out'a that washtub, crawling after that squirrel and grabbing him by the tail before it could crawl up the side of the house. Damn thing bit holes in his arms and nearly scratched off an ear.

Six months old, he was famous for being the only person in North Carolina ever to crawl after a squirrel and catch it.

Three years old, he threw himself down the well because he was thirsty. He was famous again; the whole town knew he was back to being brainless.

That boy wasn't entirely human. He hadn't said a hundred human words his whole life. Folks said he didn't have the brains to fill up a bait can. They said his brains got plumb fried before he come a-shooting outta Ma. Funny thing about brains. Some folks need 'em. Some don't. Having no brains didn't keep him back at'all.

All his young mysterious life Squirrel'd been able to make things happen, magical things. That nobody knows about him doin' because he only did them way out in the woods by himself. And no Johnson boy or man has ever had the gift of magic before Squirrel. Not a one. But Johnson men sure have had the gift of drinking, or loafing, or adultery, or running off, and some of killing. And some have all that and plenty more.

More times than not, Squirrel Martin, leaving the comfort of his woodshed, just crawled in through the kitchen window in the morning while we were having breakfast. Not saying inathing, he curled up at my feet on the floor next to Boolie.

The boy had always been peculiar in his ways, making no sense to anybody but him and me. I'm not what you call your average human female, with my magical ways. Truth is, like me, he scared people. Scared me sometimes, though I'd never let him know that for fear of wounding that sacred heart of his. The boy's tenderness and lack of meanness or anger was deep and pro-found. At least, I hope that's the correct fancy school word for it. I never did one thing but accept him as the half boy, half something else that he was.

I believe he had a special place in this world, an important place somewhere.

When Squirrel Martin Johnson was seven years old, he performed an honest-to-God miracle. It may not seem like much, I reckon, when you consider what Johnson women have been doing since God was a boy. Squirrel and I were out under the willows up by his holy murple woodshed and Model T ensemble, sitting in a hot pale yellow breeze. The willows were right next to a huge settlement of honeysuckles losing their pollen in delicate clouds each time the wind picked up the branches.

I was happy and content that day. One of those magical days where the air is soft and the wind carries gorgeous secrets and wisdom. Squirrel Martin was examining the ground, his face almost burrowed right into it.

The older kids were helping Granddaddy rip down the old outhouse, clean out the slop down in the hole, and then build a brand new one. This new one had a little glass window and green curtains for privacy on an actual door they found up in the attic. It even had a brass knob.

It was such a lovely no-account day. I was playing my fiddle and singing some of the old, old songs like "The Preacher's Sorrowful Daughter" and "Who Kilt Agnes Sloane?" Suddenly, the willow tree was full of mockingbirds, nineteen or twenty beautiful big ones. That was something 'cause everybody knows those Godly birds are loners.

Squirrel Martin was noodling around in the grass, and up above mockingbirds were singing their hearts out. It was just as lovely as can be those singing birds, singing every bird song there ever was. And some I reckon that never were but shoulda been.

Under the bird symphony, Squirrel Martin was searching the grass for dead bugs. Dead ants. Flies. Beetles. Wasps. June bugs. Lady bugs. He made a pile of stiff, curled up insects throughout the afternoon. Around an hour before suppertime, after the others had finished the last touches on the new outhouse, including painting it bright yellow, I stood up and started walking up to the house. I noticed Squirrel wasn't with me after several steps. I turned around. He was kneeling in front his dead bug pile, holding his hands over it, breathing on the backs of his fingers.

The bugs woke up. Every one of'm. They moved a leg, and then another, stretched out their bodies, and looked all around in buggy shock. They just couldn't believe they were alive again. After fighting a little among themselves, they crawled or slunk or flew away. Just alive as can be.

Another time, me and Lonny Dale were stringing up a new store-bought clothesline rope between a couple of trees. The funny-feeling rope was white and soft and spongy.

I didn't think inathing of it then, but the white spongy rope came packaged up in a tight noose knot, almost like a hanging noose. Lonny Dale wouldn't touch it. Just refused. Almost like he knew what was waiting for him a few years down the line.

While I strung the rope out from tree to tree, he was trying to sneak his hand into my loose shirt. Laughing and just enjoying being young, we both at the same time heard foot scuffling coming down the dirt path that heads up the mountain. The path that doesn't ever git you anywhere. We watched Squirrel Martin wander down into the big side yard, scuffing his feet, looking happy as a clam.

He had a snake tail in each of his fists. Two good size rattlers passively allowing themselves to be dragged along.

We couldn't believe it. Lonny Dale for one second forgot about his raging hormones. I for one second forgot about Lonny Dale. Over by the collard and beet garden, Bobby Lee was tinkering on a seized-up Buick he bought for six dollars from a man that was going blind. Bobby Lee was stripped to the waist and parched thirsty. He bent up straight to stretch his back, sweat all over him. Looking plumb evaporated, he reached into the Buick's front seat and took out a big jug of lemonade and gulped down about half of it. Still gulping, he saw Squirrel Martin come out'a the woods dragging the snakes. He dropped the jug and grabbed a good size wrench. Another look at those two five-footers, he dropped that wrench and grabbed a bigger one.

He was on his way over to the boy in a hurry, as were we, when it hit him right the same time it hit us. The snakes were willing companions. Squirrel Martin, dragging his snakes, set himself down under a willow on a patch of soft grass. The snakes immediately crawled up and lay at his feet like puppies. Squirrel was talking to them for about an hour. Me and Lonny Dale had finished with the clothesline, and Bobby Lee had given up on the Buick. The three of us were sitting out on the wrap around porch in the shade, watching the seven-year-old stroke the snakes' heads and laugh every so often, talking to them snakes.

In time, a soft wind blew down from the mountaintop and crackled the dried willow leaves. The diamondbacks rattled their tails along with it. When the willows stopped rattling, the snakes crawled away through the cool late afternoon grass back to the trail. Squirrel couldn't say five words to a human being. But he sure could engage a rattlesnake in a deep conversation for the good part of an afternoon.

And that time he brought a dead cat back to life, something the whole town still gossips about. Thinking it was me that done it. The dead cat come alive again was true. But I didn't do a thing but stand there with my mouth open hearing about it. From Macy.

Squirrel found Macy's yellow cat behind the sunflower garden, all dead and ripped up by a coyote or a raccoon. After a few days under the hot sun it was already decomposing into a strip of smelly ripe carcass. Macy told me, without much fuss, the boy picked up the cat's body and carried it into his holy murple woodshed and slammed the door closed. A minute or two later, she heard what sounded like hysterical scratching on the door coming from inside.

Then, the door flung open. The yellow cat shot out and scrambled up Boolie's huge cottonwood, making that weird high-pitch then low-pitch cat whiny sound when they're so scared and angry they hurt. Macy said Squirrel come out'a his shed a little scratched up but smiling.

None of us ever did see that resurrected cat again.

And, shoot, for years, I've been telling people about Squirrel Martin floating fast over the ground, walking on pond water, walking up the side of trees, and just sailing up into the sky. Even though I had seen him do these things, and me being pretty supernatural myself, I still only half believed it. But I had belief enough to confirm that Squirrel Martin just was not entirely human. None of us are. We *are* Johnsons, after all. But Squirrel…

And perhaps most astonishing, I saw him crawl through the grass that day the coloreds came up the mountain to lay that dead family at the entrance to the spirit field. I swear he went invisible to all but me. I saw him lay his palms over each of the wrapped up dead ones' faces, no one else noticing, and one of'm, a little girl about eleven, started twitching. Squirrel, quick as cat, unwrapped her face and her body and then he slowly got up. He grasped hold of her hand and pulled her to her feet. Then, he walked off with her into the spirit field and right into the middle of the brilliant red light and swirling lady kin ghosts. He walked out the back and into the woods, still holding the little black girl's hand. Being a Johnson, I never in my life believed that some of Jesus and His ancient old Biblical tricks was such a big deal. This was one reason why.

With Squirrel, you had to go from being struck dumb and senseless from amazement when he did something more than unexplainable and more than just a little supernatural, to rolling your eyes when he forgot to unbutton himself and pooped in his pants.

CHAPTER FOUR

Most important man in Squirrel Martin's life was black, hasn't hardly ever worked, and isn't entirely human. Once just by simple lips put together whistling, he knocked the teeth right out'a a white tobacco farmer's head. A crass old man named Willis Tallmadge who ran down a colored boy's old dog with a tractor, a boy the old black man didn't even know.

This old black man whistled Squirrel Martin back up out'a that well he jumped into when he was a sprite. The old man was just passing by when he heard all the commotion. He saw Bobby Lee and Tom Sawyer getting frightful nervous when Squirrel wouldn't grab hold of the rope they were dropping down into the darkness.

Up the black man strolled like a country gent taking his sweet time getting there.

"Hey boys," he called to Bobby Lee and Tom Sawyer real friendly like nothing in the world was wrong. "Jump down offa there."

Bobby Lee obeyed, but Tom Sawyer stayed kneeling up on the edge of the well, peering down into it. When he looked up to see who was talking, he rose up in the air about a foot and just floated slow and soft and landed on his bare feet in the warm red dirt.

Eyes big as truck tires, he had never been floated away by anyone before.

Done removing the obstacles, the old man sidled up a couple of feet from the well and took off a brown checked suit vest that didn't have a suit to go with it. He swung it over his left shoulder, and just left it laying there.

He took out a long, delicate smoking pipe from his deep overall pocket and brought it up to his mouth. It was already smoking. Soon as it saw the light of day, it lit itself. Mockin'bird Man, his name because of his magical whistling, took a long draw. He let the smoke circulate in his lungs for a short time. Then, raising his eyes up some, as he exhaled that smoke, he put his lips together in ways only this one man knows how to do. Out'a him came the gentle mournful call of three or four different types of warbler and a cardinal, all singing at the same time, riding out'a his whistling lips on a slow river of smoke.

He repeated the whole thing.

Then he did it again.

Three times he puffed up smoky warbler and cardinal calls. As his lips were closing after the last one, and his exhaled smoke was rising in the air a bold color of red, Squirrel came a-floating on up out'a there. Just sailed slow right outta that water and darkness into the full view of us all, the whole family.

He didn't cry or shock or even wet his drawers. He was hanging there a short spell about three feet above the well. The old man cleared the phlegm outta his throat and spit a doosey into a big blue hydrangea bush. A bunch of bees blasted out'a the deep petals like they were shot out'a pistols.

Mockin'bird chuckled a nice sing-songy thing at the sight of those bees blasted out'a their flowers.

He said, still like there was all the time in the world, "Y'all might want to pluck that child outta thin air b'fore he twists some and goes plunging back down into that there."

Wearing her lovely deep red silk shawl that she always wore, Mama had come down from the house to see what all the yelling was about. She walked over and took Squirrel Martin right out'a the air. She slung him on your hip, smiling at Mockin'bird. Trying not to show how impressed she was, with a shy knowing smile, she floated over to him a burlap bag filled with ripe ears of corn.

"Thank you, Mr. Mockin'bird," she said. Then she walked up to the house with the wind lifting her long black hair and the ends of the red shawl.

That wasn't the last time that old man saved our hide. Once he whistled up a pile of soft hay just as Granddaddy was falling off the roof of the barn and was six feet from crashing onto the still frozen early spring ground. *Smoop* went Granddaddy into the suddenly appearing hay that wasn't there two seconds earlier. He rolled around a little and sunk into the pile, not sure what just happened. Then he popped out, scratched his head and spit into the hay as he walked back to the big, long ladder leaning against the barn, trying like hell to remember what he had gone up there for. After climbing up a few rungs, he couldn't remember.

Confused, he jumped down, spit on the ladder, and ambled away, scratching his head.

White folks know that old colored man as the Mockin'bird Nigga Man. He could whistle the tune of any bird that ever drew a breath. But most white folks didn't know magic's put deep in every single note he whistled up.

"Listen to that lovely whistling from that ugly old nigger over there," hateful white women said harsh about him. Some of'm after they were cruel to the Cherokees or to black folks, and Mockin'bird saw them, when those ladies git home their barn'd be all burned up to pure smoke and char. Their old Civil War KKK grandpa was leaning dead over a fencepost. Or their mean and violent husband's feet were sticking up outta the cow-watering trough.

Colored folks knew a lot better than whites on such things as charms and bird whistling being far more than just bird whistling. Colored folks knew him as the most powerful charm-making man this side'a New Orleans. They called him Mockin'bird Man, without that dread word in the middle, from here clear down to Louisiana.

I never thought much about white folks and blacks being inathing other than just folks since I was little. Maybe deep down somehow I knew our family was full of both. Cherokee, too. Didn't matter to me. Folks were folks. And being honest, I have always felt deep down heart and soul comfortable being in the company of the blacks more than the whites in this town. The blacks see us as who we really are—magical folks who ain't out to do anybody any harm.

Who don't deserve it.

Speaking of those who *do* deserve it, that frightful Tolbert Greaves had begun following me like an angry wasp. I don't know what provoked him after all these years since Mama lit him on fire with magic. He's everywhere I went, a treacherous shadow leering dirty at me, not saying inathing. Last week, I was in town buying some new plates and glasses 'cause ours git broke so easily by Squirrel Martin taking them out into the woods to use as targets for his little old bird shooting rifle. By Tom Sawyer being careless. By Dahlia Rose trying to be careful. And by Granddaddy being drunk or senile. I came out'a Miss Lillian's Thrift Goods loaded down with two boxes full of pretty light green plates, teacups and saucers, and drinking mugs made of dark blue glass.

Tolbert Greaves, that fearsome man whose pants Mama lit on fire by just pointing at him, was standing at the front of my truck with his foot up on the bumper, his arms crossed on top of his knee. He was wearing a black suit, a dirty white shirt, with a black tie all covered in gold horse heads. On his feet, he had on bust-up leather telephone pole climbing boots with the spikes. He wears them no matter what he's doing or who he's with. He looked like a man turned into a horror story.

Not giving myself even a moment to think about being scared, because if I did I would never git over it, I walked right up to him, stopped, looked hard into his face, and then I kept going. Saying mean as I could muster as I passed by, "Unless you're here to help git these here into the back, git off the truck."

Greaves was looking me over good. I felt his harsh eyes touching me disrespectful in all my private places. He didn't say inathing as I walked to the back of the truck, shaking my head and hefting the boxes into the truck bed. Trying to look disgusted, not terrified. When I turned to walk back to git in the truck, he was gone.

A few days later, when I trucked down a load of raspberries, he was down to Mr. Jesse J. Brown's. As I parked the truck and was opening the door to git out, the kids were all jumping out'a the truck bed or streaming out the passenger door to unload our delivery. But they didn't have a chance to git started. Mr. Jesse came out to greet me with a hangdog look on his face. It was hot as blazes, and my bare feet were sticking to the hot tar in his parking lot.

"Ruby," Mr. Jesse whispered, "I'm gonna pay you right now. But I want you to git in that truck of yours and drive away. Never mind about leaving raspberries." He stuffed two five-dollar bills in my hand a little too rough and saw that he startled me.

"Girl, I'm sorry for being all rude, but I'd like to see y'all come back later on. There's a good girl, sugar."

I stood there with my eyes all stretched open, wondering what I had done to make that nice man treat me so. Then I saw Mr. Tolbert Greaves way out in Mr. Jesse's tobacco field sniffing the tobacco leaves. I swear. The man was walking along the rows all bent over like an ape, running his nose over the plants. I'm not sure how Mr. Jesse knew of all the trouble brought to us by that horrible man, but he did, it was plain to see. He wanted me out'a there before Greaves took any notice. Maybe the whole valley knew that man and his kin were out to git us.

Maybe this was so, maybe it wasn't. A few years ago, when he was still alive, Lonny Dale told me that he heard Greaves tell a fella, "We Greaves thought we murdered all them black magic Johnson bitches once. Next time, no weak-hearted ones of us are gonna screw it up. They'll pay for bein' what they are."

What was he talking about?

He was the only one doing inathing to anybody.

***

One thing that man cain't touch: what's done was done. Is it Silas or Hardy? Thank God I wasn't sure which was the daddy of my baby.

I was pregnant for sure.

And I was okay with it. The having a baby part. And the Hardy as the daddy part. The Silas part, forgive me, fuck him and his brutal ways.

One afternoon Hardy and me was together just sitting on our front porch swing. Hardy, who comes up here to visit me a couple of times a week, when Silas is away, told me he loved me. Always has, he says, since he was fourteen and I saw him and Lonny Dale peeing off the old bridge along Red Hand Creek. Hardy started laughing. He said, "Ruby, I loved you up and down since that day I saw you walkin' by on the path and all I could do was pee all over myself."

I was flattered some, and even admitted to myself that me and Hardy seemed more suited to each other than any other boy-man I knew. But I answered, "What more can I say to you, Hardy Jessup? I'm married. I'm pregnant. And if I hadn't married Silas, I probably would'a married your sassy twin brother. This doesn't say much for how I choose my men."

"Doesn't change inathing, Ruby. I'm in love with you, girl or woman. Pregnant or skinny. Twenty years old now or one hundred years old later. It's makin' me crazy."

"Hardy Jessup, I reckon there are more girls to love around these mountains than you can shake a stick at. They're everywhere. More girls than men. A whole lot more. You could have any of'm, or probably all of'm…at the say time," I said , hoping to make him cool down and laugh.

"Don't want any of'm, Ruby…" But then something inside Hardy seemed to tell him to shut himself up right there. And he did. Maybe that something was telling him I was getting uncomfortable. Maybe *he* was getting uncomfortable.

Maybe, just like a man, his brain up and went to thinking on something else without warning, leaving a woman there by herself next to a man's empty body.

Hardy wanted to hold me, so I let him. For a little while he rubbed my behind, but I wouldn't let him touch me anywhere else. And I didn't touch him anywhere at'all.

CHAPTER FIVE

I was pregnant all right. The belly I had then wasn't too big, and it wasn't too small. The morning sickness came for a time but passed on.

Silas said he's happy that we were going to have a baby. But he wouldn't be happy at all unless the baby was a boy. He kept asking me to tell him if it was a boy or a girl, and when I said I don't know yet, he looked at me as if I was lying.

One good thing—he stopped the intercourse with me altogether. He was scared of putting himself up in me.

He said, and I laughed out loud, "Ruby, I ain't putting my thing in y'all until the baby is out. That baby's probably got a mind to bite my thing off, not having no play toys in there besides…" He stopped right there because he had no idea what he was talking about.

Having a baby in me was a peculiar thing. I ain't never had one in me before. But it felt like I been carrying and enjoying carrying this child all'a my life. I know that a woman has hormones and chemicals inside her that make such things natural and good feeling. Until the birth—when the baby stretches out a woman's vagina nearly as big as when a foal as big as a porch swing drops out the rear of a field horse. I wasn't looking too forward to that.

And I wasn't so sure about traipsing down to that damn town to find Doc Turner when the time came. The hating folks down there were likely to shoot me and go on bragging for years how they got two Johnsons with one shot.

But then, nothing exciting happened here anymore, except the kids falling down or crashing outta trees and needing stitches or splints. Or Granddaddy wandering off to town telling folks he's Abe Lincoln's brother come to make all the coloreds slaves again. Sooner or later, the Cherokee sheriff, Mr. Dog and Two Crows, hauled Granddaddy up the driveway road asleep in the back of the big black police car.

"Ruby," the sheriff said to me this last time, "it sure scares me that your granddaddy can say such crazy things when he ain't even drunk. You want to tell me what's going on?"

But he knew I wouldn't say inathing about Granddaddy. The sheriff just smiled and helped me lay Granddaddy either in his bed or plonk him on his decrepit old yellow front porch slider.

"Thank you, Sheriff…Mister…" and I never knew what to call him. "Dog…Two Crows…" So I never finished.

This last time the sheriff hauled Granddaddy home; he lingered a moment in a kind of awkwardness before he slid back into his fancy car. At first, I thought he was trying to git up the nerve to say something secret and romantic, but when he said what he said…I was wishing for inathing but that. Inathing.

"Ruby," the sheriff sort of mumbled low so I could hardly hear, "I know you're pregnant and all…but I need you to do a healin'…"

At the thought of that and because I am not willing to lead folks into the spirit field at all anymore, never mind while I was pregnant, my whole body rushed up into that floating in midair feeling. My mind got hazy and yellow and I fainted right there in the red clay dust at the top of our driveway road, with Sheriff Two Crows and a Dog not sure if he should try to catch me before I fell or wait till I fell so he could not be sure if he should pick me up or let me be.

About a week after he come up the first time, the sheriff came driving back up the driveway road in that big black car of his, trailing a long tail of red dust. He looked like some kind of earthly shooting star. Going real slow, hitting every bump and rock.

All I could fathom was that he was coming up to tell us the U.S. government had finally delivered the "final ultimating," as Granddaddy called it. Telling us to git the hell off the mountain so they could begin flooding the world under seventy feet of river runoff.

When he finally got up here and spilled out'a the car, he had red dust all over him. Red dust on a red man. There was something spooky about that. With his big boots scuffing through the red dirt and kicking pebbles out the way, he came up to the front door.

Even though Granddaddy was sleeping on the porch slider, the sheriff tipped his hat and said "Good mornin'" to him inaway. Granddaddy hawked up some spit, turned his head to the side and let it loose into the pink rosebush without ever waking up. I don't think the sheriff was sure how to respond to that. When I answered the door, the sheriff was all full of "Don't mean to be bothering you, Ruby." He must have said it ten times until I reached out and put my fingertips on his chest and said real slow and sweet, "You ain't bothering me, Sheriff…Dog…Crow…"

And then I said to him straight, "You want to bring your baby son up to the spirit field. That right?"

It startled him I could read that right off him so easy. He nodded and said, "I do. Yes'm."

I thought about that a moment. The story goes, after a few years of the Cherokee sheriff and his Shoshone wife trying to have a child, they finally have one. But the boy is like Squirrel Martin. He's not right in the head. But unlike Squirrel Martin, that baby boy, about five years old now, cain't do hardly inathing for himself. Just yells and drools. They carry him around in a papoose-looking contraption even though he's a boy almost forty pounds. The sheriff's wife is so pained over it, she stops eating altogether. For weeks, they say.

Sheriff was mighty pained, too. He musta been at the end of his rope to gather the nerve to ask me to take the brainlessness out'a his baby son.

"I can pay you cash money, Ruby," the sheriff said sincerely.

I looked at him a bit. "I know you can pay me, Sheriff, in cash money. What I'd prefer is you continue to make sure my family is always safe against the Johnson hating folks in these parts."

His head is down and he was a-studying the ants crawling over his big black boots.

"You don't have to pay me nothin'," I said, "except this here keeping the rednecks off. But if I do this healin' for you, you cain't breathe a word of it to another living soul. Not one. Except for Mrs....Sheriff...Crow.

If the town knew I was changing idiot boys to normal boys, I don't know what kind of reaction they'd have. But I know one thing: whatever it was would eventually turn hateful, add more danger to us and our legend, and do us no good.

He thought my not knowing whether to call him Dog and Two Crows or Sheriff Dog and Whatever was pretty funny, but he didn't say inathing. Just a smile. A lovely soft tender smile on the scarred, rough face of a big, haunted man.

"Okay," he said. And I believed him.

"Tomorrow then," I said to him. "Come about an hour before sunset. Bring a little bit of your boy's Mama's blood sealed up in a glass jam jar. Not much. Just enough to drip out once in a while when I need to drip some.

"Go home now, Sheriff," I said, gentle and pure. "You bathe your baby boy in warm water tonight and then again tomorrow afternoon just before you come back here...with this in it." I reached out my hand and poured a fistful of dry red mountain dust into his palm.

The sheriff knew a second ago there was nothing in my hand. Nothing at all. He was about to make a startled face, but remembered he was up in Johnson country, talking to a Johnson woman. Then he smiled a little nervous and said, "Thank you, Ruby Lee. See y'all tomorrow."

Just before the sheriff climbed back into his car, he stopped and turned on his heel, with the valley all misty now and the ridgelines slicing delicate and blue across it. He came shuffling back. He reached into his shirt pocket and took out a folded piece of paper. "Almost forgot," he said, and smiled again. "I brung you this." Then he left for good.

As he and his big dark car bumped back down the driveway road, clouds of red dust sailing everywhere, I unfolded the handbill and read it:

Redemption County Fiddle Competition
All Fiddlers Welcome—Amateurs or Legends
Young 'n Old
Big Prize Money. Gals OK. No Bribed Judges No More.

I sure am no legend. But I sure am no amateur either. I smiled because providence, the family spirits, or just plain everyday life just found a way for the sheriff to pay me...in a way I was not uncomfortable to accept. I had been competing in that competition since I was ten. Better than all but a couple, but never once winning inathing. Not even third place.

But with our plight with the U.S. Army Corps of Engineers getting close to dire, I plumb forgot about it this year. Maybe at long last I could win this thing.

About an hour before the time I was expecting the sheriff to come back that next afternoon, Mr. Jesse J. Brown came driving up the driveway road completely unannounced. I thought it was the sheriff and his family coming way early. When he finally got his truck all the way up, Mr. Jesse turned off the motor, stepped out and walked right up to me. He was smoking a Viceroy, as usual with the filter torn off. Why he never bought unfiltered Viceroys had been something I wanted to ask him for a long time.

"Ruby," he said, "I feel right disgusted with myself. And I don't blame you if you're disgusted with me, too. I ain't gonna tell you why, but I have to stop buying your raspberries for a spell. But I am gonna advance you one hundred and fifty dollars until next summer. You deserve that, girl, after all these years we done business so good together. And don't you even think about turning me down. I won't have it. No, mam. I just won't have it."

Mr. Jesse, a huge bull of man, looked like he was about to hug me like his long-lost daughter. But he didn't. Before I could say a thing, he tromped back into his truck, gunned the motor, turned around across the front lawn, and started back down the mountain.

Just like that, our livelihood rolled away.

I was still standing there in shock when I saw the sheriff, right on time, driving up the driveway road about ten minutes later, an hour before sunset as requested. He and Mr. Jesse had to pass each other. Our decades of livelihood and good fortune going down. The one thing on earth I would rather die than do on a steady basis coming up.

Rain had poured all morning and the humidity now so thick Squirrel Martin was a-traipsing around trying to cut through it with his pocketknife. Never paying much attention to him when he did these secret things of his. This time I startled and jumped.

"I done it!" he yelled like a banshee.

I looked over at him, puzzled, because he didn't talk much. Then, Squirrel Martin ran off toward the woods, slicing his little knife this way and that, yelling, "Look Ruby, I done it."

Right then the sheriff's car lumbered up to the top of the driveway road. Smiling hello to me, he was pulling his brainless son out'a the back seat. His wife was standing in the dust next to him, looking strong and pretty. She was also looking clear through me; I mean right through my body at the spirit field a little ways up the slope.

Squirrel Martin was still slashing his blade through the muggy, thick, burning air, yelling "I done it!" Granddaddy was pissing on his pissing tree with his overalls all the way down around his ankles. You cain't see the kids, but you can hear 'em off in the woods laughing and calling to one another.

And me, I was standing in the red dust in my bare feet and blue Wrangler men's work pants. As Silas said, "Them pants is too tight on that Hollywood beautiful body, Ruby Lee. Way too tight for a married man to abide outta his wife." He never said nothing more about me changing into something else, though, because he liked looking at a female's shape as much as any man.

And when he was with me in town and damn near every man on the sidewalk spun around after I walk by, Silas didn't even give 'em the dog protecting his property look. He walked around Redemption with me like I was his personal Queen Cleopatra.

Mama used to tell me that cemetery grass is just as lifeless as the folks lying beneath it. It doesn't grow much. But it doesn't really die in drought time. It just stays there, half-alive and half-dead, waiting for us.

Emrald Jean, the sheriff's Injun wife, was nice and agreeable as she could be. When I led them to the spirit field, Emrald Jean knew right away that her family was crossing the line between this world and the next. She lowered her eyes, stopped right at the entrance, and started whispering. The sheriff stopped, too. The brainless boy was wailing.

I do believe the brainless boy was already feeling his new life was just standing there in the spirit field waiting for him. He was about to become a boy empty of his old brainlessness. And he wasn't too sure he was gonna like that.

As he stood there holding his son at the entrance, the sheriff was nervous as a turkey in holiday season, a-lookin' at me with a crazy expression. He was surely thinking: *Ruby, you ain't done nothin' but lead us up into your Johnson family two-hundred-year-old cemetery. Ain't you supposed to mumble or shriek voodoo? Be standin' there dressed in animal skins holding a deer skull? Lay on your hands or bark at the moon? Turn into a crow and peck all'a my boy's misery away? Ain't you supposed to split into three separate women—the white part, the red part and the black part, like all you Johnsons are? And dive right into the boy just like kids bringing their hands to praying and jumping fingertips first into* Red Hand *Creek?*

Somethin'?

As he was thinking this, late afternoon passed and a big, bloody, red as a beet setting sun was dripping down the backside of the hills.

It was huge, and the shades of red were like nothing we had ever seen. The sheriff and his family, scared some, took a step into the spirit field to come over closer to me. I didn't mind because I was scared some, too. I haven't ever been in the cemetery field with a sun bloody and huge like that before.

Not saying inathing, I turned and walked out into the middle of the graves. When I got there, I held up my arms as I always do. This calls up the lady kin ghosts. All around us began appearing the whole bunch of our lovely old ghost women. Every one of'm was glowing in garnety red light and floating around the old gravestones so smooth you'd swear all this was a glistening red dream from under the sea.

If you looked close, you could see that all'a'm were bloody and beat up, still looking like they were just butchered by those Civil War soldiers. All kilt together on the same night, almost sixty-five years ago. But if you didn't look close, all you'd see is twenty-five beautiful Johnson women kin, all ages, infants to grannies. All floating around us gentle and loving as can be, knowing we was up to something.

But as quickly as they started to appear and as the red light started to shine, they were just gone. The whole place went quiet. The kind of quiet you just know is there for good. To my knowledge, this was the first time ever that one of us led someone in and the lady kin ghosts decided to be uncooperative.

I don't know who looked more forlorn—me standing there all alone, or the spirit field lonely and empty like any old up mountain graveyard.

I didn't know what to do. We all stood there a while.

Then, like I had been doing charms and chants all my life instead of avoiding them like the plague, I narrowed my eyes. I turned slowly and looked at the sheriff and his wife and their drooling boy, who was screaming and squirming now. He saw those ghosts for a split second and even though he was brainless; he wanted nothing to do with them, or me.

I called the three of'm into the middle of the spirit field and had them climb up on the aboveground grave of Effie Trueblood Johnson, the one hanged for being a witch in 1692. I held out my hand for the jar of the brainless boy's mother's blood. Not much in there. I screwed off the lid and flung my arm out like I was planting seeds, sprinkling the blood out everywhere. It fell on the grass, on the sheriff and Emrald Jean, on the graves. And especially on the brainless boy who had whipped down his drawers and was taking a pee against the grave of Evangeline Johnson. Long before the Civil War, she gave up witching and healing to fall in love with a town boy named Harlan Lee and moved off the mountain to live clear out'a Redemption County—one of the few Johnsons, male or female, ever to do so. But like a magical fairy or something like that who is a special magical and tender creature, the outside world did her no good. Her boy left her. They found her drowned and somebody a Johnson had to fetch her and bring her back home.

When the jar of blood was empty and the sheriff was hauling his son's pants up, I threw the glass jar down against the gravestone so it broke. I held my hands out, palms up. I closed my eyes and saw in my mind a little boy lost in a big dark cave. So lost, he was just lying there sobbing.

I raised both my arms and said loud and firm, words I had never said before in my life. Words that just spoke out'a my mouth:

I charge this Mother's blood to aid my spell,
that this here boy will be well,
that by free he will be blessed,
with total health and happiness.

I ask you spirits to hear my call,
that it may be correct and good for all.

After a pause, I finished:

I call upon a breath of wind,
empowered by the Spirit of Air,
to carry my spell toward my dead kin,
and gracefully deliver it there.

By all the power of three times three,
this spell bound to truth shall be,
to cause no harm, nor return on me,
cure this boy's addled brains, so shall it be!

The woods groaned. Our lady kin ghosts appeared again, looking all shocked and alarmed and not at all expecting me to call a charm, let alone as powerful as I just did.

Then, long heavy gusts of air blew in on us from all sides and in the middle of the field where we were it blew straight up like a fountain of wind. And every one of those women ghosts shot right up with it. Like fireworks. All twenty-five kin ghosts exploded above the field and sprinkled down on us like brilliant red sparks. Falling slow like snowflakes. And when the red chips of light falling down touched us, the sun dropped down behind the horizon so fast it was like an apple falling out'a tree. Sunset was over before it began, and the four of us were lying down on the ground in the pitch dark.

Everything began to spin.

Feeling a strange sensation on the skin of my left palm, I clenched it into a fist. Without me making any effort, my hand opened up slow and graceful like a blooming flower. There on my palm, regally, sat a glittering red stone about the size of a chokecherry.

The beautiful thing just materialized there. I felt shock waves of pure electricity and light coursing from the palm of my hand, up my arm, and into my shoulders. Right up into my brain and then shoot straight through the length and breadth of my body.

I was a bright red light. I lit up the darkness.

Covering the distance between me and the boy with my feet never touching ground, I grabbed the brainless boy by the hair and pried his mouth open. Words I cain't remember came floating out'a my mouth and gathered all around us like little different color bubbles. He was protesting up a storm, the brainless boy, screeching. Calmly and firmly, I stuck the red stone in his mouth. I pushed his gape jaw closed. I grabbed him by both ears. I brought a long deep scream from the beginning of time out'a my soul and let it fly out'a my mouth. Right at his face. I threw the brainless boy to the ground.

That's all the Johnson ghost women needed to see. And just like that, they formed a long, floaty line and trailed right through each of us.

Starting with me.

Then Emrald Jean.

Then the sheriff.

And last, the boy.

A moment later, the sheriff, his wife, their boy and me were waking up lying on the ground. The next day sun was rising like a pink and orange blurry eye over the mountains to the east. We all looked at each other. The whole night passed.

Shaking their groggy heads, all'a sudden the sheriff and Emrald Jean remembered something and look quickly over to their boy. But the boy wasn't crying or drooling or shitting his pants at all. He was quiet. He was just sitting there smiling in the dewy grass along with the rest of us.

I cured that boy. I woke up his damaged brain so that although he isn't a genius by far, he's smart enough to play and smile and learn and talk. I must admit that I enjoyed what I did. And how I did it. I didn't do inathing I was taught. I didn't say inathing I learned. I just made up what I did as I went along. And it worked out fine.

Okay, so I admit. Charms and spells might come easier to me than I thought.

But bringing me back down to earth in a hurry, when the sheriff and his family left, and I went back to the house, Macy told me Bobby Lee's gone and done it. He'd gathered up some clothes and his banjo and walked into the woods. He never came out.

Granddaddy and me suspect he'd gone to that military life he'd been yearning for since he was a sprite. But we cain't know for sure.

CHAPTER SIX

We just had a little scare. This morning I felt blood dripping down my legs. Before I dared touch myself there to see what it was, I said a little made up spell to keep my baby from bleeding out'a me. Before I could move or yell for anybody to come running, Macy walked into the kitchen wearing nothing but a man's shirt, not her own, just a couple of buttons holding together the front. Grass stains all over her knees. And her hair a mess, like a little hurricane full of bits of dry grass and dandelions just blew through it.

"Ruby!" she screamed loud as a girl can scream. "You're sloshin' blood all over. What's got into you?"

I cleaned myself and the floor up and lay down for a while. The bleeding wasn't that much considering my usual menstrual time, which this couldn't be, me being pregnant and all. I don't know what it was, and hopefully, it wasn't nothing harmful to my baby.

And I plumb forgot to ask Macy why she was walking around like she just fell out'a a hayloft with a couple of naked boys.

***

The Redemption Mountain Musical Society Fiddling Competition crept up fast. They were holding it at the Redemption Town Hall on a big wood platform they built each year right over the granite front steps. Lord knows where anybody in Redemption could git $50? But they said they had it and prize money was gonna go $25 for 1st place, $15 for 2nd, and $10 for 3rd.

Silas was never happy about my fiddle playin', even though I can outplay almost every man in the county. "Ruby, tappin' your feet with that thing juttin' outta your neck makes you look hillbilly," he always said. But I know what Silas really meant is he thinks his men friends will tease him because his wife can do so many things, and all Silas could do is hack coal out'a the ground, hold his liquor and poke his wife from behind whenever he had a mind.

It was a nice sunny day and the heat wasn't bad enough to make playing a chore. "Ruby Johnson," one of the judges growled to me after I pulled up in the truck to the parking area with all the kids hanging off. "Ruby Johnson, gals and fiddle playing competitions never sit right. Why don't you go park your behind in a church or somethin' more girlish? Better yet, go up yonder an' play fer them dead Johnson ghost a-yours. Folks don't want you down here no more. An' sure don't want you winnin' no fiddlin' prize."

The man was grinning at me big and toothy so everybody nearby would think he was wishing me good luck.

I smiled back at him, thinking, *Go to Hell, you fat stupid redneck bastard.*

"I think fiddle playin' and females is as natural as squirrels up a tree," said Hardy Jessup in a low whispery voice right behind my ear, sneaking up behind me with his ma.

"Ruby," said old Miz Jessup straightaway. She was wearing a pair of men's big work boots that had been painted bright blue, some kind of orange shirt dress and a Boston Red Sox baseball hat, probably with no idea what the *B* stands for. "Girl, you come from the strangest folks I know. Not a full-blood white among you. All that kin blood so mixed up I swear it must be a different color. How are you and your granddaddy, Ruby? Your pregnancy goin' smooth?" she asked polite enough.

"Fine, Miz Jessup. And the children are, too."

I knew she heard about Bobby Lee running off, but she didn't say inathing about it. Nobody said inathing since he lit out, because nearly every family in the hills had at least one son or daughter who crept out in the middle of the night for greener pastures.

"Where did y'all git the two dollars they're chargin' this year for the entry fee, Ruby?" Miz Jessup asked in a nosy way.

When I didn't answer, both Hardy and his ma knew I hadn't read the handbill close at all. "Oh my Lord," I said and put my hand up and covered my mouth. "Two dollars? I didn't think that far," I answered soft and upset, "I was too excited by the notion of playing in public and maybe winning something for my effort. They never charged entry fees before."

"Two dollars…" I said again, as if I were really saying two million.

Miz Jessup pressed something into my hand. "You go play your heart out, Ruby *Jessup*. If you win somethin', then pay us back. If ya don't, my family owes you somethin' on account of all them years you tried to be girlfriend to Lonny Dale."

Both the Jessups smiled at me. Hardy's smile reminded me of the one he gets when I know he's about to try to kiss me.

Then in a brief time delay, Hardy and me shot a look at each other. His ma just called me Ruby *Jessup*. Miz Jessup could see me blushing, not knowing what she said that caused it.

Hardy, smiling that same aroused smile, said, "You kill 'em, Ruby Lee."

Then, he went wandering off to say hello to the folks that had known him, and hated me, for all our lives.

When I was warming up, the other fiddlers were warming up too, standing under trees or out by themselves somewhere on the grass. I was surprised. For not playing too steady, my fingers felt good and nimble. I couldn't feel the thorn scratches or the finger wound under the black fingernail. My bow hand was smooth. I felt I was running it through silky water.

Twenty-five people were there to compete. Mostly it was the fiddling folks from our part of the mountain. We all know each other. Some old hundred-year-old granddaddy down to eight-year-old Ricky Sprot, one of Squirrel Martin's sometimes friends.

And our young cousin Carter Addison was there, too. And a few strangers who said they come from places most none of us had heard of.

The first fiddler to compete at the Redemption fiddling contest was a stranger.

He walked out on to the stage like he been on a million stages, smiled once, and proceeded to leverage the fiddle sorta against his armpit. Looking strange like that, and all us others standing there with ours shooting out from under our chins, we almost started to laugh. Until the music that came a playing out'a that young man and his armpitty-held fiddle washed over us like beautiful waves from the River Jordan.

He played a lightning fast breakdown number. Then a sweet and aching love song. That fella's playing peeled people's souls right off their bones. Not a person moved. People even seemed to feel that clapping and hooting would cheapen what the young man had just done with a mere fiddle. Leave it to Miz Jessup and Hardy. They got the crowd a-going.

Before the day even started, this amazing player had already won. Question was - who would git 2nd and 3rd?

After he finished, I stood listening to the first ten contestants play their two songs. Most were powerful players. Born and raised with fiddles in their fists when they were still waddling around in burlap diapers.

It all went fast. At my time, I walked out on the stage trying to posture like I wasn't pregnant, and, just for no reason I can tell, I dropped my bow. I dropped it right in front of me, and my left foot kicked it somehow end over end like a long, skinny football. It sailed clear over the end of the stage and landed on the bosom of one of the White sisters. She had been standing ten feet back from the stage with her three spinster sisters. And she's just as spinstery as they are. This was Pernie White, I believe.

Pernie was the White sister that sat behind the wheel of their old black Dodge touring car doing the steering. While another sitting beside her worked the gas and made the windshield wipers flap when it rained. But they never went out driving in the rain. So sometimes that old lady made the windshield wipers flap back and forth just for the hell of it. That one was Elsie. The other two, Pearl Jean and Hortensia, sat in the backseat and sang hymns.

All around the valley they drove, four old biddies who owned most of the land on the east end of Redemption. Four old sisters who never kissed a man. Who had probably never been anywhere alone except the outhouse for their whole lives. They were not mean, especially. More mannerless and crotchety. Had to many opinions and would spit them over everyone they saw. I saw all four of'm screaming at a tree once. They were like some four-headed creature from ancient times that was so disturbing folks were too scared to talk to it, even if it knew every secret in the world and would tell anyone who asked. Fear of unfamiliarity sure is a powerful threat to the way so many folks want to believe how daily life should be.

With my fiddle bow resting on the old lady's big old droopy bosoms, the reverend from the Church of Christ the Carpenter walked up to her and just stood there. *What do I do?* he's thinking. Wouldn't do at'all for him to reach into the bosom of an old Catholic lady to dig out the fiddle bow for not just a young lapsed-Baptist gal but a full-blood witch.

None of us could hardly believe it. That old lady was at least eighty-five years old. She reached up her hand, swiped the bow off her big chest, grinned at the reverend, and flung it back my way like a bow-shot arrow. Was surprising enough she could find the bow on those big things, let alone fling it hard and straight about twenty feet. My bow was scooting smooth back across the stage and in a moment I had it in my fingertips, poised to begin playing.

Our first song was supposed to be something everybody in the audience was expected to know well enough to hum, sing or clap along to.

I hadn't given my selections any thought at all right up to the time I was standing there ready to play, seeing I know so many tunes. Hundreds of tunes. Mountain music, church music, flat land country music. I know maybe one thousand tunes.

Before I knew it, I was playing a number by a young man named Dickson Shaw from up Oklahoma way. It's called "Appalachian Fire," and it is a mess of lightning fast bowing and fingers moving faster'n the eye can see. I musta been doing good because all the folks, including other players—and the stranger player—stopped whatever they were doing. Every one of'm turned to the woody old temporary stage to listen to me. Half of'm even started clapping and hooting.

When I ended with a flourishing bunch of flashing bow strokes, they all started yelling and whistling. Even the armpitty player nobody had seen before was clapping a little.

Land sakes, I began thinking. *Maybe I can actually win this thing.*

Then, I raised my bow, getting ready to play the tune that nobody was supposed to have ever heard before. This was the judges' way of seeing if any of us could write our own songs 'sides just playing songs already writ by others. But I didn't see it that way. Not at'all.

All my life since I first picked up Daddy's legless brother's fiddle when I was a witchy little toddler, I been playing tunes that just come into my head while I play them. Things I never heard before. It's like somebody else was playing these tunes and passing them through me like a breeze lifting the curtains through a springtime open window.

I gently touched my bow to my fiddle strings, and *mercy me*, I began to cry. For five minutes, I shut my eyes and let all my tears fall as I played a slow sweet lament that city folks call a ballad. Making it up as I went. My playing reminded me of all the folks I had ever known. All the folks I ever loved. Who have lit out or died or just plumb one day turned up missing.

When I finished, my eyes were still closed. But my ears were hearing the whole of Redemption County whistling and clapping loud and yelling my name. It felt so good. Playing for people always feels good. But playing so heartful and sweet and having folks who usually spit on me think my playing was the ovation kind, I felt wonderful. Even if my black fingernail was throbbing now.

After the last fiddler played, surprisingly, the judges were done with the judging faster than anybody felt comfortable about. The whole county had made a great effort to conduct the competition fair and square, with no giving mares and milk cows to judges on handshake promises to vote for kin. In no time at all, one of the judges stepped up to a place at the front of the stage and held up his arm. Immediately the people, about four hundred, shut up.

"Ladies…and gents…on behalf of the Redemption Mountain Musical Society"—he grinned big and dumb—"it is my pleasure to announce this year's winners."

He paused and looked around a little as if he were having trouble believing anybody out there gave a damn about what he had to say. No one was screaming at him to "Get the hell off the stage, you Presbyterian bastard."

Looking pleased with himself, he continued.

"Sometahms…" he said slow as mildew building, "sometahms things go not according to the plan. And this is one of'm sometahms. We have a winner. And we have a third placer." He puffed up his big red ripe tomato looking face and spit out, "Trouble is…we got a mess of second placers, too."

"So let's just mosey through this. Third place - Jacob Lee Dickason of right here Redemption, North Carolina." Not many people liked Jake Dickason or his hide-tanning family. They clapped cordial enough for a soul to feel good about himself for a few seconds.

"First place, Arnold Ploy from over Nashville, Tennessee." The stranger with the armpittish fiddle holding style. He got fewer claps than Jake Dickason, but unanimous and respectful "man 'o man!" head twists and whistles from every single person in attendance. Including me.

"Now here's the tricky part, folks. We have us a few second placers. All of'm fine fiddlers. All of'm coulda won if a certain fiddler here had …stayed …home …in …Nashville," the tomato looking fella joked, drawing out his words like they were made from stretch material, getting a few small chuckles.

"So here's what we got.…in second place number 3, Clancy Meter from Red Hand." There was some choppy clapping and no hooting at all.

"…In second place number 2, Carter Addison." Carter, our cousin, got a thunderous response because he is truly a fine young fiddler, and folks cain't figure out why he hasn't left the mountain to go be famous somewhere. Or why he only scored a second place tie?

"…An' tied for second place number 1, Ricky Sprot, eight-year-old prodigy son of Piny and Muldoon Sprot from Bulls County*…and…Ruby Lee Johnson*!"

Little Sprot got all kinds of whoops and whistles on account of him being two feet tall.

And me? That's all he said. The judge whiffed out my name like it was a foul smell and he wanted to git away as fast as possible.

Nobody could tell who they were clapping for—Sprot or me.

Hardy Jessup and Miz Jessup came rushing over to me, not sure if they should be reacting because I got robbed? Or thrilled to death I finally took home a prize? "My Lord!" cried Miz Jessup. "Clancy Meter and an eight-year-old Sprot same as you for second place? Judges been gargling with sheep dip? Don't you think, Hardy? Them judges drunk or somethin'?"

First place or a confusing tie for second was all the same to me. Fact is, I played my heart out and my heart was glad I did. Keeping my record going, I'm still the only woman ever that played in the fiddle competition. And now, after five times, finally winning something.

When they tallied up the winnings, the Ploy fella from Nashville went home with $25 cash money. That little kid who won third went home with his $10 happier than a pig in shit. Me and the other three, we split up $15 three ways. I got my $5. Half the boy third placer got. He got talent, but no soul.

I have all the soul in the world. But clearly passion in playing and me being female is only worth a little more than half of nothin'.

***

I had another bad scare. Because I was carrying a baby, I had to go to the outhouse three or four times during the night. I loved lightly skimming my bare feet in the dark through the cool damp grass, the blades all full of life and happiness and moisture sliding across the soles and between my toes. It felt like the good angels there to protect us in the darkness were kissing my feet.

One middle of the night, I found my way across the grass, went into the outhouse, closed the door and did what I had to do. I was singing in there. When I was coming back out, I walked right straight into a dark figure standing there waiting for me. The fright knocked me right over. There wasn't a moon. We didn't have electric lights. For one split second I saw a face. A face all scarred up that chills me dead cold. Tolbert Greaves. He didn't say inathing. He only stood there with a hateful grin looking down at me all spread-eagle in the grass. Then, he slowly turned around and took his sweet time walking back into the woods.

That man just wanted me to know how easy it was to git to me. And that he coulda done inathing to me he wanted. And even me only being a couple hundred feet away from the house, there wasn't much I could do to save myself had he set his mind from surprising me to hurting me.

I didn't tell anyone about it. Not even Hardy Jessup. I don't know why. Then, we Johnsons and everybody else in Redemption got a big dose of harsh reality that made such things as fiddling contests and danger in the dark seem not quite so important.

CHAPTER SEVEN

The facts were the U.S. Army Corps of Engineers and the U.S. Government were coming in. No ifs, ands, or buts anymore. That reservoir project was finally right up the front of the line. Those jaspers were scouting out the local boundaries, starting with our land. Surprising me one day, a few of'm were just standing in the front yard when Squirrel Martin and I were stepping out the front door. One of those fellas said, "It don't matter to none of us which'a these valleys git the flood, you or them over there to Red Hand. Both are near perfect places to put the new reservoir. But the State of North Carolina wants to git a little somethin' outta this, too." As he ended that sentence, he was looking all around like he was casing out our property to figure out where he was gonna build himself a house.

"Thing is, Miss Johnson," the USACE fella said to me, "the State of North Carolina wants your land. Every twig and stone of it. Fine land this is—3,957 acres. More trees per acre on your mountainside than anywhere else in the state. And that's a fact."

I was too dumbstruck to even blink. The heartless man went on. "So how we're figuring it, you sell us your land and we'll help you git resettled someplace else. Wherever you want in Redemption County."

"That all?" I say, mocking him. "You buy our land right out from under us. And all you're gonna do is fix us up somewhere we don't want to go? And you git all'a this here?"

The man took out his handkerchief and mopped his face. He blew his nose, shooting a little snot out into the air. "No, mam, Ruby, that ain't all at'all. If your land's being logged and loggin's creatin' all kinds of jobs for folks, who on earth would want to flood out such a thriving town?"

He took a long look at his snot achievement on his faded yellow monogrammed hanky. "You'd be rich in pride knowing you did the folks in this town a service not none of 'em'll be able to repay. Yes, mam. The whole valley will love you Johnsons like no others."

I stood there, frozen. Out'a nowhere, a big, long blacksnake came moseying out'a the tall grass and crawled on by not three feet from where we were standing. All'a us forgot where we were and what was happening for a time as we watched the huge thing slink off through some more tall grass and slither right up the side of Squirrel Martin's holy murple woodshed. And disappear into the old Model T up there on top of it.

Squirrel Martin stood there with his mouth open. Slow as sap dripping, he says, "Holy crap, look at that bastard."

Even the USACE men snapped out'a their snake fascination and shot startled looks at me, that said: *that touched boy just spoke human words, ain't that somethin'*. I *do* believe I had an expression on my sweet face that looked like that snake just crawled right up my leg, singing church hymns.

Squirrel Martin had spoken sensible human words.

And man oh man, I could tell he didn't like the feeling of those things floating out'a his mouth. For him, human word talking springing out'a you feels like your mouth is full of worms.

Hanky man got back to business.

"The way we see it, Miss Johnson, you don't sell, the town you live in is gonna be underwater by next spring. You keep you your place but you don't have no town to go to. And no people to know. Everything below'll be full'a fish and snappin' turtles. Ain't much of a choice. But know one thing, if they was really playing dirty, the U.S. government could empower the State of North Carolina to take your land by eminent domain."

"What's a-ment domain?" I asked, a sad look on my face.

"Mam, it's when the government sends in a fleet of trucks and a bunch of cops to pack you up and drive you out—not paying you a damn thing. Or payin' you two turds an acre. Next day the big Caterpillar tractors and men with them big, huge tree cuttin' saws come. And it ain't no home after that. It's progress. For them all around, getting jobs cuttin' down all your trees, a buncha folks will be workin' and won't starve. Progress is in dyin' need in this area, mam, in dyin' need...and progress in Redemption County is...well, up to you."

He went on to explain, but we never understood his point, that throughout the country in 1929, especially in the South, especially in Appalachia, especially here in Redemption County, the economy was collapsing. That's what he said. Straight-faced. Hell, even I know the only economy we ever had down here beyond tobacco and fruits and vegetables and still whiskey was when the picture show theater opened up in Quigley's old barn in 1925. He named it The Time Square Thee-A-Der after a picture postcard of New York City he saw once. He painted the name on a marquee of a big hunk of plywood in red house paint. They made $127 dollars that year, three cents a ticket. Economy, my ass.

***

Beyond Tolbert Greaves staring me frightened that time and looking at me like he was raping me right there in public, I got another reason to hate and fear that man.

One hot day Squirrel Martin was watching a big black tin can of a car with no roof and four tires all looking like they were spinning in different directions. It was traveling fast on the valley road right toward where he was standing at the bottom of our two-mile long driveway. He had gone down there without telling anyone. I think he was so curious after hearing for so long about the flood that was coming, he went down to see it roll on in.

Him being down there at all, never mind alone, was something we just never did. He knew better.

Unless we were going to town in my truck, none of us would cross that line of our land's red dust giving way to the black tar all full of stuck frogs and honeybees of that road. White Southern Protestant civilization at both ends. Folks living on that tar wanted nothin' but nothin' to do with us unless they was ailing bad enough to need healing. And we sure wanted nothin' to do with them. I reckon 'cause of his brainlessness Squirrel Martin really didn't know why.

That black car a-zooming his way, long rifle barrels and men's hats was all you could see setting in it. Nobody had told him of no year-round open season on Johnsons. He just stood there gawking.

The big ugly car slowed and stopped right where Squirrel Martin was, under a big old ancient chestnut tree. Heat had the road tar melted up and bubbling in little black tar pools. The black car's backfiring and farting gas stank like an old drunk Rebel grandpa. For almost a minute, all those men did was stare at him. Sun's beaming down. Car engine sounds like it's about to grind dead. Little gusts of summer breeze are kicking up red dust devils that spin glorious until they git stuck and collapse like disintegrating dust ghosts into the moist tar. And the worth or pleasure of hurting the boy was being evaluated by four ignorant men. One of'm setting in the back seat holding a buckshot rifle said slow as dry rot, "You the retard Johnson, boy? Named Squirrel or Beaver or somethin'?"

It was Tolbert Greaves doing the talking.

Feeling the hot red dust on the bottom of his bare feet and wondering if he should just plain git and fade away right before their eyes, no human words were festering in Squirrel Martin's mind to say inathing back to that mean fella. 'Cause he didn't speak in words. He was going over those fellas and figuring them out as if his eyes was a bloodhound. Not much to 'em. Farm hands. One was a gravedigger. Tolbert Greaves was sitting way back so you couldn't see his face. Squirrel Martin didn't need to see no bastard's face to know who he was. He was the only dangerous one, Squirrel could tell. The others were numbskulls.

They sure thought they had themselves a retard to push around though. The fella, Greaves, with the buckshot rifle, sat forward and grinned, slow. One of the other jaspers told him, "White retards are just as bad as niggers. A Johnson retard is worse than niggers. Shoot that little bastard."

Still grinning a smirky looking thing, Greaves raised the rifle up and took aim right at Squirrel. Not two-feet away. But then he twirled it around and smashed the butt against the side a Squirrel's face.

Next thing Squirrel knew, he was hanging upside down, his ankles bound up tight. A long rope all ragged and thin bound his feet and slung all the way up about twenty feet over a branch high up a tree. One of the men had hold of the other end. Squirrel Martin was swinging upside down. He was scared to death.

Those men had him swinging over a little inlet of marshy pond in long slow swings like a feather floating back and forth through the thick summer air. His hair hanging down, running over the surface like a bird skimming for catfish.

A few more swings, and lowering him after each one, his head was plowing through the water just below his upside down nostrils.

"Hey, you men," Squirrel Martin screamed as water was pouring into his nose. "Please dona do this. I ain't but a boy. I truly ain't."

But what came out'a his mouth was "I done it. I done it. Trash bastard whites."

One of the men standing on a big old red dusty bluff on the side Squirrel was swinging toward yelled out, "Squirrel boy, you done it all right. Squirrel boy here's so spooked he's pissing them filthy overalls. You a disgusting piece of shit, Johnson boy. A real piece of Johnson turd." All the men whistled and whoooweeed.

As he swung back and forth, water was now rushing into his ears and more poured into his nose until he spun and crashed to the side of the creek where Tolbert Greaves was waiting for him.

Greaves was lifting his leg up sideways like he was gonna stomp a snake. That man's what God himself would define as pure evil.

"Done it, trash bastard!" came screaming out'a Squirrel's brainless mouth. Then, "You done it, bastard!"

"We done it, all right, retard boy. I know you ain't capable of words. An' nothin' sensible comes shittin' outta your dumb ass mouth." The bottom of Greaves' boot was heading toward Squirrel's face. "But ya know what? Being a retard ain't no reason to pity a Johnson like you. No, it ain't indeed."

Tolbert Greaves tried three times to stomp Squirrel in the face as he swung up over the bluff. Each time he barely caught an ear or missed altogether. Didn't hurt him like he wanted. When on the next swing Squirrel swung toward Tolbert Greaves, the big boot heel didn't miss this time. It came crashing down and broke Squirrel's nose. Greaves had grabbed hold of the rope instead of kickin' the air and was trudging on him with his foot. Being upside down, blood couldn't flow out and Squirrel's nose. He couldn't breathe. Then, Greaves let the rope go.

But this you won't believe. Not in a million years.

When Greaves let go of the rope, Squirrel Martin Johnson hung there, swung all the way over, like Greaves still got a hold.

Defying gravity.

Squirrel hanging dead still in the air, way over to the side. Even though he walked straight up the side of a cottonwood tree once, Squirrel Martin was a might shocked himself.

Tolbert Greaves got angry. He's thinking, *What's this here Johnson devilry? What is this scary ghosty boy gonna do next? Float me in the air? Turn me into a runt hog?*

Then, a loud gunshot. Squirrel felt his face burn like it burst into flames.

Back at our place, Me, Tom Sawyer, and Lonny Dale Jessup knew something was wrong because right at sunset the spirit field starts to shine up brilliant red and the lady kin ghosts are flying all around tearing out their hair. One of'm was showing us a smoky outline of Squirrel's face right over her own face. It was Lonny Dale who thought to go to the old swimming pond on the far edge of our land just off the valley road toward downtown Redemption. I never had a chance to ask him after how he knew to go there and why so self-confidently. He just walked straight there fast down the mountain through the woods with me and Bobby Lee trying to keep up. There were times, I swear, I didn't know if I was more than a lifted-up dress and a lie down in the grass to Lonny Dale Jessup. But he loved Squirrel Martin. Lonny Dale went out'a his reckless, selfish, cocky way to look after him, and spend time with him when he was up our place and was supposed to be visiting me.

"Ruby Lee." Lonny Dale would cock his head, whistle, and say, "That brother of yours is the most terrifying and interesting boy I ever did see. You'd think he was a right moron by the look and sound of him. But take him out into the woods and you'll see him lord over the animals. Talk to 'em. Make 'em laugh. I swore I saw him fly right up into the air when he thought I was far behind."

We found Squirrel where Lonny Dale brought us. Right off, I was squeezing tiny pellets of buckshot out'a the skin on his face. My hands were all bloody. So were Bobby Lee's. Squirrel Martin's nose was broken and Bobby Lee had to grab it square and move it back straight. Squirrel Martin howled.

Once we got him home, he couldn't see very well or touch his face for two weeks as all the little holes healed. He had nightmares about it for a long time.

Those men having their fun with Squirrel Martin got all over Redemption. The story got jazzed up some. Folks said he was swinging back and forth and those men were taking target practice on him. Trying to see how close they could git without hitting him. Tolbert Greaves lost because he hit my little brother square in the face with a load of buckshot.

Strange thing, because Squirrel Martin was a Johnson folks didn't know if they should pity him or be glad he was almost kilt. 'Cause he was the retard Johnson; folks were leaning toward "too bad Greaves wasn't shootin' shotgun shells instead of buckshot. Would'a taken the kid's head clean off."

Folks liked the sound of that. But those men only told half the story. Folks would've shot them for sure for being insane if they had told the full truth.

After he got face-shot, Squirrel went swinging back across the pond. The man holding on to the rope got startled, he let it go. Down plunged my brother into the creek. The rope was roaring over the branch. For almost two minutes, the men didn't see him. Then, just as a couple of those boneheads were wrestling with their conscience whether to dive in after him, he came up. He shot out'a the water like a big jumping catfish.

All'a him shot out. He was a foot above the water. All'a him. Right side up. He was just floating there in the air with the rope still tied around his ankles. As the birds were calling and branches were swaying, slow as a feather Squirrel Martin floated down little by little. His bare feet touched the surface—and stayed there.

The men saw Squirrel Martin Johnson, most brainless boy in North Carolina, standing square on the water like the Lord himself. He was even rocking a little on top of the turbulence he made.

"You see this?" the rope-letting-go man asked the huge fat fella in the bust overalls. The fat fella fell down hard on his knees. "Holy Mother'a God," he was muttering slow in a stupefied trance. "Holy Mother'a…"

Folks say Squirrel Martin Johnson stood there looking from shore to shore for a while. Not liking this one damn bit, Tolbert Greaves took aim at him again, this time with the other fella's loaded shotgun with real shells.

His face bleeding all over, outta Squirrel's mind came "No more of that, Mr. Greaves. Time you boys went along." But outta him flew: "I! Done! It!" He said it so fierce, the men heard, "Git now, you mean bastards. You ain't gonna like what happens here next if you ain't gone in no time flat. Git now."

The man on the red dust bluff with Tolbert Greaves grabbed Tolbert two fists by the shirt and dragged him into the bushes and then to the trail back to the car. Over on the other side, the skinny jasper that had been holding the rope suddenly whomped him up a load of fear strength. He grabbed old fatty under each armpit and lifted him right to his feet. Then, one trying to carry the other, they stumbled off the big rock and fell into a formation of jagged stones and boulders before they could clear the place and find the car.

Last they saw of Squirrel Martin Johnson was him looking like Hillbilly Jesus walking on water with fifty feet of rope like a monstrous beaten snake under his toes.

And honestly? It took him till he was five to realize that all folks don't stand on water. Not even I can do it. But when I'm standing in the spirit field with the lady kin ghosts flapping and storming around, I can look into you and make the cancer in your black lungs just plain go away. But walkin' on water? I wouldn't even try it for fear of offending God. But Squirrel Martin? He did it all the time.

After that, I put a hex on the bottom part of our driveway road. Unless folks were coming up to receive our hospitality, folks scared to death of us but needing a healing, you'd just drive right past the dusty old entrance up to us a million times. "Damn thing used to be here, right next to that huge old chestnut," they'd all steam. But that's all they'd do, steam. And eventually, shaking their heads, knowing black magic was afoot, they'd drive their old clunky car, Johnson hate, and half-flat tires away.

Granddaddy and Tom Sawyer didn't know what to do about those men nearly killing Squirrel Martin. Tom got so angry he took a big tree chopping axe and whipped it right through the wall'a the barn. Granddaddy swore up a storm and then got drunk.

A couple of days after that, the USACE men came by to give us a date for when we had to decide what we were going to do. Six months. Next spring.

Nothin', not even the State of North Carolina hanging Lonny Dale Jessup, then dumping him all stiff on his ma's front yard, was more on people's minds than the flood. Hell, most'a North Carolina never heard the word *reservoir*. Flooding folks out'a house and home to make a monstrous huge drinking water lake, folks heard of that.

On the other side of Seminole County, the U.S. Army Corps of Engineers rolled in one day. Told a whole town it had to move up the valley five miles. An' if they didn't, was nothin' to the USACE. "Y'all just wake up drowned sixty feet underwater one mornin'. Do whatever the hell you wanna do, you dumbass hillbillies."

Some of'm wouldn't clear out. Dynamite leveled dams on three rivers cutting through over there. Within two hours, cows were floating around and them folks that refused to move up to the new town were floating around, too. Some of'm had dumped some bacon and cider in rowboats and sat there holding the oars ready to go, thinking the flood was gonna wash over the ground nice and polite. The water came roaring over the hills and thundering down to flat land so fast and so powerful, them rowboats was crushed and broken like a bunch of boulders dropped on Coke bottles. Over a hundred stubborn ones drowned. Found most of'm tangled up in trees that one minute were sixty feet above the ground, and next were ten feet of treetop poking outta turbulent water looking like more ragged steeples than a person can count.

A couple of days later, those treetops were ten feet under and disappeared forever. The old town was named Cicero. The new town up on high ground they built in a month. Named it City of Progress, even though it was a town of only six hundred folks with nothing resembling a mayor. And they didn't build enough of it. There was a lot more of'm folks homeless than them *cheap old come in slabs you nail together* shacks could accommodate. A bunch'a them homeless folks said fuck y'all Mr. USACE and moved to Red Hand over the mountain from there, moved here, or moved up north to Virginia.

Pretty soon them USACE men are gonna come rolling in and choose which'a town, us here in Redemption or them over Red Hand, will be on the bottom of a lake six months from now.

And all seemed to be leaning on me: who gets the flood? I'm surprised we ain't been overrun by mobs from both towns trying to bribe us or force us or kill us.

Every other week, a few of those empty-headed looking jaspers wearing suits with sleeves too long and pants too short came traipsing up sweating their asses off. Those ragged suits got 'em thinking the suit made 'em look important, better'n mountain trash like us. They looked plumb destitute after hiking up the top half of our two-mile driveway road 'cause their USACE company car got beat by curves and hills and potholes way below.

What made us laugh, every time: one or the other of'm would always step in dog shit. In their heads, they'd be swearing at old Boolie dead asleep under his favorite tree. But they'd be smiling false and generous to us.

A course, them looking at Boolie, we'd all look over and smirk at Granddaddy. A man who believed in doing his business wherever he happened to be when his bowels, as he said, *started to sing.*

Those men never did find out they was always scraping Granddaddy off their shoes.

The men'd hand me a bunch of papers and rattle off a few numbers, hoping to plumb stupefy me with a million writ down words. So I wouldn't realize they was offering us two pennies and a bird turd an acre. Just like Mama used to do, I smiled, not sayin' anything. I handed the papers back. I'd just smile, call Boolie or Dahlia Rose and head up to the house, leaving the men flat-foot up a mountain just as hard traveling down as up, and me hoping Granddaddy wasn't up to something more ambitious and direct. Like shooting at them.

CHAPTER EIGHT

One morning, the sky was all full of traveling black birds. Hundreds of birds all gliding and dancing here and there like big feathery black snowflakes, filled the sky.

With my shirt open enough to show my belly, I was sitting in the kitchen with all the windows open. I was feeling the mountain breezes whispering against my skin and spreading all around the swirly sweet smells of lilac and hot red dust, farm smells rising from the valley of manure and tractor gas. I ran my hands all gentle over my belly, telling the tiny one inside to be patient about coming out here into the world. I told my unborn that this world can be beautiful and blessed just as it can be ugly and hateful and murderous. And that most folks if given a preview would choose to stay right where they are rather than git born.

I was asking my unborn child, "Baby doll, you want your Mama healin' folks and runnin' all around a famous ole witchy healer? Or do you want a Mama that lives happy off the land and finds some nice gentle type of fella to marry and stays up the mountain happily ever after?"

As I was trying to think of some pleasant things to say to my unborn about human life, Squirrel Martin crawled in through the window, not saying inathing, and curled up at my feet on the floor next to Boolie.

Then, at last, that next week, the baby came. Two weeks early. On Halloween—October 31—about five minutes after midnight.

First Johnson gal ever to have it as a birthday. With our particular magical lineage, that's hard to believe.

She came fine and happy as can be. A couple of days before she came, I was having trouble tolerating the ride down the driveway road to town. Taking all the deep ruts and bouncing over jutting rocks, I was suddenly sitting in a pool of water that just burst outta me.

I heard about a woman's water breaking, but I had never seen it. At first I thought I peed myself. But woman's womb water isn't pee, that's for sure.

Since I was already in the truck and heading into town inaway, I just kept on a-going, letting the old truck practically drive itself to Doc Turner's. Only the doc wasn't there, and the note he nailed onto the front door to explain where he went, rainfall washed off the ink. Not a legible word left.

I grabbed the blue ink rain-washed note and stuffed it in the pocket of my pregnant lady's dress. I wanted to show my baby child someday that even though Doc was not there and the note he left was as useful as a bare fork to a starving man, we Johnson women will always find a way to git things done right and safe as possible.

Back in the truck with Squirrel Martin in the front seat with me, him not at all certain of what to make of me big as a cow, sitting in water that sprung outta me like a mountain spring, the truck drove us to Miz Jessup's.

Sitting on one of their crazy old porch sliders in the front yard facing the road, Hardy saw us coming from about a mile away and knew right off what was happening. When I pulled up in front of their house, Miz Jessup and the three crazy old Jessup aunts were standing there waiting for me. They were carrying all kinds of clean sheets, white porcelain water bowls and other stuff I cain't make out.

And on account of the contractions were coming and sucking me up painful from the inside but somehow I had to git the contractions to push my baby outside, I didn't want to know what they had in store.

The Jessup women said I didn't scream too bad. But from Hardy's look of terror when the door opened once, and he was standing out there in the parlor white-faced and his mouth hung wide open, I think I had been doing a lot of "Sweet fuckin' Jesus, I'm dying" screaming.

But then finally, me all plumb tuckered and sweaty, there she was. An angel wrapped in white linen bed sheet cloth and lying in my arms more peaceful and quiet than I imagined even the Christ child was, him lying sleeping and resting before he had to start worrying about all humanity.

When Hardy would finally come in, I said, holding her up a little, "I'd like you to meet Safire Dignity Johnson." Hardy reached right down and gently took her in his arms.

Silas won't be too thrilled about the Dignity part, or that she is a girl. But since I don't think he knew what dignity means or is, he'd just wag his head around some. Saying under his breath in moderate disapproval, "Ain't you something, Ruby Lee. Ain't you something."

Safire wasn't like other babies. I knew that already. She was just like Mama, me, and maybe Dahlia Rose. She had the healing gift and she got it big. A person can feel it in Safire as soon as they picked her up. That happened right off when Miz Jessup scooped her up for the first time. Safire resting against Miz Jessup's chest, sleeping, Miz Jessup's eyes nearly bugged out and bounced across the floor. "Man alive, Ruby Johnson! This new child is making my whole body tingle and feel like the Lord is gonna walk right outta my mouth!"

She called for one of the Jessup aunts to hold Safire and have the same experience for herself. But the pinkish-haired old woman wearing a mothy ole stole of minks champing into each other's tails wouldn't go near.

She mooed out something like, "No…thank…you…I kin feel that child's power from right where I is." Then, she ran right out'a the room to go find a salt mine or something to start shoveling like mad over her left shoulder.

That night, in Lonny Dale Jessup's old bedroom, in his old bed where me and him woke up the old aunts a hundred times when I climbed in the window at night (but they weren't ever gonna say inathing to Miz Jessup about it 'cause they're Methodists, an' Methodists cain't mention sex), Safire Dignity Johnson opened her tiny mouth and gently attached it to my waiting breast.

My baby drank the milk of life from her new Mama all night long.

That next morning Doc Turner and Reverend Pine Gregory Angelle came by to see how me and Safire were doing. The doc, he poked and rubbed me. Looked up me, put fingers into this and that. Had Miz Jessup boil up a batch of curing roots and bitter leaves into a compress I was to keep between my legs for three days. And drink some of it that was still in the boiling pot every four hours, with one eye closed.

He was serious. City medicine and hill medicine were clunking into each other, but I didn't think they liked each other very well at all.

The reverend mostly peered into the room with only his baldy head showing, smiling the crooked Alabama smile of his at me, saying such things as "The Lord helps those who help themselves, Ruby." Then he'd zip his head out again.

Finally, mostly to shut him up 'cause with a vagina still the size of a fencepost hole, I wasn't in no mood for the Reverend Pine Gregory shoving his head up me, so to speak. I said back to him, "Reverend, there ain't a Johnson woman in all'a history who didn't have monstrous inner strength. We have been helping ourselves to deeply led, eventful, even blessed lives for decades and decades and need no help from you."

Then I added, maybe because I was tired and my nipples were sore and swollen from Safire's enormous appetite. And I was sad because eventually Safire and I would have to go home. And Silas wouldn't say inathing sweet and gentle to us. And Hardy, who would say soft and gentle things all day if you let him, and who could maybe be this child's daddy, but as long as I was married to Silas we couldn't even pretend. And because Squirrel Martin stayed right there with me every moment totally quiet and sitting in the corner like a loving family dog…I added, "Reverend Pine Gregory Angelle, the reason this beautiful and special Johnson baby girl child exists at all is because I ain't afraid to help myself."

I said sorta joking and sorta not, "So now, ain't it about time for the Lord to hold true to them hopeful words an' keep his damn promise to us Johnsons? And help us some in this world of ours that don't want us in it?"

Not sure why this comes to mind now. Probably because he was supposed to be daddy to my children, had we any. One night about a year before Lonny Dale committed his awful crime, he and I was out on the front porch of our house all curled around each other on Granddaddy's rusty old porch slider. Smoking Lucky Strikes. Pretending the bats skittering all over where unhappy pieces of night that wanted to git themselves relocated somewheres else. It was one of those nights that are darker than most other nights. Not just moonless night darkness, which they are, but even darker than usual moonless nights. "Eyes closed nights" I think is what Mr. Mockin'bird Man called 'em. Dark so thick it slows you down when you walk through it. Makes your eyes water. It's a little harder to breathe.

"Darlin' let's go pick some flowers or somethin' out in the woods," Lonny Dale said sly and sexy, meaning "Let's go do it, girl, it's been a couple of weeks."

"I ain't so sure about any flower-pickin'," I said back to him priggish and kissed him on the cheek all playful. "But I would like to take a walk. Come on…"

Giving him a little shove backward, I jumped up quick as you please and ran around to the back of the house through the cool damp grass toward the back rise. It was tough seeing a damn thing, and I stepped on sharp pointy rocks in my bare feet a couple of times. Lonny Dale caught up quick enough. On the hill overlooking the cemetery field, he came up behind and tackled me playful. Laughing and swearing, we rolled down some of the hill through the daisies and black-eyed Susans and stopped with me spread-eagle on the ground and him on top of me. "This your idea of pickin' flowers?" I asked him, giggling. "Crushin' 'em?"

A'course, Lonny Dale had my shirt unbuttoned so quick I could feel the mountain breeze rolling over my breasts before I felt him undoing the buttons. I was deciding if I was gonna let him touch me there for a while or push him off and run through the dark some more. Just like that, he was dead still and not there. Well, there, but powerful distracted, like he been turned to stone. Which, I reckon, in some ways he did.

The cemetery field down below just exploded into an enormous flash of red sparkling light. As if a crimson shooting star just plonked into the side field. Hardy was suddenly cat-brained, watching it happen. 'Cause he was blocking my view; I could only see the sky directly up above blaze red for a moment.

He was so startled he didn't say all fake mystified his usual, "What the crippled Christ…?" Dumbstruck, I reckon, is the word I'd use.

When I sat up and the big burst of red toned down, standing down there at the entrance to the graveyard, glowing pale and spooky in pink light that practically ain't there, the little singing gal named Eve Morning Glory Johnson we've heard stories about all our lives, one of the three sweet little old singing sisters murdered by the Yankees with the rest of our Johnson ladies, was floating about a foot off the grass. I just knew it was her. Watching us. Looking sad and mournful and seeming like she ain't ever seen a young boy and girl having fun before. Kissing in the grass at night. Having not a care.

Lonny Dale, although partial to not believing his eyes in matters of the supernatural like the rest of Southern Christianity, whose lack of basic worldliness and with god fearingness overruling their senses, as in: *Seen it right there in front of me, by God, but I still ain't believin' I seen it*, and, to his credit, never scoffed at or teased me about my "witchy" gifts or my family's place in Southern magical lore ever again. After seeing little Eve and then the ghost ladies rise into a red wash of blinding light, in his own way, he treasured me even more. He was wild and full of himself. But he was a sweet, loyal soul. I reckon that one otherworldly experience changed his whole understanding of the balances between the physical world and the one you can put your arm straight through.

In less than two years after that sweet, mysterious night, Lonny Dale was accused, convicted and hanged.

Back at the Jessups', my baby girl was sleeping all cozy on my legs, and I was sitting up in Lonny Dale's bed.

Not sure why I was thinking about this, either, I know what those two gigantic explosions were we heard that time we took the truck down with a load of raspberries to sell to Mr. Jesse J. Brown. They were huge old things. Birds a mile away got thrown right out'a the trees.

Cousin Jim Addison got himself all blown up. His brother, Cousin Carter Addison, our fiddle playing cousin, got his eyes blown right out'a his head.

On the other side of the valley, there's a big government work site where they're supposed to be clearing a hillside of trees so they can build a factory of some kind. That's supposed to "bolster our diminishing economy." Everyone in Redemption knew they were taking down the trees now in case our side of the mountain got the flood. That's where the big hydro doodad that turns water into electricity would sit.

None of us could fathom why those two, Cousin Carter and Cousin Jim, went to work for the U.S. Army Corps of Engineers. They went down there for log-clearing jobs even when they knew there was a damn good chance the State of North Carolina was gonna swipe our land no matter what it promised.

Down they went. Two up mountain teenage boys that have never even been all the way over to the other side of our valley, ten miles away. Boys who had no clue about how somebody organizes a square dance never mind trying to understand the U.S. government and the U.S. Army Corps of Engineers flooding valleys. And building three-mile across lakes with hydro something and drinking water for a thousand years. Or logging out and selling a whole mountainside before the water rises up it in the name of progress. And that mountain is our mountain, including Jim and Carter's. But, yes sir, down they go. And got jobs. Tearing down and killing their own mountainside. Taking all the life and beauty and magic away from their own home. None of us could git it. But all'a us were kind and never said inathing, hoping those boys had a secret plan to redeem themselves. Somehow. Someday.

They were down there a long spell. Learned how to cut down trees that the State of North Carolina calls "forestry." Learned how to dig big holes and call it excavation. Hell, Dahlia Rose could dig a hole and saw down a tree, and she was six.

Do it on a big scale for the U.S. government and they call it a budding career. And they think *us* folks up mountain are brainless.

But that dread day come. And it came horrible and cruel. Till then, those boys had been having the time of their lives.

Before the accident exploded him into human liquid, "I cain't see a damn thing, Carter," were our cousin Jim's last words. I swear.

Jim Addison, twenty or so then I reckon, was sitting in a Caterpillar tractor with tires bigger than Squirrel Martin standing on my shoulders. Jim pulled back on the sticks to jitterbug the big scooper out'a the hole, with a rock big as the up mountain Church of the Second Coming in it.

Under all that heat and machinery noise, he was swearing at the big digger. Swearing at the hole. Swearing at that damn rock that had the better of him. Carter, a year younger than Jim, was leaning on a shovel right there six feet away, holding his ears. All that he could see was Jim's lips moving.

"I cain't see a damn thing, Carter!" Jim screamed at Carter. Carter could only see Jim's lips moving frantic.

The big, overworked Caterpillar was steaming up fierce. Sputtered some. Sputtered some more real loud. And then exploded. A huge thing. Felt and looked like a bomb crashed down.

It exploded Jim into pure liquid.

What was left of the big blown up and smoking yellow disaster was hissing real loud. All that was left of old Jim was human juice splashed everywhere for fifty feet around—trees, stone walls, men…on everything. Standing there so close, Carter was bathed and baptized in all'a Jim's goriness.

Before this horrible thing happened, Carter and Jim grew up here with us almost like they were brothers to the kids and me. Then, they went down the mountain, thinking surely the mountain loved them. Ever since they was kids, the mountain told them where wind came from. Taught them how to change the course of streams to flow down to dying pastures. Showed them where to fish, where to hunt, where to pitch a lean-to and sleep safe on its hallowed ground under a black ceiling of stars. In summertime, they lit candles in the mountain caves. Fed flower nectar to hummingbirds landed on their fingers. In wintertime, they poured honey in the snow. And made hundreds of snow angels with ice halos. All acts of love for the mountain.

So when it punished them severely for digging holes and clearing trees for living money, none of us could understand why the mountain took exception to their young, careless minds. Those wild mountain boys never meant no disrespect. Not a lick.

Caterpillar tractor parts were splashing everywhere around. Every man within twenty feet's eardrums were blowed in and bleeding. Men were on the ground.

The flaming debris, all sorts of big chunks and slivers of metal and rubber smashing down, lit fires in the underbrush. Then, the other explosion, this one all sizzling and hissy, sent the water left in the Caterpillar's boiler a-raining all over, and put all the fires out.

Bits of Jim's bones were in Carter's mouth. Specs of his skin were in his hair. Carter raised his fingers to his eyes to rub something out that was beginning to sting. Throbbing pain skipped right up to fiery agony faster'n a rock busting clean through plate glass.

Reaching in there, he felt his fingertips clawing into raw terror. His fingernails were scratching against the backs of empty eye sockets. Cousin Carter feeling his sight gone, his brother gone, and his future gone, he just melted down to the ground and wanted to die. But even though the pain of blowed out eyes was horrendous and unbearable; death was nowhere near.

Several strong men picked him up and carried him over the ground with their fists full of his clothes. One thing was for sure: There was not enough left of our cousin Jim to put in a tobacco tin. Jim was blowed up to kingdom come.

Days later, Carter woke up. His head and face all wrapped up in bandages like an A-rab. He had lain there on a cot in the little work site doctor's office that long because they were afraid to move him. Seeing he was awake, some men stomped into the little room. After tossing him around, they lifted him up, and carried Carter on a stretcher out to a big car with a big swinging door hinged on the back.

As they're doing this, one fella said, "Ain't right to put this boy in a funeral car. Bastards coulda used a truck to git 'im down to a flat country doctor. Jeez Christ, it ain't right to put this blind kid into a funeral car."

I spose every person's life has one big powerful moment where nothing is ever gonna be the same again. Churchgoers call "seeing the light" an epiphany or something. Not sure what they call a disaster interfering on your life. Having his favorite person on God's green earth turned into human liquid. His own eyes blown out. And then hearing that those men were going to cart him down to the hospital clinic in a hearse must'a made Carter more angry than he ever been in his life.

On the way down the steep and treacherous Back Path, as it was named, the bumps and twists making Carter's eye sockets and head throb in horrible pain, that death car hit a hairpin turn too fast and reckless. It smashed through a long row of rocks lined up along the side of a decline and plummeted almost straight down a couple of hundred feet into a ravine.

Glass was shattering. Big rocks were shooting in the broken windows. The car was tumbling loose and roaring like mountain lions as it crashed down. The car finally stopped rolling and slammed into a bunch of boulders.

The driver, his head mashed to pulp, was back up the hill a-ways all busted up in a chokecherry bush, lying with his mouth open and flies already buzzing in and out. The other fella was lying on the floor of the front seat with his chest crushed down to two inches thick.

Carter, with his head still all bandaged up over his eyes, now had another head wound. A big chunk taken out his forehead by a flying rock, and even more bloody than he was before they put him in the death car. He crawled out a busted window and passed out in the dirty orange grit and dust.

Carter woke up in his own darkness. Black, directionless, mindless darkness. He woke up hungry, not sure if he was dead or alive. He knew what had happened. And knew he had to git himself somewhere. Blind and weak, he was trying to git a fix on which direction he should haul himself. Each time he came back to consciousness he pulled himself to his hands and knees. Then, he willed himself back to unconsciousness; it was safer, his dark inner world.

After a couple of days of waking and then willing himself back to the dark, singular realm inside us all, he took a couple of awkward steps. His arms and hands feeling for something to touch in the air. He tripped hard over a good size missile of granite jetting out'a the ground. He lay still for several minutes, fallen into a little island of pure white azalea flowers. Then, gagging on blood, gravel, bad tastes, and bad thoughts, he stood, shakily. Disoriented, he bent over to clear his head. Straightening up, Carter reached out into the air with his hands, again, and took a step forward into absolutely nothing.

It was Squirrel Martin and Mockin'bird that found Carter about two miles into the woods, way south of where that hearse crashed down. That boy was out in the big woods for maybe a week, stone blind and looking none too prosperous. He was kneeling by a dried-up creek with his clothes all tore up, his face all dried blood, and Lord above, his eyes plain gone right out'a his head.

Those two did something unusual; they sat there on a big ugly rock jus' watching Carter for a while. Jus' watching him. They couldn't believe their eyes…Carter was holding a mess of black eels in his arms, all sliding and squishing around. The eels were trapped in one of the only pools of water left on an evaporating creek bottom. They were one squirming weave of black knots and loose ends, slimier than eels usually are on account the water being all brackish. I reckon those eels breathed all the air plumb out'a it, and now were panicking like snakes breathing smoke in a brushfire.

Finding the one he wanted, Carter dropped all the eels but that one. He handled it, then took a big bite out'a that poor eel's stomach. Then a few more.

With his hands all full of the struggling, frantic black mud eel, and kneeling in thick green-black mud with some of the eels still slithering around with nowhere watery to go, Carter fell back on his butt. Right out loud he screamed, "Jesus Christ, Jim, why on earth did you git yourself all blowed up to nothing left but red slop? Why'd you leave me here like this!"

Then, Carter threw up.

Setting on his ass in creek mud, Cousin Carter Addison, with eel blood and goo all over him, fell over on his face. Squirrel Martin and Mockin'bird leaped off the rock they were sitting on. They turned Carter over and started rubbing the puke off his face and out'a his empty eye sockets. Those eye sockets, more puss sloshing around in 'em than puke. And after biting into a live eel five or six times, there was a-lota puke. Eel puke. So recently et, some of the pieces were still moving.

For three days, fearing to move him until he showed more signs of life, those two did everything they could to keep Carter in this world. Mockin'bird caught, skinned, and roasted up rabbit and squirrel. One time a deer. Squirrel Martin found roots and berries galore and mushed him up some turtle soup. Carter drank it right out'a the upside down shell.

Mockin'bird gently placed rolled up balls of some variety of soft green moss into those empty eye sockets, along with some healing herbs and pollen, and changed them four or five times a day. At every change of moss, either him or Squirrel Martin would scrape out the puss and shit with their own fingers. That they dipped in whiskey first to kill off the little germs we humans cain't see but will kill a man as slow and painful as a slow-turning screw right into the gut.

When he finally came to, Carter never complained, even one time, even with whiskey drops spilling into his eye sockets to disinfect them and stinging so bad, his face turned gray. He lay still while they cleaned up those hollow eyes. He ate whatever vittles they made. Time was passing sideways.

But he never spoke and didn't seem to know who was attending to him so quiet and mysterious. Maybe he thought it was our women kin ghosts, since he was related to them, or just plain ghosts. If he knew it was Mockin'bird and Squirrel—his little retarded cousin with magical gifts, and the most famous conjuring black man in North Carolina—he never let on.

Until one day he heard, "Guess what today is?" Mockin'bird asked, kneeling beside Carter in a stand of tall dense pines they had him lodged snug and dry under.

Carter lay there, his gone eyes looking straight up through a sizeable space between the sweet-scented, swaying pine boughs into one of the bluest of azure summer skies. Right into the damn sun, big and soft as a steaming tomato. Them big green wads of moss making him look like he had them round, see-ever-damn-thing fly's eyes.

Real soft Carter said, "I mean no offense. I don't care what today is, sir."

He lay there quiet again for a spell, still staring unblinking into the sun with those big ole green eyes.

"Course you don't, son," Mockin'bird said back to him. "But Ah'm gonna tell ya inaway. It's bin one full month since you blowed out them eyes."

A defeated look of a drowning man conceding to his fate crossed Cousin Carter's face. A look of somebody who wishes he had died after all rather than be in the predicament he's in.

Right then Squirrel Martin kneeled down beside Mockin'bird. Without speaking, and without hardly breathing, Squirrel Martin put his two palms on Carter's two blown out eye sockets. Quietly, slowly, Squirrel whispered, "I…done…it."

He took his hands away. Carter sat bolt upright, clawing at the green moss in his eye sockets. As the moss fell and met soft the ground, Carter felt a stinging pain in his eyes. He blinked hard and rubbed them. When he opened his eyelids, he had eyes again, and he could see.

Mockin'bird told me this himself. I have known his whole life that Squirrel was more than a strange magical boy. But what he did wasn't magic. I suspect if I had to I could help somebody with near blindness to see better. But nobody, not even Mockin'bird, not even Mama when she was alive and at her best in magical doings, could somehow conjure blown out eyes and put them back into a person's head and make them work again.

After all those years of knowing him better than any other human being, I still ask myself, "Who is this boy who cain't talk and sleeps like a dog curled up on the floor beside my bed every night but can make blind men see?"

When the time came, I wasn't averse to leaving the Jessups anymore because of all the comings and goings by those crazy aunts acting crazy as hell. Sometimes washing the hallway walls with lemony tonic water and reciting some prayer in French. That was when they weren't parading around the house in single file, wearing nothing but their old lady underwear and dime store flowered Easter hats, singing "We will come rejoicing…" and "Do dah do dah…" until I was close to pulling out my hair.

CHAPTER NINE

Then, the devil himself come. The devil himself.

That bastard devil come and kilt everything pure that I'll ever know or feel love for in this life.

After four days lying around the Jessups being waited on hand and foot and Safire sucking milk from out'a me and already looking like she was growing, Hardy finally came back from wherever he was.

"Drive you home now, angel girls?" he said on that morning when both me and Safire were napping just before lunch. All sleepy, I said, "Hardy, no man ever drove my truck before. 'Cept the fella that sold it to me fair and square five years ago."

Hardy smiled. He touched Safire's nose with his fingertip, and replied, "What's that got to do with the price of tobacco?"

"Nothin'. I just like it so when I can see you smiling."

Hardy was running his fingertip along the edges of Safire's tiny face. "She looks fine, Ruby. Really fine."

I can tell Hardy's convincing himself a little that Safire was his baby girl. Could be, you know. Maybe Silas had weak seed or something, and all those from standing behind me ruttings didn't git it where it's supposed to go. And me and Hardy, we done it laying down with him gentle on top, kissing me. Maybe the seed flows better when a man's on top of a girl. Her legs wide open and waggling up in the air joyful and full of the heat, making her gasp and twitch and lose control of her dignity for a time.

But when the right man is inside'a the girl, it's a beautiful time. And her dignity always comes back. Every single bit of it. That's what gave me the idea for plunking Dignity in Safire's name.

Miz Jessup and the Jessup aunts got me cleaned up. They put me and Safire in the truck. Squirrel Martin still had never left my side. The Jessups plumb forgot he was a-sitting there with me in the bedroom room. They just waddle past him all day long. I even forgot about him sometimes until I saw him there all curled up in the corner, looking up and smiling at me.

I called him over gentle to see Safire a couple of times. But Squirrel Martin wasn't ready to be an uncle, apparently. Squirrel Martin wasn't even ready to be a brother. He only paid mind to Dahlia Rose and me. Has no time at all for Tom Sawyer, Macy, or Bobby Lee when he was still here.

Hardy Jessup got us driven home in fine style. At every street corner in town, he pulled the pickup over to the side and called anybody that's there over to see Ruby Johnson's new baby girl. It was strange: Instead'a fearing me, everybody was laughing and cooing and congratulating me. Some even congratulated Hardy, and every time they did, he took quiet pride in not saying inathing back about who the daddy of Safire really was. For a time, I was even imagining that it was Hardy who was my husband. And the three of us there in the truck, with Squirrel Martin all confused but happy in the back, was showing everybody our fine new family.

And not once did a person look at me cruel or say inathing' meant to imply they hoped me an' my new baby girl would be dead an' gone soon as possible. Could hardly believe it.

After Hardy drove the truck up the driveway road, he finally understood how downright tough it was to drive her being ornery as she was. The two miles up being orneriest. "Shoot, girl," he said, when we came up over the last rise before the house comes up into view…" But he didn't finish. I know he was thinking that most men he knew couldn't drive the truck up that driveway road at'all, let alone drive it us as good and overall smooth as me.

Hardy swung around the front yard and backed the truck right up to the front door, sending gravel and dust a-flying. "Hardy," I said, "For God's sake stop the clownin'! You're shakin' the Bejesus out'a Safire and me."

He said he was sorry, but he was still smiling and prancing like a new daddy. I let him take Safire in his arms, while I stepped out'a the truck by myself.

"Hardy, I don't want to go inside yet," I said to him. "Me and the angel girl want to breathe some pure mountain air. I been birthing and sleeping for four days. And she's been living upside down in a little warm bath of birth water for almost a year."

Then, I told him to ready up the bassinet the Jessups gave me with the soft baby blankets they gave me, too.

"Put it under the cottonwood there next to Boolie."

For his one minute a day, old Boolie woke up from his sound sleep and gave the air a sniff. Smelling something he ain't smelled for a long time, he got up and ambled over to Hardy still holding Safire in his arms like he been holding her comfortable all'a his life. Boolie lifted his old head up and sniffed again. This time Hardy hunkered down and presented Boolie with the newest addition to the long, long ancestral line of magical Johnson kin women.

Boolie was very happy to make her acquaintance. His tail was wagging. His old legs were hopping around a little. With me and Hardy watching, and Squirrel Martin climbing out'a the back of the truck and then getting in behind the wheel, Boolie gave Safire three or four big approving licks with his tongue.

Hardy looked over at me and smiled big as a barn door. "Seems angel girl passes the ancient Johnson dog test with flyin' colors," he said laughing, his eyes twinkling in a way I ain't never seen no man's eyes twinkle before.

I was still smiling as I walked out back to use the outhouse. I could hear Hardy singing church hymns in a humorous kind of way as he got Safire all fixed up in the bassinet. Then, he put it under the old cottonwood. The beautiful old tree was dropping fine yellow pollen down on the white netting Hardy stretched over the bassinet to keep the bugs and sun out.

All this time, Safire had been sleeping or looking around happy and peaceful. Not one bout of crying. Not one.

I was walking back around front, feeling good about relieving myself here at our place after relieving myself elsewhere for a time, when I saw Squirrel Martin sitting behind the driver's wheel of the truck pretending he was driving. Until then, I hadn't thought of the kids or Granddaddy at all, but as I was coming around front I started to hear them laughing and a-singing, coming up the driveway road. Probably they came out'a the woods on to it a little farther down after we drove by and after a morning of raspberrin'.

They probably knew that me and Safire were home now.

There's a special spiritual moment when you show a person a new baby for the first time. The person kind of goes away somewhere and only his soul is standing there all opened up and washed over in delight and wonder. Even grumpy old ladies who have had or seen tons of newborn babies turn into their souls for a while as they fuss over the infant. And want to hold it against them so they might feel what Heaven on earth really is, one more time.

I was looking forward to giving the kids that experience. Most especially, Dahlia Rose, who as the youngest of us, an' never saw a close kin newborn in her whole life. Maybe this new baby girl would help Dahlia Rose become happy again.

They could be like sisters seeing there was only seven years age difference between them. And there was thirteen years' difference between Dahlia Rose and me.

Hardy was walking back up the downward pitch of the front yard toward me, still smiling, hoping I'd notice what a fine job he did getting Safire all laid out and napping under the tree, the one that was sprinkling little bits of yellow pollen like fairy dust down on my baby girl every once in a while.

Happy as a bluebird, I was about to call something out to him—but I never did. Never got the chance.

Right then was when Squirrel Martin decided he's learned enough about stationary truck driving, and he thumped the door open, climbed out, and then slammed the door closed. Tell him a million times not to, he still loved the sound of slamming that truck door. And he did it every time. But this time, the truck started rolling. Nobody in it, or even near it now that Squirrel Martin finally decided to introduce himself to Safire and was on his way over there.

The truck was suddenly just rolling over the ground, gaining speed like somebody was pressing down on the gas, only the truck ain't on. Just rolling. Fast.

Both me and Hardy made a beeline toward it from the different places we were standing. I was closer but on account of just pushing a baby out'a me, I couldn't run worth a lick. Horrible pain boiled out'a my privates and I felt warm blood begin to flow down the inside'a my legs.

Hardy near left his boots behind, sailing right out'a them he was running so fast. Squirrel Martin was standing there frozen, watching the empty truck rumbling down the very top of the driveway road—just as the voices of the kids were rumbling up, and any second their heads would pop into view.

I was screaming for Hardy to catch it. He was screaming for the kids to git out'a the way. But they had not cleared the rise and were standing down there frozen, too, wondering what was going on because they cain't see no runaway truck yet. An' cain't hear Hardy clearly.

Squirrel Martin was so distressed; he took out his pocketknife and was dancing around a-slicing at the hot humid air again, screaming, "I done it! I done it, Ruby!" Only this time he was full of fear and misery.

The "if onlys" in this life, if you lined them all up from here to kingdom come, they still will never git you anywhere. Watching all this, the "if onlys" started to descend on me like a huge black flock of starving crows.

But the "here and nows" was still in its horrible present tense progress and hadn't even started yet.

It was heroic, and I believe he knew what he was doin'. Old Boolie transformed himself into himself ten years younger and threw his whole body in front of the runaway truck, trying to stop it or trick it or something, as it was heading straight for the kids. There was a loud clumping sound mixed with Boolie's weak, frightened yelp. Then, Boolie stone dead in one second was thrown through the air, right at Hardy. Hardy had to stop his running and duck out'a the way.

The truck was almost at the dip where it would plunge over and steer right into the kids unless through some Jesus miracle they could register what they couldn't see yet and jump out'a the way.

Something happened at that moment—the truck whacked into a pothole and curved over just a mite. The runaway truck was still heading down the driveway road. But it was traveling on the far left side rather than down the middle like it had been doin' before.

I knew—as the pickup was just about to roll past me—I couldn't jump into the cab and fish for the brakes. I couldn't reach in and give the steering wheel a good yank to send it harmless out into the field.

But I could jump right in front of it myself. Shift its direction to a better place.

I was running the last bit, intending to jump when I stubbed into a big heavy tool right at my feet half hidden in the grass. It knocked me down to my knees. I was crying now. I wasn't scared of dying. I was panicked and horrified at the thought of leaving Safire so soon.

Whatever that big heavy tool was, something told me to grab it. I hefted it up effortless like it was a little ole length of plumbing pipe. It must have weighed fifty pounds.

Holding it like an Injun chucking a spear, I took the old iron digging tool and sent it flying straight and true. Landing in the dust just ahead of the pickup, it bounced again and hit its mark—the left front tire, square. The truck shot off the driveway road and bumped down the grassy side yard bank.

We were all so damn relieved; we broke out laughing. Fear laughing. Hardy turned to me with an expression chiseled on his face that I could never describe. But then, Squirrel Martin began yelling again, "Ruby, I done it!" Then he adds, "It was me that done it!" And he's crying and screaming for he already knew what was gonna happen.

Directly in the path of the truck, Safire Dignity Johnson, four days old and sleeping quiet and sweet as an angel. Sleeping under the more than one hundred-year-old cottonwood tree, showering my baby angel girl in yellow fairy dust, was clenching her tiny eyes shut, preparing to die.

The tool that changed the truck's direction was that old fencepost hole digging thing. Not knowing a thing about the quirks of my old truck, Hardy set the hand brake when he parked it, but didn't tie it off with the handkerchief I use to keep it stayed put. Squirrel Martin slamming the truck door jarred the hand brake free.

Hardy was on his knees under the old cottonwood. He started screaming and screaming. The kids were slowly filtering up to the yard with their hands covering their mouths, all in shock already.

I was kneeling on the dry dusty ground, with baby delivery blood running down my legs. Knowing I had just done something horrible. Deciding, how I did, to throw the tool left instead of right, probably saving the kids by doing so. But I just kilt my own baby.

Right then, Granddaddy stuck his head outta the barn. It was clear by his beard all full of sticks that he just woke up from a long doze in the fresh-cut hay. Scratching his ass through his drooping overalls, he called, "What are you kids standing there a gawking for.

Ruby and that new girl baby will be home inatime, an' I want y'all cleaned and washed." Then, he squinted, and stopped scratching his butt.

"That you, Hardy Jessup?"

With Safire lying there bloody in the grass, I tried to wipe the blood gently off her face so I could see her. Hardy tried washing the blood off her with gentle scoops of well water from a bucket Granddaddy brought us when he finally got it through his hair-all-sticking-up head what was going on.

***

I don't remember much at her burying. The breeze was sweet. Fall sun was tired and just barely able to touch down on us. Silas jumped down into Safire's burying hole with his arms full of the baby girl he never even seen alive. She wrapped up in sheet linen. Then him leaving her down there after he climbed back out to help Hardy and Squirrel Martin with the filling in…that's when I fainted dead away, floating right out'a this earthly life.

Thinking, *My baby is dead, and I'm the one that kilt her.*

Just like in some old fairy story, they put me to bed and I went into a deep sleep. I had dreams. So many dreams. It was all dreams. Even I was a dream. I had no idea that I had a physical body lying back on planet earth in a feathery bed, with Safire's blood still caked under its fingernails.

Where I went, all was soft and floaty and people came and went who said things that made no sense, and they didn't have to. Dream people communicate in languages that really ain't languages at all. It's done through feelings and knowings that pass right from them to you and back. Most times, you already know what dream people mean before they open their mouths to say inathing.

I remember a beautiful little sparkling ghost girl takes me by my hand. I know her in a way I cain't describe. It's like that in dreams. Then she's gone, and I am bathing naked in a cool high country river with nothing around it anywhere. It's a beautiful place full of tall green grass, white bark trees and big funny-shaped flowers only one color: different variations of red.

The little ghost girl appears again. She's standing on a big round rock plugged into the riverbank.

"Ruby," the girl said so sweetly I began to cry, "you will need to make your choice by and by."

And even though nobody told me inathing about the choice, I

knew what it was. It was the same choice they gave Mama. Mama was tired of everything: the town, the people's hatred and meanness. By the time she was thirty-one, she had two stillborns. Six children. Squirrel Martin's brains never came along with the rest of him. And then, Dahlia Rose's twin, Gracie Marlene, who at one and a half years old got left outside all night by Pa and was plumb gone in the morning. 'Cause Pa was too drunk to do more than carry just one of the babies into the house before he passed out.

When they discovered the baby was gone, Mama just went into a kind of strange coma. She lay down in the spirit field. The spirits of our kin asked her if she wanted to stay in this dreamy death place permanent. And without a second thought, tired of body and mind, Mama said she did.

Then, everywhere I went in this long, long dream, the flying Johnson women kin ghosts were asking me if I wanted them to teach me how to fly. And the little ghost girl would appear to tell me I had to make a choice.

So I made one.

"I ain't staying here," I said to the little sparkling girl. "Maybe your grandma didn't want to live as a human female no more. But I do."

At first, she didn't say inathing to me. She looked confused, and I reckon nobody here in the Johnson women's place of all dreams had just plain said, "I ain't stayin' here. Send me back."

Then the ghost girl, my Safire, said soft to me, "Mama, that truck kilt you. Run over you and left you twitching like a run over dog. Then, it run over me."

"Did it run over Hardy Jessup? Or the kids?" I asked.

The little ghost girl took her time answering. "No, Mama, they're all just fine."

"Safire Dignity Johnson, please send me back. 'Sides bearing you, I ain't done nothing on God's green earth yet I'm proud of. Not a blessed thing."

They say for someone run over by a truck; I had very few injuries. In my memory of what happened, I threw that big heavy tool in the way of it. But even with "fear strength," I could not have thrown that big steel tool. Later they told me not thinking twice I threw myself in front of that truck tire like I knew what would happen, the truck hurtling off in a new direction. It sure did. But not the direction I had in mind.

I slept like the dead, and maybe even my body and brain did die for a while. But my spirit wasn't dead by a long shot.

Once again, Squirrel Martin stayed in my room for all'a that time. He was the only one who I would open my mouth for so he could feed me a little something. The only one who could git me to use the bedpan or clean me up after. The only one who could brush my teeth.

Just like he did at the Jessups', at night he curled up in the corner of the room on the floor and slept with one eye on me. Lord only knows where Squirrel Martin's other eye went!

***

From out'a my million miles away dreams, one afternoon I felt Granddaddy shaking me rough and tender together, saying, "Ruby, wake up. Wake up now, girl. We got trouble. Bad trouble."

An hour or so later, I woke up, smiled at him and said without him telling me a thing, "They'll never git it, Granddaddy. Don't you fret none. Nobody's going to take our land away."

Truth was, that wasn't true. With one stroke of the pen, the U.S. government could appropriate our side of the mountain in a heartbeat. And that's exactly what they were fixin' to do.

Granddaddy was surprised I knew about our trouble before he even told me inathing about it. When I said that—"Nobody's going to take our land away"—he stared at me for a while then scratched his head. Two minutes before…I was in a coma deciding if I wanted to live or die. Then, there I was clear of mind and full back into life.

"I hope you're right, girl. I surely do. But the U.S. government ain't someone we can take lightly. No, sir."

"I know that, Granddaddy. We won't take inathing lightly."

The day before I woke up, a bunch of men appeared in the front yard, taking Granddaddy and everybody by surprise. Hardy had been on his way home, walking down the driveway road after spending the day sitting quietly by the side of my bed. He bumped into these fellas sweating and groaning, an' swearing at each other because the car they were riding in couldn't negotiate its way up the rough terrain.

Because Hardy is Hardy, he turned right around and walks back up, sensing something was dead wrong.

If Hardy hadn't been there, I believe Granddaddy would'a croaked straightaway with a coronary. Granddaddy cain't read. And he trusted no one but about two people in all this world to tell him the truth. When the men handed him the fistful of legal papers, he had no idea what they said exactly. But by the stiff expressions and fake attempts to be friendly, and hearing those men say they would be looking out for "you and your fine family's interests every step of the way," he knew he was up a creek of deep shit.

And after Hardy spent thirty minutes reading every word of the papers three times just to rile them, he looked at Granddaddy and frowned.

Sensing the cruel fate lurking ahead was beginning to sink into our rotten apple hillbilly minds, the men started smiling back at forth to themselves.

"How long they got?" Hardy asked to no one man in particular.

"Two months," a skinny one with holes in the soles of his shoes answered, trying to beef up the sound of his authority. "Maybe less."

Granddaddy, silent for the last few minutes, scrunched up his eyes when he heard that.

Very slowly, he teetered over to the skinny man. Granddaddy, in a strange showing of gentlemanly acceptance, poked out his wrinkly old hand and offered it to the man. The skinny man backed up a half step, looking at Granddaddy as though he was extending a reeking skunk carcass. The skinny man had dealt with these dumb ass hillbillies before. Shoot you just as soon as they look at you. After looking around at his colleagues, the skinny man decided it was safe. He produced a stony little smile on his face and reached out to take a hold of Granddaddy's invisible, rotting skunk.

The next thing anybody knew, Granddaddy whipped out his ornery ancient penis and started to piss all over the skinny man. Not reacting with lightning-like speed, the skinny fella finally put some distance between the arch of steaming piss and himself, screaming, "I knew this old mountain maggot was up to somethin'!"

Granddaddy swung around and managed to git at least a squirt of his watery condolences on every one of'm. Even a little of it on Hardy, who didn't care in the least. It was a story he'd enjoy telling in town for weeks to come.

The U.S. government had decided to flood Red Hand and spare Redemption. But that just made it worse for us Johnsons.

Starting with us, the U.S. government intended to buy up all the

Redemption Mountain on this side of the mountain. They want to strip it bare of trees for plank wood to build homes up north. Somehow, our trees were better than their trees, and this was what was gonna spare us and put the town and valley around Red Hand seventy feet deep.

They are planning to sell half-rites of ownership of our 3,957 acres to the big logging outfit that had already stripped huge sections of mountainside all over the county. They were using one of their deceitful phrases all over the place again: "Progress is in dyin' need up here. This'll help keep your economy from collapsing."

Even if we had understood what it was, none of us still wouldn't have given a hoot about the economy. None of us down here in the Deep South gave a damn about what went on in the rest of the country unless it had something to do with tobacco or music pickers from this area that made it to Memphis or Nashville.

We Johnsons was getting our lives stole right from under our asses. The U.S. government would conjure up two thousand labor jobs by destroying everything alive we owned and everything we ever knew.

Granddaddy relayed our sentiments precisely when he pissed all over the fancy pants and dirty shoes of the U.S. Army Corps of Engineers itself.

But that wasn't going to stop inathing.

To save Redemption, we had to destroy ourselves.

And after all that had happened to me, I felt destroyed already. How was I ever going to find the will and the strength to fight for our rights after my new baby getting kilt her first day home? And since the government didn't think we Johnsons had any rights, fight for our lives?

This might finally be the end of us. Wasn't the town that finally kilt us. Wasn't fear, hate, or superstition. It was *progress*. And even I know the word for that is irony. Us Johnsons just seem to have been fighting with quirks of fate from the very beginning of us. The very beginning. And it ain't fair.

CHAPTER TEN

Christmastime brought me no joy. Our troubles were everywhere...the Army Engineers. Pa not around since last spring, which seems for good. Lonny Dale hanged. Bobby Lee left for the military or somewhere. Boolie run down. Granddaddy mush brained as a pumpkin. My beautiful angel child leaving this life before she even knew her own name. My husband not caring for me and probably never did except to rut all my Hollywood beauty whenever he could. Making winter worse, it had been snowing steady for a week. Almost three feet up there.

And now Tom Sawyer.

After many of the good fiddlers played at the fiddling competition, Tom Sawyer went up to each person and spent a long time showing them his song words, the ones he always said, "were looking hard for some good country music notes to make 'em come alive."

I watched Tom Sawyer talk a little about himself and then let the person leaf through his lyric book. Looked to me as if everybody liked what they were reading. Only thing is, few of us up here can actually write music.

Just when Tom was gonna give up, the young man who finally won the day's fiddling came ambling over to him and asked to take a look. I couldn't hear what they were saying, but the beautiful fiddler cocked his head and whistled five or six times. They spoke a little more, then the man offered his hand for Tom Sawyer to shake. Which Tom did, smiling big as a lake.

He never said inathing about it after that.

Yesterday, he came up to me and said, "Ruby, tomorrow I'm heading over to Nashville to make my fortune writing the words for songs that are gonna git music-writ. And played by some of the best country stars that ever lived."

What can you say to that? If he stayed here with us, I'm not sure he could do inathing useful to help keep our land except help load up when we got thrown off. Besides, this was Tom Sawyer's destiny. We all knew that. It was just happening a mite earlier than I thought. And at a terrible time for the rest of us. He was only sixteen and a half. In some ways, still a baby. But in others, like the rest of us Johnsons, he had wisdom and stamina come from hardship and pain. I truly believed Tom Sawyer would do what he believed he was cut out to do: become music famous in his own soft but confident way.

"What can I do to help you ready up?" I said right to him and touch him gently on the side of his face. He wasn't sure what to say, since I believe he had prepared himself for a good argument.

Used to be Tom would git Granddaddy on his side first before talking to me. No point even talking or arguing with Granddaddy anymore; he'd gone true senile and spends most of his days tromping out in the snow, throwing sticks for Boolie to fetch. Or else, he'd go off into the woods whistling every once in a while for dead old Boolie to come a-running from whatever he had been sniffing an' investigating.

Sometimes Granddaddy plays so hard and earnest with dead Boolie, I expect to see old Boolie's footprints dancing all around Granddaddy's in the snow.

***

The one important tragedy going on that didn't bother me at all: Silas was gone. And I give a healthy Amen to that.

Was just too much for him when he came home after three weeks underground clinking coal to find his new baby daughter was born strong and healthy. But was kilt by her own Ma, even if it was an out-and-out accident. And even if I saved the lives of the kids.

He didn't care. He said, "Ruby, you have always been a strange one, with strange spiritual ways I never let bother me."

He had downed about a third of a bottle of Wild Turkey and

kept on rambling.

"But two months back I jumped down into a dirt hole up over my head, laid down a sweet child into it and covered her up with dirt. A baby girl who I ain't even seen smile once or nothin'."

He took another big bubbly swig and burped loud a couple of times.

He looked me over with that sex face he'd get when it's straight up to the bedroom time. "I enjoy sexualizing with you, Ruby, I truly do. Poor dumb mountain girl, you have no idea how beautiful you'd be in the outside world. No clue at all."

Silas' eyes were becoming unfocused. "You're Hollywood pretty, Ruby. And your figure is Hollywood fine. Man alive, you're so high mountain, you have no idea. Man alive…" he slurred and the whiskey bottle slipped out'a his hands and emptied the rest of its contents on the floor.

Next I know, Silas had me by the hair. Both his fists were full of it and he was dragging me over to the window.

"Ruby Johnson," he said with slurred conviction, "I'm leaving you. I don't want to be your husband no more. Fine body and all, I'm goin'."

He had me all twisted up, with a hand full of my hair like he was lashing up for a bull ride. "Git around now and behave yourself. Ain't like you ain't used to this."

If I screamed and fought back, I was afraid I'd scare the kids to high heavens. If I went numb as I usually did to his ignorant Bulls County ways, I had the feeling this time he might kill me.

Why he was dragging me to the window instead of whipping me around and pushing me over the footboard of the bed, while he poked me from behind, was some last straw that broke in Silas' head or just all that plain rotten meanness finally bursting out'a him like I knew it would someday, an' he wanted me disgraced in front'a the whole world.

With one of his fists full of my hair snapping my neck back rough, he pushed me up against the window. Standing there behind me, with his other hand he yanked up my nightgown, got himself ready, and pushed his pecker right up against my rear end place—the place on a woman's body where no man should ever stick his fingers or his throbbing manhood. With me smelling all his whiskey stink, and feeling his thing pushing harder into it, opening it up, shooting pain and humiliation all over me, I tried to turn around and scratch Silas' eyes out.

But from the position I was in, and held by Silas' brawny arm, all I could do was swing my arms at nothing I could touch, with my fingernails clawing nothing but Silas' evil air.

Silas pushing his thing into my rear end hurt like blazes and wasn't going in too easy. Silas tightened his grip on my hair. He spit on the fingers of his other hand and wiped it all over the head of his pecker. Then, he was shoving it in again. This time it was sliding easy.

To keep him out'a my rear, I was squeezing my legs and rear end as tight as I could. It musta done some good because he was struggling again to push in after he got pushed right out.

Next I know, my head was crashing through the window glass, and I felt a horrible burning all the way up my rear. I was screaming now. Glass was shattering all around. I thought the falling down glass had sliced my head off because of the blood flowing down my neck and dripping in big streams down to the floor.

I think Silas was shocked as me at what he done. I expected him to let me go. Throw me on the floor and slunk off someplace swearing and yelling. But he didn't. Instead, he pushed my face down against a jagged piece of glass still attached in the window. My left cheek rubbed against it, I felt my skin slice open and more blood flowing. I felt Silas pushing in and out'a me as he held my face against the glass about a nick away from my eye.

That's when Squirrel Martin bust in through the door with his bird-shootin' rifle and shot a bullet one inch over Silas' head. Silas did little at first except stop his rutting.

He twisted his head around toward Squirrel Martin and sneered. He spoke more slow and more evil than inathing I ever heard in my life: "Git your goddamn retard ass away from here or I'll kill you dead raght'chere, possum boy."

Surprising both me and Silas, Squirrel Martin just stood there grinning. Silas couldn't bear that grinning. Still holding my face down against the sharp piece of glass, I could tell he didn't know whether he should charge Squirrel Martin, shove me right out the window, or both.

He didn't have time to ponder much further than that. Squirrel Martin shot another bullet at Silas that grazed his temple, spilling some blood. The bullet kept a-going right out the broken window into the darkness and the chill that was descending on the mountain like wavy black linen.

After that, Silas Silatoe wanted no more of us Johnsons.

He dropped me to the floor and skunked outta our bedroom, still glaring at Squirrel Martin, but not too much because he knew Squirrel Martin would shoot him dead easy as so what.

Funny thing, I wasn't that upset from Silas' violence at all. I knew it was all over with that man. Still feeling his pecker up me, and blood all seeped into my eye, I looked over at Squirrel Martin holding his rickety rifle. I said with a brief grin of my own, "That man's one lucky son of a bitch to still be alive."

More or less sober the next afternoon, Silas threw his old travel bag out the broken bedroom window with all his clothes in it. Standing there in the bedroom, ignorant and silent, he narrowed his eyes at me hateful and rubbed his fingertips against the bullet wound Squirrel Martin deliberately put where he put it. A third would'a hit him right between the eyes. And Silas knew it. But he was leering at me, nonetheless.

Knowing that look from the night before, I said to him, "Silas, you're leavin' me. An' if you weren't, I'd be throwin' you out. Your dirty rutting days like you're pissing all over somethin' sweet and holy are done."

He didn't like the sound of that, and briefly I sensed he was considering just grabbing me and doing what he pleased. But he didn't. He just stood there silent. He threw up his hands in disgust and said, "You go to Hell, Ruby Lee Johnson. You burn your damn sweet ass in Hell."

Right then, I swore to myself, I would never let a man hard do me or disrespect me or keep me from being 100% my real self ever again. Silas spit on the bedroom floor, went outside and disappeared over the mountain toward Red Hand, carrying his ragged carpetbag and all his meanness and hate right there inside it.

Maybe Silas went crazy on account of his unseen baby being dead and blamed me in his ignorant way. But Hardy was truly lost and crumbling apart over it. His ma said he even cried, which brought tears to my eyes. When his twin brother Lonny Dale got dumped dead on the Jessup front grass by the guards from the prison, all Hardy did was git drunk and puke up still whiskey into Macy's white azaleas.

For my dead baby girl, he cried real tears.

With my beautiful and noble brothers Bobby Lee and Tom Sawyer gone far out into the world, all that was left of us now is Granddaddy with no more working brains, me, Macy, Squirrel Martin, and Dahlia Rose. Sometimes I know why Mama chose to give away her life and disappear without a trace into the magic of our lady kin ghosts and the magic of the spirit field. If you come upon female suffering somewhere, chances are you'll find a Johnson woman nearby.

CHAPTER ELEVEN

Then, 1929 was poof gone, and it was the Sunday before New Year's Day, 1930. I wanted to begin this New Year on a different foot. I was thinking maybe a little commiserating with the Lord would help us git over the misery of last year.

None of us has ever been churchgoers. Grandma used to walk down to the Redemption Baptist Church every once in a while. A church of those holy rollers that preach about trust in Jesus as they handled poisonous snakes and such. Grandma went down there hoping one would bite dead the Messenger of the Lord they had preaching there, a man she knew from some past occasion. She was hoping a snake would kill him dead right there on the pulpit. When that never happened after a couple of years of going, she finally stopped going.

What's left of us Johnsons and Hardy Jessup (who was coming around an awful lot now) go down to church sometimes. Still cold winter, we'd go steaming down the driveway road through deep snow in places and black ice in others, with Granddaddy curled up on the front seat floor with his eyes closed. And him mumbling to dead Boolie's ghost, who is down there curled up with him, to be on his best behavior in God's little country shack. And once we were in there, all lined up on a pew, Squirrel Martin every once in a while would stand up on it to git a better look at the Reverend Pine Gregory.

With Johnson hatred so imbedded in these people, pictures of us as devils were probably floating around in their brain cells—nobody dared sit near us. It wasn't just humiliating. It was unchristian.

The Reverend Pine Gregory Angelle, not a poor preacher, especially, is just a plumb confusing one. At one point in the sermon last time we went, the reverend said in a deep and holy voice, "Children of the Lord, when sin is in your midst, burn it down. Just as sure as I'm standing here on this pulpit, lookin' at y'all lookin' at me, waitin' for a sign, I say—when you find a place of sin, and a sign comes from the Almighty—BURN IT DOWN!"

At that exact moment, with the Reverend Pine Gregory's arm straight up, a finger-pointing to the locked Gates of Heaven above, bam!, a big black crow came busting in through the window like it shot out'a a cannon. And slammed into the pretty vase of flowers that was sitting on the edge of the reverend's altar. Most likely dead the moment his head smashed through the glass.

The entire congregation shrieked wild and sin-struck and leaped to its feet as if Satan himself, causing only minor flower vase damage and dripping some water all over the altar but nothing else of any consequence, had just made a spectacular but unsuccessful entrance.

Hardy looked over at me and desperately wanted to laugh his head off. So did I.

All at once, Granddaddy rose like a dead man come to life and stood on the pew right next to where Squirrel Martin was already standing. Up on his creaky old tiptoes, he laid his hands smack on top of Macy's and my heads to keep his balance. Granddaddy boomed out in his biggest *you can hear him calling you two miles away in the woods* voice, "Why Reverend Pine Gregory, you look like a man who ain't sure whether to screw the goat or screw the shepherd!"

Driving home up the driveway road afterward in the snow, none of us felt any closer to salvation than when we traipsed in on the Reverend Pine Gregory and his crowed-up sermon. But the idea of burning ourselves into freedom…like the reverend said about burning sin away: it was nothing we were truly entertaining. But in some strange sort of way deep down place, me and Hardy knew it might be all I had left.

Lighting a fire.

We had no legal grounds to defeat the U.S. Army Corps of Engineers from taking our land either by eminent domain or paying us a bag full of Buffalo nickels for it. Either way, we would have nowhere to live. And even if we had a legal leg to stand on, there wasn't anybody in these parts lawyer enough to know how to work his way through a complicated case against the U.S. government.

Standing around in the kitchen, taking off our coats and counting up shoes after everybody took turns pushing the truck outta the snowdrifts all the way up, we were all just gawking back and forth at each other. Dahlia Rose sang up with excitement she ain't shown in a long time. "Ruby an' y'all—we're missin' the point of New Year's Eve entirely. A new year ain't about church. It's a day for counting our own blessings and looking forward to counting some more as the New Year comes undone all year long. I ain't sad to see 1929 fizzle into nothing left at all. And we sure could use some brightening up around here."

We were all staring at her jaw-dropped just like we did when Squirrel Martin said something more than his "I done it" pronouncements. For us Johnsons, Christmas and New Years has never been about the baby Jesus so much as a time for us to sit quiet and loving by the wood stove telling stories about love and kindness and laughing. Me finally agreeing to play some old high country Christmas carols on my fiddle until the kids fell asleep.

But that year we missed Christmas. Everything was so awful, it just passed us right by. And here it was almost New Year's Day 1930, and we were all still alive. Most of us, inaway. Past Dahlia Rose's bedtime, the kids, me, Granddaddy with Boolie's ghost sleeping at his feet, and Hardy Jessup all drank warmed apple cider, each with a cinnamon stick shooting out like they do it at the pharmacy lunch counter .

To give the kids just a bit of Christmas, Hardy read Mr. Charles Dickens' big picture book of old Scrooge and his wild night of traipsing bad to good. Hardy made up someone called the Ghost of General Brocklehurst H. Bigbie instead of the Ghost of Christmas Yet to Come. He knows the mind picture each child has of the black hooded gentleman gives them nightmares till the 4th of July.

Near the end of the evening, I played mountain carols for an hour or so. Everybody was singing along to some of'm like God Rest Ye Merry Gentlemen, I Saw Three Ships, and Si-a-lent Night, except Squirrel Martin because he cain't sing. Out loud inaway.

And Macy was singing real soft because she was feeling she's too grown up and womanly to be embarrassing herself singing in front of Hardy.

Afterwards, with Dahlia Rose asleep upstairs in bed, Hardy, Macy, Squirrel Martin and me sat around the wood stove and talked until almost midnight. Well, Squirrel Martin didn't talk, a 'course. But I swear, he listened more intently than any one'a us knows how.

We talked right through Macy finally wandering upstairs to go to bed. And Granddaddy, already up there, flinging his bedroom window open over the front door three or four times to relieve himself of all'a his apple cider.

Hardy and me had been itching to talk about Rev. Pine Gregory's sermon and its implications on my life but wanted to wait until we were free of the others. Pretty quick, our conclusion was the U.S. government wouldn't pay a red cent for land that was all ashes and black stumps.

"He said it himself, the Reverend Pine Gregory," I said to Hardy, "where there's sin, burn it down. Ain't it sin when strange government men come to throw you out and make themselves feel a little better about it by shoving a couple of dollars in your hand?"

Hardy said back to me, "I ain't sure we can call it sin, but it ain't right. And I'm not sure if the Reverend Pine Gregory was inferring that we burn down Redemption Mountain." Then he took a deep breath and tussled Squirrel Martin's long, raggedy brown hair. "But was I you and your family, and there wasn't no other way to survive, just like soldiers defending their homeland I would take drastic and irreversible measures."

I looked over at him and smiled big. "Why Hardy Jessup…that's a mouthful—drastic and irreversible measures," I said, teasing him some.

"Ruby, an ignorant son of Appalachia can take it upon himself to learn more than five-letter words in his puny lifetime."

I was gonna tell him I was only fooling, and I was proud of him for trying to improve his worldview, but just then the thumps of Macy's footsteps came back into the kitchen just before she did. "So what if I'm pregnant? Most girls my age is already on number two or three."

Hardy and me looked at her with eyes all wide open and stunned. Squirrel Martin wasn't exactly sure what she just said, but he knew no good was gonna come of it whatever it was. Macy was fifteen-years-old.

Before either Hardy or me could say a word in response, Macy said, "I done it with every town boy I could find, and a good bunch of the town men. I done it lying down, sitting up, squatting, upside down, standing legs wide open with my be-hind pushed out an' me hanging on to a limb of a tree."

Again, Hardy and me just looked at Macy. Squirrel Martin wandered over to the wood stove to give some lazy embers a few nasty pokes with the poker because he didn't know how else to respond to this. Just then we heard Granddaddy upstairs calling for Boolie. Then Dahlia Rose coughed a dainty little thing informing us she had crept along following Macy downstairs and had been sitting quiet all this time in the corner of the kitchen, listening to everything.

"And they pay me good, those fellas. Some give me two dollars if I let 'em do inathing they want. And I don't mind at all because I'm getting cash money to do sex that I would'a done for free, enjoying every minute."

For the third time, Hardy and I just looked at Macy. Thinking, *Well, this is one way to tell a girl's all grown up when all the men and boys in Redemption save their nickels for getting their hands on Macy's pretty body.*

I opened my mouth to say something, but nothing in the world came out. Nothing. Words just stayed where they stay when they ain't flying out'a a person. Even Hardy was froze.

"I'm planning on havin' this baby. Then I figured I'd leave it with you on account yours is kilt. Then, Ruby, I'm goin' to New Orleans to see if I cain't find me a life worth living."

Just like that, Macy spun around with her three and a half feet of raven hair all flying and fanning out, looking like it wanted to go to New Orleans, too.

Macy walked outta the kitchen in Macy-way, with her behind moving around a little too much, and clunked up the stairs to her bedroom. We heard the door close soft. The springs of her bed squealed, telling us she just jumped on it and was probably lying there on her stomach dreaming of becoming a New Orleans whore.

CHAPTER TWELVE

I had no idea what to do anymore. Winter'd been fiercely full of snow and cold. Weeks at a time we cain't git down the mountain. And folks sure cain't git up. Now'd Tom Sawyer's gone away from us, me and Squirrel Martin and Dahlia Rose and Granddaddy were all doing okay given the circumstances. Macy, though, she took to being absent for periods of time, sometimes a few days. We were snowbound, but she found ways to git down the mountain. Squirrel was unnerved by her escape resourcefulness. Well known for his own mysterious comings and goings, he just could not work out how she was slippin' away? Where to? And how she was slippin' back home? Me, I was unnerved by her secrecy. Some days she came sidling downstairs from her room for breakfast after being gone overnight, and no one knew she was back home. I never asked where she was or who with? My little sister made her statement of emancipation and I abided it. Macy Johnson never once showed interest in spells and magic in all her life. Mama used to say she was "an earthbound soul, not one red ounce of magic in her veins." I was wondering if the Johnson magic took hold of her after all? Lord knows, maybe she could fly!

I spose newspapers from other parts of North Carolina, and our own ones, too, are saying this is the worst winter of all time. More snow and cold since somewhere in the beginning of the last century. It don't take a genius to know that no old person from these parts ever told stories about snow and cold as fierce as this.

I kept asking Granddaddy about it. But after his brief bout with sanity for that week all of us fixed up the innards of the house cause we couldn't get out, when snowdrifts were so high against the front they touched the second floor windows, you'd'a thought the clouds above all froze and came crashing down, and me and Squirrel had to dig a tunnel out the front door, using frying pans in each hand for shovels, but like savages we all preferred climbin' through the windows—Granddaddy didn't even know he was living in the 1930s.

Most days now, he called me Dandelion, which was Grandma, his dead wife. "Dandelion, darlin'," he called after me when I tried to sneak past him sitting in his easy chair. "Dandelion, you sure is pretty as a picture, and even prettier." Then Granddaddy konked off to sleep for the rest of the evening, until he got up somewhere around 3:00 AM to let Boolie out to do his business, while Granddaddy did his business right off the backdoor railing into the snow sometimes.

During our snowbound time, we had fun together fixing half-jarred out window sills, painting yellowed walls, a couple of them with what was left of Squirrel Martin's holy murple color paint. Me and Squirrel sanded, filled in the cracks with sawdust and horse hoof glue and varnished the front room and kitchen floors.

Before we painted them, me and Dahlia Rose washed down every wall with buckets of a lye soap, whiskey and sweet water concoction we made. It smelled like skunk cabbage mixed with roses.

We washed two hundred years of Johnson history off.

Then we painted ours as the family comin' apart right back on.

Dahlia Rose seemed to be living her life a little more happy, and she talks a lot more than she done when everyone was living here. Her and me spend all our time together now, with Squirrel Martin scoutin' around in his feral boy ways. And I declare there was more intelligence and knowing in that little girl than there is all the rest of us. Somehow, maybe with Tom Sawyer's help, she learned to read. As the snowed-in weeks went on, she could read almost everything there is to read in the Johnson house. The Mark Twains. The Bible. Little story books about a curious Civil War girl named Azalea Beauregard, which was a tellin' of the history of the War as much as it was stories of her bold adventures. The Dictionary. The L and the S books we had of the Encyclopedia. Even the backs of seed packets and the Redemption Chronicle two-cent newspaper that Hardy brought up every once in a while.

Sometimes I couldn't remember how old Dahlia Rose is—seven or eight? Or maybe even six. Nobody kept track of such things, including her. She right up and said to me out'a the blue one day, "Ruby, a body's age has nothin' to do with nothin'."

I stopped what I was doing and looked down into her sparkling blue eyes. Dahlia Rose thought her thoughts out some and said, "Three of mah sisters and brothers is gone out, or is goin' out, into the world of grown up people. All of'm done it too young."

"That's what you think?" I said to her gentle but not really understanding. But she wasn't listening to me very good. "What I want to know is…Ruby, what do people look like on the other side of the mountains? Are they taller than us? Can they spring, summer, and fall in bare feet and swim naked anytime they want? They smart or stupid? Why does a person like my brothers and sister find their dreams only in faraway places called Hollywood and Paris Pants?

"Why cain't people be in love with their dreams right here?"

Why not, indeed. Our youngest-born may just turn out to be our wisest born. Then, she said, "You ain't left, Ruby. You walk around in your real life right here, not Hollywood or that other Pants place. We love it here, don't we?"

Like a condemned man about to learn his fate, Squirrel Martin Johnson looked up from where he was sitting on the floor, cutting out magazine pictures and eating most of the glue he had intended to use to glue the pictures on a piece of cardboard to give to Granddaddy for no reason at all. Squirrel Martin just wanted Granddaddy to have something nice to look at while the old man teetered into the dark place for old people of complete and sometimes humorous dementia.

Squirrel Martin put his scissors down and got up off the floor. Like a little toddler boy, he walked over to me and smoothly and instinctively put himself on my lap. Squirrel Martin knew full well that his life and future and mine were weaved tighter together than cord strands that made a length of rope.

While he was sitting on me, and while Dahlia Rose was still standing there wondering about what human beings that ain't Appalachian look like, I ran my hands as soft and gentle as I could over both their backs. Then I hug us three close together.

I didn't need to say nothin' to them. Both of the little ones knew I ain't goin' anywhere. And neither are they. Until they have a mind.

For right now, all we can hope is that this cold, blasted winter gets a mind to go blow cold and icicle-up people's lives somewhere else. Food's running low, but not too low. Me and Hardy bought all the winter provisions thinking Tom Sawyer and Macy would be here with us. And Granddaddy ain't eaten hardly inathing but the boxes of Milk Bones we had stored up when Boolie died.

So, isn't it interesting that we're having an easier time of not starving after our family left us cold, than if they was still living here?

When my birthday came at the end of February, instead of turning twenty, I felt a hundred years old.

That morning, without saying another word to anyone except Dahlia Rose Love Johnson, Macy Irene Johnson walked down the front steps carrying an old carpet suitcase, and something all wrapped up in bed sheets that looked like a birdcage. Slipping around in the ice and snow covering the driveway road until you git down to where cars can climb up to, Macy descended Redemption Mountain still swearing she'd only come back one time to hand over the baby.

There was a car there waiting for her. She hopped right into the front seat of a brand new Chrysler rich folks automobile. After dumping her stuff into the backseat, she scooched over to sit right up close to one of the Caton Brothers from Caton Coal and Oil over in Kentucky. How Macy got noticed by a Caton from so far away? I'll never know.

Just before Macy left, Dahlia Rose asked her why she's going away from us. Not even blinking, Macy huffed all dreamy, "Long last, Dahlia Rose, mah ship is comin' in. It truly is."

When Dahlia Rose told me about what Macy said, Dahlia Rose said with her darling, sweet face all lit up, "Ruby, Macy kept a-sayin' that her *shee-it has finally come in.* Ah had the most terrible time, Ruby, not laughing or asking Jesus to forgive my ears for hearing such things as shee-it comin' in."

Then she said, "Ruby, where did Macy's shee-it end up comin' in to? And is that where she's going? To go catch up to her shee-it that finally come?"

***

Usually, Hardy would'a been here to hear Dahlia Rose's divine little questioning. And Hardy an' me would look at each other and share a smile, knowing we'd talk later and have ourselves a good laugh. But Hardy hadn't been up here for a while.

Not on my birthday, and not before that for over a month.

I finally found out where Hardy'd been for all this time. He got married. His ma swore. When the snow finally melted enough to make the driveway road drivable for my decrepit, old truck, his ma and me bumped into each other at the grocery.

Hardy met a girl who was passing through.

Miz Jessup said I should remember her, but I didn't. She was the younger sister of that Arnold Ploy fella, who played so beautiful and won the fiddle competition last year. Miz Jessup said the sister was with Arnold. Maybe I just didn't want to remember the girl. Miz Jessup said the Ploy fiddler and his sister came back here to look up some of our mountain fiddlers because Nashville was a-looking for fiddlers to play background on records.

"Hardy and the fiddler's sister married legal. Ashley Summer Ploy her name is," Miz Jessup said. "Pretty as a picture."

Then Miz Jessup stopped talking for a little bit and looked me over like she never seen me before. "Looks a lot like you, Ruby Johnson, but not as total pretty as you are. And not as humble as you, neither."

I'm not sure I want to think of Hardy married to some faraway girl. Shoot, I don't know if I want to think of Hardy married at all. But married to a girl that looks like me—those words coming from the mouth of Miz Jessup—upset me greatly. Made me cry.

While I was crying there in the milk and cheese aisle of the Redemption General Store, Miz Jessup gave me a second good going over. She wanted to say, "Ruby! I had no idea you had feelins' for Hardy that weren't just friendship and brotherly!" But Miz Jessup knew what she needed to know and just quietly pat my arm a few times and left.

As I watched her leaving, I wasn't sure if I was in love with Hardy Jessup. And if I was, was it because he lugs the memory of his brother Lonny Dale wherever he goes? Or that I just missed powerfully the only man in my life that treats me kind and respectful?

And knows I am more than capable of doing most inathing done by a man?

Besides, me and Hardy have been having fun, and solving each other's problems since we were little kids.

And now, they were gonna take the mountain away. And Hardy wasn't here to help me keep hold of it.

***

Spring finally came, soft and gentle, but everything up here is dry as a bone. Trees are dry. The pine needles on the ground are dry. The streams are not half as furious as I would have expected after all that white winter snow. Where did all the spring melt go?

Yesterday, those U.S. Army Corps of Engineers men came up to see us again. Same ones, only this time they brought the sheriff. He didn't look too happy being court ordered to escort the skinny man Granddaddy peed on, and all his Army engineer friends up here, so he could throw us Johnsons off land we've owned before most of the European whites even made it to the Deep South.

Our Injun family parts were here a thousand years ago. Our white family parts were up here in the mountains before the 4th of July became something to celebrate. And our colored family parts have been a-sneaking in quiet and steady into the family since slaves first started escaping from their white plantation masters.

"Mornin', Ruby," the sheriff said, tipping his hat as usual. "Fine day, isn't it."

He was looking all around out there where you can see Appalachian heaven roll on perfect and graceful for twenty miles from our front yard. That man just couldn't look at me. He wasn't gonna show it but he was as heart broke over our plight as a man can be.

What I said to him was, "Nice to see you, too, Sheriff…Crow…whoever." But what I was thinking to say was, "What the hell are you lookin' for out there?"

All the men standing there with their city suits all dusted up from climbing the driveway road did exactly as the sheriff was doing. Some shielded their eyes with a little salute even though the sun is behind us, and all'a'm looked out into our beautiful countryside view.

"I gotta give you this," the sheriff said and sorta ambled over slow and embarrassed as if he lost a bet and had to show me his privates. He held out a big stack of official-looking documents all full of red wax seals, signatures, and state and federal insignias.

"Thank you, Sheriff," I said to make him feel better about

having to do such a distasteful thing. Instead of the "Fuck you and your family, Sheriff!" I coulda said and not felt bad if it had been any other lawman from these parts up here doing this.

He didn't say inathing more. I spose he was remembering the healing we did up here last year that brought the brains back to his little son. I wanted to ask, "How is the little fella?" But I could tell the sheriff didn't want me to ask such personal things in the middle of this awful thing. I didn't want to, either.

With nobody knowing what to say, Squirrel Martin came slinking up with his pocketknife out. The skinny federal man threw his eyes over to the sheriff and glanced back at Squirrel Martin. The sheriff strolled over to where Squirrel Martin was, kicking stones and dust all over with his big black boots. He picked Squirrel Martin up and swung him around firm but gentle so that Squirrel Martin was sitting on the big man's shoulders. That was statement enough, I reckon, for where the sheriff's loyalties lay.

Until they left, the sheriff never said another word. He let Squirrel Martin play around in the front seat of his big black police car for a little while. And Squirrel Martin being Squirrel Martin, he jabbed and turned and poked and pressed every single thing hooked up to the sheriff's dashboard. When Squirrel Martin finally found the switch for the siren, and it blared so loud birds in every direction leaped out'a the trees, Granddaddy woke up.

Hearing the siren screaming all over the mountaintop, Granddaddy came a-running out'a the house stark naked, with his stretched out old dingle swaying to and fro like a milk cow's udder. He was hefting Pa's old World War I rifle.

With that dingle of his swinging like a church bell, Granddaddy started shooting up into the trees. The damn old rifle still worked. Where Granddaddy got World War I bullets was funny just to think about.

Granddaddy said little as he was defending the Johnson honor from a mysterious aerial attack of who knows what. He kept shootin' and a-shootin', killing branches and one old wasp nest that came crashing down and exploded on the ground like it was a balloon loaded with gray dust.

Right then, those damn men started laughing at Granddaddy. They laughed and laughed, while Granddaddy went a-scootin' around stalking invisible foes. He shot dead the lilac bushes. Winged big mounds of dirt. He took a bead on the yellow outhouse and blew the door off the top hinge. Then he shot my truck. Shot it right in the tailpipe, sending thick dusty clouds of rust into the air. He was shooting around so furious; he hadn't noticed when Pa's Kaiser killing weapon ran out'a ammo.

He was just starting a fresh charge over a pile of manure when he made the acquaintance of a low-hanging branch. One shot from the enemy was all it took. The branch slaughtered Granddaddy right in the middle of the forehead, and Granddaddy dropped like a bird turd.

Before long, the sheriff and the federal men were gone, and I was holding in my hand a document thick as a tabletop. All'a its thousands of fancy words and lawyer talk essentially saying ten words, none of'm with more than four letters: *Git the hell out by the end of next week.*

But as long as any of us could draw a breath, this wasn't gonna happen.

Funny how timing is sometimes. The next day we got a postcard from Tom Sawyer. Brightened things up a little. It said *Hey y'all, I'm a-comin home in a couple of weeks for a visit. I'm doin myself mighty well in Nashville. I'll tell y'all all about it whince I git there.*

Tom Sawyer had no idea yet the "Johnson y'all" was down to a senile old man who got lost for days out in the woods making himself miles of fencepost holes, never planning on erecting any fence. A little fair-haired mountain princess, too young to be inathing other than a golden child. A boy whose brains are brilliant and retarded at the same time. And me…twenty-year-old drop-dead beautiful (men say) girl-woman who ain't got a man. Ain't got a child. Ain't got a future. And in a few days, ain't got the family house. And what's worse, ain't gonna have the family mountain.

The only thing to think about was what we're gonna have to do by Sunday noon to either git off or make a stand. And worrying ourselves into three severe cases of the hives. But I had to do something. I had to think about our future, dim as it was. So Squirrel Martin, Dahlia Rose and me got out all the garden tools we could heft. Threw them in the back of the truck and headed halfway down the mountain.

At a sharp curve, most people don't see because they're too busy trying not to drive off the cliff, there's a little dirt road. It leads to the hundreds of acres of our wild raspberries that have been growing there since the first Johnson keeled over nearly dead from hill climbing and starvation in 1710. He stayed alive by chomping on the raspberries until he acquired enough strength to whack a moose over the head with a shovel. And ate that. Or so we've been told.

It was hot as blazes. I went down there thinking that maybe the kids and me could dig out a mess of raspberry bushes, wrap up the roots in burlap, and bring them with us, wherever that might be, so we could make a new start. For nine hours me and the kids broke our backs. The roots went down deep and tangled around rocks and boulders that lurked about a foot below ground.

Getting the roots out was awful. Wild raspberry plants are like wild horses. They are best kept right where they are, loose and free, otherwise they lose their soul and then the spirit dies.

Knowing all this was silly desperation but kept us fighting, we managed to drag ten big bushes out'a the ground. But we did a hacking job on the roots of four. Wild things don't like their wildness messed with. All four died by the end of the day. The rest that next morning.

Our God-beautiful blue razor-thin ridgelines, soft hills fading into softer hills fading into even softer hills. And the magical mountain mists drifting through the tops of tall pines like spirits floating through somebody's dreams. How could we leave this?

We hadn't prepared a blessed thing to move out'a the house or cart stuff off the land.

It was time now, as Hardy said, *to take drastic and irreversible measures.*

I cain't say it's easy burning a mountain almost clear to the ground. But I cain't say it's hard neither.

Close on midnight that night, after I knew Granddaddy was about as dead asleep as he ever gets, I roused the kids out'a bed. Squirrel Martin without a sparking brain in his head already knew our mission and was rearing to go. Dahlia Rose, wearing her little ole white cotton sleeping gown with the hem all ripped and thready an' plumb adorable nonetheless, was still half-asleep and just allowed herself to be led along.

We tumbled down the back steps in the dark and walked through the backfield with grass up to our waists and over Dahlia Rose's head, heading for the old pink barn. If there was anywhere safe from fire, it was there because it was built on a big rise with boulders all around it. All'a us were barefoot. As I was wondering if we should quietly scoot back to fetch our shoes, we cleared the mound out at the far back edge of the field, and into our view materialized the most beautiful thing we ever saw.

The red lights sparkled like garnets. The dancing female figures were graceful and passed over the ground without ever touching it. All the gravestones covered in long billowing lengths of magnificent white silk that caught the moonlight as they gently waved. In the middle of the lit up spirit field with her hands all glowing lovely with pretty white light stood that little ghost girl I saw just after Safire died.

At first, she waved for us to join her. Then, changing her mind she floated out'a the cemetery and over the tall grass and met us halfway. To Dahlia Rose's delight, the ghost girl reached down and offered her hand. Then, there she was, our glorious little ole Dahlia Rose a-standing in the midair of our backfield on a hot early summer night, floating like a butterfly.

The expression on Dahlia Rose's face was what I reckon folks from the time of Jesus had on theirs when Jesus brought that dead fella out'a the tomb.

Not wanting to be left out, Squirrel Martin ran up to the ghost girl and his floating little sister and reached up his hand. Just like that, Squirrel Martin rose off the ground and floated on the ghost girl's other side. The three of'm floated back to spirit field, glowing like a red star. The spirit girl was offering safety to Squirrel Martin and Dahlia Rose on the one night in Redemption County's history that may rival that awful slaughter up here. That kilt all these here Johnson flying ghosty beauties during the Civil War.

Then, I was heading over to the old barn so I can pour gasoline. A few days earlier, I drove down to Coats Gas and Repair and filled up a big metal drum with gasoline. Then, drove it up here.

It was around 1:00 in the morning when I filled metal buckets with gas and carried them out to places on the property as far away as I could git from places I didn't want burned up...like the house and the surrounding fields. The Raspberry Acres. The barn. The spirit field. None of these things I wanted scarred. I truly didn't.

In fifteen minutes, I emptied three big cans of gas in areas on the far east side of the mountain. I figured the flames would come our way, wrap around the side of the mountaintop until they reached Indian Lake and all the waterfalls. I was counting on those falls to either put it out gradual as it approached from all the traveling mist or stop it dead in its tracks.

When I lit the first torches and flung them into little hemlock groves whose needles were dry as desert sand, I expected a few half-serious campfires to emerge out'a the dark. Dead dry spring and no moisture at all since the winter snows being the case. Instead…a vast wall'a orange flames exploded. It reached up high like the arms of a fire being, ran across the ground and split in different directions like several fearsome slithering fiery creatures, leaving everything they passed over consumed in flames. The roar of'm as they shot up the sides of those dry pines was so loud, I couldn't hear inathing else. I ran through the woods the other way to the next burning place, where I had already left two big jugs of gas.

Everywhere I ran, barefoot remember, I could smell gas and feel gas seeping and stinging into my cut and bleeding feet. I flung the torches end over end hard and angry like tumbling demons, furious the only way on this earth for a family in Appalachia to keep their lives and property was to destroy it.

In three hours, the north side of Redemption Mountain had walls of flames sixty feet high traveling faster than a person can walk. By daybreak, the fire had crept down into the Raspberry Acres and ate a good swath right along the driveway road. A wave of flames and pine smoke rolled over the back field, ate and collapsed the barn, and destroyed half the house.

Just before the back half of the house went, and it was still night, I was running back home to see about Granddaddy when I saw him fly out the back door holding a broom. I brought my hands up to my mouth to make a megaphone to tell him to go to the spirit field but I tripped over a pile of logs and cracked four toes before I could git a word out to him. I saw the fire roar over him with the force of an avalanche that consumed every living thing on all sides of him. Far from polite campfires, they had grown deadly. Granddaddy was just…gone.

Before I could even think let alone feel the horror, the fire I set now turned its murderous eyes to me.

As I was trying to pick myself up and limp over to the safety of the spirit field, my four broken toes, one with bones exposed, and the pain making me scream, waves of fire descended on me. Like it had on those colored chain gang men I saw as a little girl. That I saw the first time I remember anybody ever bringing me down the mountain, besides for school and church, to see the world beyond our driveway's red dust and the old chestnut at the bottom. Three black men on a Penitentiary work detail burning to death.

The field they were burning clean so it would be ready to take a new crop the next year turned on them in a sudden shift of the wind. All chained together, they couldn't move fast enough to git out'a the way. The huge flames rolled right over them like these ones just rolled over Granddaddy. Flames huge and furious and alive.

I saw them men when me and Pa, him driving a Dodge he had just barely working enough to roll down the driveway road a few times before it croaked, were driving to Foster to buy our little raspberry baskets wholesale. He was still in charge of our Raspberry Acres operation then. On the way back, we saw those fiery men.

Thirty minutes after we left that horrible scene, I was so traumatized from seeing men burn; I was still lying on the back seat with my dress over my head, screamin', when the car exploded on us. Pa was bumping along on a back road when the engine ka-banged and shot right up in the air. It busted through the hood and landed like an unexploded bomb on the roof of the car.

Pa got out and stared at it for a time. He opened the back door, hauled me out, and we walked the eight miles back home. That car sat on the side of that nameless back road in Redemption gathering dust for three years. We saw it one time when we were driving to see if Pa could git relief checks from the county's poor fund.

Ever since then, I often see one of those burning men in my mind. He's a nice looking black man with a peaceful face and nice eyes. This man, still on fire but seeming not to mind it much, has a way of walking through my mind and walking through my dreams like he wants to lead me somewhere.

I even gave him a name; he shows up in my brain so frequently. I call him Mr. James. No reason, I suppose, except I like the smooth and strong feeling I git when I say or think of his name.

I call on him sometimes, all fiery but calm and tender to me, when I need soft thoughts when I'm scared. Mr. John always comes, flames all over him, and holds me in his arms. It feels so, inaway.

As I was limping along, behind me the heat was so fierce, my skin was burning under my clothes. And the back of my hair was smoking like a big pile of red smoldering autumn leaves.

I was breathing pure smoke. I could feel myself passing out and falling. Taking a hell of a long time to do it, all slow motion and dreamy. The fire was so close; I felt like it was going to blow right through my body, keep on going, and reduce me to just my blood hanging there boiling in the air.

But just like that, I'm being led along by someone saying to me, "Ruby, my sweet girl, it just ain't your time to die." That someone spoke in Mama's voice. Then, by some kind of enchantment, an invisible wall shot up behind me the fire just couldn't roar through. The flame and heat just lay down behind me and died.

But stars above, my life had often been nothin' but a big ole horrible test and I was surprised I made it that far.

Then, I heard Dahlia Rose calling me in her sweet girlish voice. Then, I was in no human world that I can recognize, and I didn't know what to think anymore.

CHAPTER THIRTEEN

After the fire, the town did not exactly declare us dead. But it did not declare us alive, either. Which when I think about it, considering where me and the children went and stayed for that long, long while, was exactly right.

We were gone a full decade.

Just gone.

People are going to have to believe. That's all.

Everything was beautiful and slow moving and peaceful where we went. It was like a dream; where everything that was ugly and dangerous and sad and hopeless while you are awake is dreamy and soulful and like being alone in a quiet, joyful church when you were there. I am not at'all sure people who are not magical, who are not Johnsons, inaway, know about this place. Maybe it's just for mountain folks. Flatland people would ugly it up.

I don't think we were dead. And if we were alive, it was nothing like living our daily lives in Redemption. Time was slow *and* fast, right on top of each other. Can't explain it any other way.

The biggest surprise, Squirrel Martin could talk. And he did. He talked up a storm. He talked about everything. How the stars were so far away a person would be a million years old by the time they walked to one. He talked about why people are so scared of life and in need of believing in God to tell them how to live. How easy a time preachers had of convincing churchgoers of almost inathing. For a long while, he talked about what threatened white folks so about blacks. He said black folks have a deep soulful connection to something white people will never know. Scares them. Makes them feel disconnected. I never could git him to tell me what he meant by connected.

I spent my time making fiddles. Beautiful ones from types of tree wood we don't have here. I made a thousand of'm. Had them all hanging on little hooks right in the air. Folks would come and I let them pick one as if they were pieces of heavenly fruit, sounding and feeling in their hands nothing like one another. We could feel ourselves getting older but it was of no consequence. Somehow, we knew that. We would never die there. If we did, it was because we had had enough peace and beauty. Imagine that? Deciding to die because your life was perfect.

Then, one day, we *did* have enough of peace and beauty. We did not full-on die though. We just thought it was time to come back to Redemption. Any folks that knew us from way back may be gone or else we hoped wouldn't have a care about Johnsons anymore. Maybe we did die. Maybe all this earth is is a waystation for pain and misery. And women carry most of it.

When I talked about things like this, Dahlia Rose squiggles up her pretty face and says something like, "My stars, Ruby Lee, no wonder all your men left you. You ain't at all dumb and demure as they want you to be."

Like a big ole Godly hole just opening up in thin air for no real reason at all, one fine sunny morning me and the kids just come a-traipsing' outta the spirit field. We felt happy and normal as can be.

After ten years and being back home in Redemption, we were right back where we were right after the fire. Feeling a mite unsettled. But we also felt changed, more worldly, although where we just came plonking out from after so long a time was...otherworldly. When you come back from a better reality to the one you needed to escape from, you never feel settled with your decision. I'm not sure about the kids, but I asked myself every day for months, 'Why the hell would someone want to leave close to perfection?" For me? One reason. Perfection doesn't teach you inathing. It doesn't have rough surfaces and sharp edges that make you determined, passionate and curious. To be honest, perfection is damn boring.

Mr. Henry Ford's old rusty boned Model T dinosaur, which was the first thing Squirrel Martin wanted to see, had come crashing down when the fire ate Squirrel Martin's holy murple woodshed. For all these years, it'd been sleeping peacefully out back under the willows.

If you look close, some scar damage to the trees caused by the fire was right there in front of your eyes. And some gigantic old oaks and pines are not where they're supposed to be. But standing back and looking from a distance, the old place was the same old place, minus half the house. And enormous pile of burned timbers where the barn used to be.

The fire almost made a clean sweep past the house. As if it had good intentions, only pulled off the back addition of bedrooms that nobody used but Granddaddy once in a while when he was on one of those mattress testing things of his. It also ate the back porch.

We had no idea what day it was. Or what year it was. We were all too scared to find out.

Me and Squirrel Martin and Dahlia Rose spent nearly a week sweeping and washing and ripping out burnt parts of walls. We scrubbed the mildew off the ceilings and covered up the rodent holes as best we could. When we finished the cleaning-up, it wasn't half bad.

"Ruby," Dahlia Rose said, brushing sawdust off her shirt over her breasts, "Ah'm sure there's some kind of piney fluid that will help take away the smoky smell. But I cain't think of the name of it."

Seventeen years old now, she hooked her thumbs into the belt loops of her jeans and scooted her rear end around a little to git her underwear out'a her bum crack. When she was done, she laughed and was smiling her sun shiniest and said, "A gal's gotta do what a gal's gotta do."

Plenty of small things were still wrong, but we didn't care. Smoke drifted out'a the walls when the wind was blowing hard outside. I think Squirrel Martin liked it all smoky. Helped him sleep at night for some reason.

Before long, we got new screening we found up in the attic on most of the windows. Also from up there, we lugged down five gallons of white paint so old we guessed it was gleaming new on store shelves during Reconstruction. Not enough to paint the whole house, all three of us splashed it around on the sides, more on the front, that from a distance made the whole place looked fresh painted.

We got pretty flowers in glass vases all over the house, too. That was Dahlia Rose's doing. Every time I turned around she'd found another glass vase. And a new arrangement of pretty wild things would be on a window ledge or the corner of a bookshelf.

She was seventeen. Grown and drop-dead Hollywood beautiful as Silas used to brag about me. But I ain't bragging. She was gorgeous.

Squirrel Martin, he was twenty-two. Tall and skinny and gangly as a long stem of wild grass. He still didn't talk, but spent his days doing more thinking and listening than the rest of the world put together.

Somebody, I suspect it was Sheriff Dog And Two Crows, buried what the fire left of Granddaddy under the old cottonwood that Boolie used to dream his dreams under for days on end. I liked that man. Outside of Hardy, and Mr. Jesse on a good day, the sheriff was the only other man in Redemption with what I suspect is called integrity.

Me and the kids had a little service for Granddaddy. Dahlia Rose brought loads of flowers to sprinkle around and Squirrel Martin dug a little hole right in front of the marker the sheriff stuck in the ground. Squirrel Martin buried his favorite pocketknife probably right over Granddaddy's nose. It was the pocketknife that Pa gave him with the mother-of-pearl etching of Robert E. Lee looking fine in his spotless gray uniform, still looking like he believed the South might win the war.

But a funny thing about Robert E. Lee: folks say he was one of the greatest generals the USA ever produced. He led the South far more victoriously than any other general coulda done. But Lee did not believe in the Southern cause. He wasn't a bit fond of states' rights, or the South seceding to form its own bunch of confederate states under Jeff Davis, whom Lee was not especially fond. And Lee was against slavery. Pa used to say that Lee was the perfect Southern warrior gentleman. He stayed loyal to his home folks and kin even though he didn't agree with them. Lee raised a banner of belonging and loyalty over the rest of the South's banner of ignorance and cruelty but joined their side inaway.

Squirrel Martin's kind offering of something dear to him in the memory of his granddaddy gives me a respectful feeling I cannot explain. He and Granddaddy had a special Robert E. Lee attitude toward each other. It was quiet. No long philosophical conversations. No bear hugs and hand squeezing. They just got on with it. It was all in their proud looks back and forth, thinking a few seconds ahead of each other.

I reckon Granddaddy was the only Southern man over eighty years old who whittled only one stick of wood in his whole life, my fiddle bow. That's why Tom Sawyer got all those pocketknives Granddaddy seemed to make appear every other week. Granddaddy never used 'em.

All Squirrel Martin liked to do with knives was carve up humidity and heat into pieces of something fantastic only he could see.

And me? When we were through honoring Granddaddy and the kids were walking back to the house, I stayed and lay my body over Granddaddy's grave and rested that way for the rest of the afternoon. I never had the chance to mourn him after he died in the fire. When we left this earth, the children and I were only aware of ourselves and a few spirits, such as the Ghost Girl and Mama occasionally.

***

That next week I'd be thirty years old. I didn't mind, really. Being a lady instead of a gal made my thoughts more interesting and my view on things a little more deep connected. But deep connected or never mind, since we three come home, I only been down the driveway road once, to go into town.

That was after I found Granddaddy's stash of buffalo nickels in a tin box he kept buried on the north side of the big cottonwood tree, right where I knew they'd be.

Good thing, too. We were broke as sin with no Redeemer comin'.

Finding them made me feel luck or providence or some damn thing hadn't abandoned me entirely. If Sheriff Dog And Two Crows had done his grave digging there instead of the south side of the tree, he would'a plonked Granddaddy's little pile of ashes into the hole and found himself a reward.

Not sure why, my truck just wasn't there. Thought we'd find it all burnt up and melted into a big heavy blob in the driveway some place. I was really hoping we'd find it all gassed up with a brand new set of spark plugs and a Sears battery good for the rest of its life. The little ghost girl settin' in the driver's seat smiling great big zings of red light. Maybe even some fresh paint and a hand brake that worked when it was supposed to had found its way into the old truck's guts somehow.

Unfortunately, somebody carted or drove the old truck away. First thing on the list, after getting some better food up here than what Squirrel Martin had been bringing in from the woods—possum, rabbit, chokecherries, wild carrots and lima beans he's picking up from somewhere—we needed a new truck.

It took all morning, but I walked the eight miles into Redemption. Squirrel Martin was almost speaking in tongues he was so upset and determined not to let me go it alone. He relented finally when I explained to him he had to stay and protect Dahlia Rose. I was sure the wood stove fires we been lighting up here all week, with smoke billowing out the chimney, had more than a few folks riled up down there. Being the family protector appealed to Squirrel Martin's sense of family honor, a 'course, and he stopped yappin'.

Sides, after ten years without us, I had no idea what flat land folks or mountain folks thought of us Johnsons anymore.

Pretending I was invisible to every passing car and truck, I pretty much made it into Redemption downtown with a minimum of men's hoots and whistles shootin' out'a their car windows and diving under my clothes. I arrived early afternoon to a deserted town. Come to find out the annual Town Founders Day festivities were being held somewhere close. The town population was all over there, speaking highly of men who come into the mountains three hundred years ago with wagonloads of slaves. Rifles to kill the Indians. Leather belts to beat their wives who milked the cows, hid the whiskey bottles, warmed the beds, and reared the children.

New stores were everywhere, but I didn't pay them any mind. I marched straight into the old General Purpose Clothing store. Before I even got to the counter, I said to the sales boy in one long breathy, sexy exhale, *"Hello…how are ya I got these here nickels to spend on clothes and such for a twenty-two-year-old skinny boy no hips about six feet tall and a seventeen-year-old gal with bosoms and shapes just like mine two inches shorter'an me and git me hair ribbons and a bra for her…for myself who you can plainly see right here in front of you needs a bra too please include shoes underdrawers for the women three overalls three pairs a'jeans an' work shirts for each of us three two yellow and two green cotton ladies' dresses even though we ain't gonna go anywhere a buncha headscarves a workin' boy's hat three towels six sheets three blankets a boy's dress-up white shirt and tie we all need dungaree jackets work gloves a razor and razor blades lots of lady's panties some of that hard candy ...I gotta carry all'a this six miles on flat ground and two up the mountain so jam it all into some big parcels with twine I can use to heft 'em somehow back with."*

I smiled nice and lovely and struck a beauty pose, my Hollywood beautiful breasts knowing exactly where they were pointing.

The sales boy, a muley, red-haired kid of about twenty, stood there like Ice Boy, froze still, with confusion and exhilaration melting all over him. I could see he was appreciating my Hollywood beautifulness. He nailed his eyes to my chest and my face at the same time. An expression like an old hangdog hound smelling a unicorn for the first time on his dirty face, he was trying to understand a word I just said.

Then he went to calculating his ass off on how much all'a this would cost on account'a him being on commission.

Costs for clothing goods were more than they used to be, but still dirt cheap. After he counted all the nickels, and, tapping his twitchy fingers on the counter, and after a lengthy inner discourse, and some loopy penciling on a piece of cardboard, he determined I was $2 short. And now I owed him. He drawled slow as an old hound taking a hard crap, eyes twinkled up some, "Spose you'll need a hand fetchin' these here awful heavy thangs home."

What the hell? I was thinking, and I nodded, smiling my ass off.

The kid smiled back, teeth a mess of ground pepper and cabbage from his lunch. We rounded up all the items, and he wrapped up the purchases, then told me to go wait outside on the sidewalk. The front door slammed behind me.

The *Open...Y'all Welcome* sign on a string in the front window flipped over to *Closed...See Y'all Tomorrow.*

Two seconds flat the kid came sliding around from the behind the building in a death trap-looking vehicle with not a speck of glass in any of the windows, and the radio blaring "Blue Moon of Kentucky." The radio took turns coming on and going off all by itself. After telling me he named his car "Old Craphead," for obvious reasons, thirty minutes later we were sitting at the bottom of the driveway road, parked behind two willows whose branches swept the ground.

"Mam," he said. Then bold and ignorant as can be, he skiddled over, wrapped his arms around me so one of his palms was squeezing my breast. Then he slipped it under my shirt and was touching it. Quick as lightning he was kissing me. Hard.

I just let go to it. We squirmed out'a our clothes right there, sitting in a sorry-ass vehicle behind a blind of willows as dusk fell. A woman now, no girl, I was squatting on top of a bumpkin boy as he pumped up into me in the back seat of Old Craphead. With his big old redneck pecker inside the most Hollywood beautiful woman in all'a Appalachia, North Carolina.

He kept it going longer than I expected. I had two short orgasms before he took both my breasts in his hands, mashed up his face and grunted like a hog with its nose stuck in a tin can. The boy was detestable. But the physical contact with a flesh and blood human man, even one most people's family dog can out-think, was a beautiful and intimate experience. In a way nobody but me will ever understand.

We didn't say a syllable to each other when we were finished. Cool mountain wind blowing down from the mountaintop was perking up my nipples and giving me gooseflesh. We got dressed. I hefted the three big parcels and stepped out'a his disaster car right into a night so loaded with stars the sky looked like it was drooping in the middle.

I ran my eyes over his face without them touching it, and said, "Baa baa now." I walked right into the dark, knowing not a sane soul alive would follow a strange, mysterious woman up the driveway road to where the Johnson witches used to live. Took two trips to get the parcels up. But I didn't mind. Being born again, for real, back from ten years lost and back into human life, not no holy roller gibberish, I was craving the dark expansive feelings of our endless woods and the silence but for the soft echoie rustle of night branches, occasional hoots of night birds and the magical rhythms of nightnoise. Home wasn't much anymore. But it was alive and vast and mysterious and ours.

And I knew not a sane soul alive would believe this boy when he pounded the bar with his clenched up fist, insisting he ain't drunk or a goddamn liar, that he fucked a woman more beautiful than Lana Turner right here in Redemption, and right in the back seat of Old Craphead.

Other than Old Craphead's owner, not a Redemption soul knows it's us living up on the Johnson place again. Some just think it's stray mountain folk thinking they found themselves a castle to live in. Not knowing inathing about Johnsons and if they did, they would'a never crossed our front yard.

Dahlia Rose and me were talking about it. Before we went down again, we need to create a hell of a good story explaining our whereabouts for ten years.

And we need to make money somehow. We need canned goods and sacks of flour, rice, beans and coffee to add to what Squirrel Martin's been bringing in from the woods. As Granddaddy used to say, always drooling brown chaw down the side of his face, "I ain't got one red cent to call my own." With Granddaddy's lifetime collection of buffalo nickels spent on new clothes and supplies, we could do him one better—we didn't have a copper cent let alone a red one.

CHAPTER FOURTEEN

It was not a difficult conclusion to come to. Our future lay with Mr. Jesse.

And it was mighty clear folks are gonna need some time to warm up to me and the kids being back after so long a time that nobody saw hide nor hair. One morning, Dahlia Rose and me grabbed two shopping boxes and walked down that snaky two miles of driveway road. I had had an idea, and I wanted to talk to Mr. Jesse about it, if he was still alive.

"Ruby, they gonna know us?" Dahlia Rose asked me three or four times. Each time I answered, "They may not know us. But they damn sure will remember us."

Walking down the mountain to a reception by the locals that could be joyous as much as deadly, I said to Dahlia Rose, "Honey, this reminds me of all them times black women and Injun women had to hike up their dignity, hide their fear and walk straight into some whites-only place. They had no idea whether they would be spoken to or shot at."

We reached the bottom of the driveway road and crossed over to the other side of the valley road and stuck out our thumbs, hoping somebody not a serial killer'd give us a lift to Mr. Jesse's. First car that came by was full of young college men.

"Where y'all headed," one of'm asked Dahlia Rose after they hit the brakes so hard the car nearly did a somersault. Then he answered himself not waiting for us to reply as so many men are prone to doing. "Heaven? 'Cause you two are the prettiest damn women I ever did see. Man alive, girl, where did you come from?"

Both me and Dahlia Rose could recognize right off that these boys weren't threatening. Just young.

"Why…" said Dahlia Rose, "I been living in fairyland for the last ten years."

She was smiling back at the boy with her sparkling purple Elizabeth Taylor eyes, bewitching the young man who couldn't think of a thing to say after that. None of'm could.

At first, they wanted me and Dahlia Rose to sit on their laps because there wasn't much room for two more. Then there was a gentleman enough in most of'm that they did some scooting over and rearranging so all'a us could sit on our own place and still breathe a little.

"Y'all from around here?" I asked the whole car.

"No mam, we're from Bulls County on the other side of the valley. Y'all been over there?"

I was trying not to think of those burning colored men I saw as a child my first time out'a Redemption. Or about Silas and all his crudeness and meanness, who I was still married to, and, I reckon, I'd'a just have to pretend we got a divorce because I had no plans to see him again. Or he me, I suspect. I was beginning to answer in Southern gal dumbbell speak in case I needed to trick them with intelligence later on. "Why, a 'course I have. Other places, too."

But Dahlia Rose said quicker than me, "I ain't never been nowhere but here and fairyland, Mr. Asks A Lot Of Questions." The way she said it was just like a brat princess saying, "I own the whole damn world, with you in it, Mr. Fancy Pants."

The college boys thought that was funny. A lot of whew-wees and mah-mah-mahs bounced around in there. Our conversation stumbled on like that; nothing said worth thinking twice about.

Then, up ahead, Mr. Jesse's place was looming large. "We're goin' over there," I said, pointing.

The college boy driver careened over the yellow line and whipped up a weather front of red dust as he blew into Mr. Jesse's parking lot.

"There you go, fahn ladies," the driver said like a limousine driver. "I hope you enjoyed the rahd."

"Oh we did," I said with more cheerfulness than necessary. "You handsome boys have a fahn day now."

Just as they dust-clouded in, they dust-clouded out and peeled off down the lonesome old valley road. Mr. Jesse was standing in the doorway of his little office with his hat off, scratching his head and looking horse-whipped. Whether it was from damning the college boys for their recklessness or trying to figure out if me and Dahlia Rose were who he thought we were, I could not tell.

"Who were them hoodlums," he said, but really wanting to ask who we are? as we walked up to him.

Dahlia Rose answered real nice and sweet, "College boys from Bulls County. They were gentlemanly enough to give me and my sister a ride."

Mr. Jesse was stalling from having to make his brain come to a conclusion about us. He said, staring after those boys as their car was now no bigger 'an a bug in the distance, "What are Bulls County college boy smart alecs doin' around here?"

All the while, he was giving us a good going over. Up and down, real slow.

I became immune to men crawling all over me with their eyes since I was a bitty little girl. I wasn't sure how Dahlia Rose was feeling. Mr. Jesse's eyes touching us in all our private places. I didn't reckon he meant to be disrespectful or too sexual. He just wasn't believing what his eyes were telling him.

Real, real slow, a voice came out'a him like somebody who flings open their front door wearing their pajamas, and to the glowing man standing there smiling back, they say because they cain't believe it, "Jesus…? That really you?"

"Ruby…? Ruby Johnson…that you?"

As Mr. Jesse was acting like he seen a couple of female Jesuses, I was trying hard to think of something to say that would put his mind at ease. I couldn't think of inathing except, "Good to see ya agin, Mr. Jesse. How are you and all your vegetables doin'?"

"We're just fine," he said slow as dry rot, "we're just fine."

I ain't never been one for beating around the bush. I come right out with it. "Mr. Jesse, I came here hoping you and I can talk business. You got some iced tea or something we can drink somewhere quiet? Maybe a condiment?" I was starving hungry.

Only place he had to talk business in was his scrawny office that only fit him alone standing up, or right there in the sizzling, dusty driveway. At first, he made a nodding gesture and signaled me and Dahlia Rose to follow him. After three steps, Mr. Jesse realized he ain't got iced tea and for all he knew a condiment was some fancy *when company comes callin'* fish dish. His expression was going all wrinkled and rubbery like a big old possum. He wanted like hell to ask me where we Johnsons had been for a full decade.

But he held his tongue, and I'm not sure why. Maybe he just plain didn't want to know or was afraid to know. He was from an old Redemption County family who are full aware of the Johnson supernatural legends. So instead of asking us inathing, he stalled some more. And we stood right there in his parking lot.

"You cain't tell me this here beauty is that little gold-haired sister of yours?" he said to me, meaning Dahlia Rose, a 'course. "That fine, fine child has sure growed up…"

Dahlia Rose is such a beautiful young woman, Mr. Jesse went blank as a preacher with his pants down. "Has sure growed…up…growed…fine," he said finally.

I was thinking now all this Mr. Jesse awkwardness probably ain't doing our fledgling business relationship much good. Sweet but firm, I said, "Mr. Jesse, you've known my family all'a your life. And you've known me all'a mine. Am I right?"

He looked at me like I just said, "Mr. Jesse, that sky up yonder is blue on a daily basis, am I right?" It was a stupid thing to say, but I done it inaway. Business negotiating takes a skill I ain't sure I have tucked in under my belt yet.

"I'm nervous, Mr. Jesse. I ain't never done a thing like this. Tellin' you that just lost me my advantage of mystery, I know. But I'm not lookin' for mystery, I'm lookin' for a business partner."

Now he said something. And he didn't mince words either. "A raspberry business partner?"

"Yes, sir," I said short and simple.

"Keep talking."

"All of our acres that got burned away in the big fire years back are mostly all grown back. The Raspberry Acres for some reason have almost doubled. Cain't say why. Maybe because they've been growing wild and unpicked for all'a this time. Inaway, sir, these days only Dahlia Rose, Squirrel Martin, and me live up there anymore. The job of pruning and picking and hauling all those berries is just too much for us. We never really cracked into making real money with them inaway because all we needed was day by day living money. Things aren't so simple anymore."

Mr. Jesse was absorbing all this with a deep-thought look on his face. Pickups skedaddled up and down the valley road out front as we talked, but none of us looked up when they passed by, until one full of men came barreling down the road. First they honked the horn as the truck flew by, which I expect was to explain to Dahlia Rose and me that these men were thinking how nice it would be to rut our brains out. They turned around and drove back slow and honked a little more. Then they just gawked silent, with all their heads leaned over, looking out the driver's window.

"Key-rist!" Mr. Jesse said, annoyed but understanding perfectly what got into these boys. He'd been sneaking peeks at us the whole time we were standing there, only he thought we didn't see. Why is that? Men sneaking penetrating looks at your breasts or rear end think if they look right into your eyes for a few seconds before and after, the women doesn't know what they're doing?

Soon enough the men whipped around in another U-turn to head back in their original direction. Heads all sticking out the other window now like they were watching the end of the world with beautiful breasts walking around over here.

"Let me see if I'm understandin' this, Ruby," Mr. Jesse said calm and friendly. He's wiping his sweaty brow with a pocket-handkerchief that must have mopped the sweaty brow of George Washington. It had less cloth to it than a rock.

"You're askin' me if I want to buy into or share the business runnin' of your Redemption Mountain raspberry pickin'. This so?"

"I'm more interested in selling you half interest to the Raspberry Acres. Which means you can hire anybody you want to work them and haul away as many you please to broker to all the folks you want to broker to. Only you own 'em outright. Or do inathing you want. The acres are half yours. Berries you take out of'm are all yours."

Mr. Jesse knew there was money to be made by somebody who takes over the enterprising of those berries on a basis more professional than just the kids and me loading up the truck when we needed to. And then crashing down the mountain. Granddaddy, when he could think clearly way back, and me were always curious why no land developer or business schemer or just plain local farmer didn't hike up the driveway road, smile huge, and throw a price in our face for picking rights or owning rights.

I suspect people around here had enough of their own troubles trying to stay alive during lean times that never ever got thick. And if you plonked all the cash money from the whole county back then into a cigar box, there would still be room for most of the cigars.

All this time I was thinking about these things, Mr. Jesse had been factoring. "How much?" he said.

"I knew a 'course you'd ask that. And, my stars, I don't know. What's the price of a mountain acre these days, Mr. Jesse? And because you're practically kin"—(he didn't like me saying that too much. Although he recognized the implication that I appreciate all the years we done business together before this, and how fair a man he is)—"I'll leave that for you to factor out. And when you pay me, I want you to do it in installments so it will give me and mine a living wage for the years to come."

I reached out my hand and he took it right away, although my female sense told me he wanted to touch me and think about rutting more than think about a business deal.

"Can one of your farm hands drive us into town real quick? Me and Dahlia Rose jus' need to buy some things at the grocery. And maybe even an entire wardrobe of new clothes."

I said this less as a real request or outright lie, more as a little business strategy of my own. I wanted him to think that we Johnsons weren't entirely broke. If he knew the truth, he could offer me dirt balls for the Raspberry Acres and I'd have to be half-serious about accepting them.

A boy named Jackson Pike drove us into Redemption proper and waited for us in his truck out front as we walked up to the grocery with no idea what we were going to do. We didn't have any money. I went to town with the vague notion that if I could git a positive response from Mr. Jesse to think about my business proposition, maybe I could mention that to folks and open up some credit somewhere. I even had a brief fantasy of Mr. Jesse saying all jolly and respectful, "Ruby Lee Johnson, I been waitin' twenty-five years for one'a you Johnsons to ask me that." I see him reach into his secret pocket and produce $500 like a carnival magician taking a rabbit out'a a hat.

Standing there on the sidewalk in front of the grocery, Dahlia Rose said low, "Let's just thank that boy and git him outta here so we can set a spell and think out a plan. Without him chewing on grass, thinking dirty thoughts most likely, staring at us."

"Girl, how are you thinking we're gonna git ten miles home?" I asked her.

She replied, "You done it once. Question is Ruby Lee Johnson Silatoe Whoever Else You Might Be Someday, how are you thinking we're gonna git even a lima bean when we ain't got a cent?"

Just then, the carload of those men who were gawking at us earlier pulled in next to the Pike boy and were immediately right in our face, standing in a circle all around us before we could blink twice.

Not liking the look of this, the Pike boy backed the truck up. As if he'd been just setting there alone and bored for weeks and just this instant the time arrived for him to disappear around the corner by the Church of Christ the Carpenter.

Crackers that they are, one of the men, a corn cob-headed looking guy, stepped into the circle the others formed, pretending he was wearing a big old fashion Three Musketeers feathered hat or some such. He made a grand gesture of taking it off and bowing to us. "Well, if I never…" he said real sarcastic. "Maidens from them old Greek myths right here in our little ole town. 'Magine that. 'Magine that."

Besides him, there were five of'm, all closer to forty than twenty-five as I thought before. "Would you lovely, amazin' mythology bee-utees like to join us for a small, refreshin' late morning appointment with Mr. Jack Daniels?"

Before any of'm or any of us could say one word, a fat one in overalls with a blue bandana hanging like a dead bird out'a his back pocket said loud, making all his friends startled, "Shoot man, I know them! That red hair one is that Ruby Johnson. Remember her? The half nigger who shows white? That family of crazy Johnsons with a retard boy named Chipmunk or something. All those stories of their kinswomen getting knocked-up by ghosts. This one here burned down her own place up on Redemption and five thousand acres of mountainside one night for a reason not a soul knows why. Then, all'a'm except a burnt up old granddaddy just up and disappear in all that smoke. Just gone into all that smoke. Nobody seen 'em since.…till now, I reckon."

The fat man was talking so loud, and the spectacle of the two of us surrounded by a group of threatening men drew a crowd right quick. "Ruby," Dahlia Rose whispered under her breath, "you think we kin go home now?"

First a few people came over to lend a hand to two defenseless females. But after listening to old Fatty blabber, and seeing us for themselves, in a few minutes we had twenty-five or thirty people standing there glaring at us.

Glaring us stone cold dead.

They had such strange looks on their faces. Like at any second some silent signal was going to tell them to start smiling and welcome us home. Or mob kill us once and for all right there on the sidewalk outside Tompkins Bros. Grocery, est. 1864.

Never in my life have I used the spirit to hurt anybody. Cain't even recall a time I even thought about it seriously. But there we were. Dahlia Rose trembling. And so was I but I think I was covering it good.

Not sure what got into me; I took Dahlia Rose's dainty hand and backed us up against the grocery store window. Then, I let her go and took a full-step forward by myself. No words. No threatening looks. No swearing.

I just held out my arms and showed these folks my palms.

Little by little all the Johnson stories they ever heard went a-clunking around their dry old cow-flop brains. Then, every one of'm started to come down with a touch of amnesia. By magic, in less than a minute, I had their brains empty as a big ole room with nothing at all in it. The people that came over to lend a hand, and then were considering becoming vicious at the sight of us, quietly started greeting each other like they was coming outta church. Then went about their business. Not even remembering me and Dahlia Rose were standing there.

It was so easy to do.

Soon, all that was left were those six crackers.

"You ain't gonna kill iny'a these here, Ah hope," Dahlia Rose whispered.

Just as I was holding out my right palm an' pointing it at old Fatty, trying to think up something to do to him that won't 'cause too much stir or injury, and just like the law always does in movies, a big black sheriff car pulled in slow. Using this as a good excuse to save some redneck dignity, the crackers slid on outta there, Fatty knowing he just narrowly avoided getting his testicles roasted. Or probably worse.

After getting out'a the police car, standing there looking at me half excited and half like he was seeing dead old Robert E. Lee himself with red hair down to his ass, Sheriff Dog And Two

Crows, saying nothing, opened the back door to his vehicle. He waited for us to climb in.

The sheriff drove us over to Pattersonville and gave me eight dollars to buy groceries. He said very little. Every few minutes he's drawl on about something plum obvious, like, "Them trees over there are sure dry and thirsty. Look at'em. You can almost see their roots clambering down deeper. Ain't rained here since April." When we had our grocery bundles setting in the backseat with us, he drove us home, with his gigantic car spewing torrents of red dust all the way up the mountain.

Just as he was getting back in the car after helping us carry in the groceries in, he turned to say something, but did not. Too many things were on his mind. His brainless son was now brainful and married to a nice colored girl who helped him in his bait business. His suspicion that we set the big fire ourselves because they found used and unused torches and burned up gasoline cans. Granddaddy getting in the way of it and burned alive. Maybe that was a crime for the fire starter, maybe not. Not a Johnson in sight for ten years. Not a soul down country who would dare come up to the old house on account of Civil War ghosts and crazy ladies fixing to skin them alive.

The kind man, looking old now, too, smiled at me, said nothing, and drove away.

Over the next week, with Mr. Jesse not driving up like he said he would, making up his mind real slow or else playing *git you nervous business games* with me, me and Dahlia Rose discussed our options. Squirrel Martin was coming in from the woods once in a while to cart away cans of food from the pantry, half burned candles, old paper bags, empty Pepsi bottles, and other stuff to some secret place out there. He wasn't hurting inathing so I let him alone to do his secret mission.

All that week Dahlia Rose and I talked about our options a million times. But we sure didn't have a million options. Truth is we had three. One…stay put. Work the deal with Mr. Jesse and take our chances with the local folks. Two…move away. And to where? And with what? I didn't even have a truck anymore. And three: Stay put in a different way. Live here on this side of the mountain but do all'a our people interacting on the other side of the mountain. The Bulls County side.

Johnsons are just make-believe ghost stories to scare little kids over there.

CHAPTER FIFTEEN

But before we even had a ghost of a plan, one night, rocks came smashing through the windows like a hundred huge hail stones spit in at us by a pitch-black night.

Dark figures gripped tight to raging flame torches paraded around outside the house and chucked rocks in at everything they saw. Rocks bounced in all over, breaking windows, breaking mirrors, chipping plaster off walls, smashing Dahlia Rose's flower vases. What cups, glasses, and plate ware we had all came crashing to the floor when two big bricks hit the kitchen pantry shelf at the same time. The broken shards spread out across the kitchen floor and bore deep into my feet when I ran in trying to find Dahlia Rose by following her screams. For the rest of the terrible night, I limped around leaving a trail of bloody footprints everywhere I went.

I'll never forget this: my fiddle was resting on the sideboard calm and composed as can be. Rocks just didn't seem to want to hit it.

Five huge Kluxers, one of'm Tolbert Greaves, in white robes and wearing those ghouly hoods marched right into the house with their torches. Not caring at all that one small careless action could burn away the rest of what we owned.

I knew I couldn't reach Dahlia Rose before they did and since one of us had to escape to save the other, I hid in the storage hutch under the stairs. Dahlia Rose was screaming, so she was easy to find. Two of the men grabbed her rough and dragged her fighting hard out the back door.

Once I knew they had Dahlia Rose, I was ready to give up so I could git with her and try to git us out'a there. But then I thought if they couldn't find me, I'd be able to git Squirrel, who was out in the woods somewhere, to help sneak Dahlia Rose out'a whatever captive place they had her.

All that planning didn't matter. My trail of red footprints led the Kluxers through the living room and right to the hutch closet and me, where I was waiting with a kitchen knife to hack off whatever any of'm bastards put toward me.

But the brute strength with which they smashed in the door stunned me. The stairs above came crashing down. On me. My knife was just suddenly in one of their hands. As they were hauling me out with their hands dug in my hair, all their other hands were traveling rough and deliberate into my clothes.

But I still managed to scoop up my fiddle as they hustled me outside.

Almost to the exact second the bastards threw me up against the outside wall in the backyard next to Dahlia Rose, rifle fire came out'a the darkness and bullets hit two men. A Kluxer hit the ground looking a mite stupid, thrashing around like caught fish on dry land. Trying to git a hand to his gunshot ass to check the damage. Another was hopping around on one foot like he just stepped on a nail but was too embarrassed to tell his ignorant friends the bullet hole in his thigh hurt.

Several more little .22 rifle shots pinged around, scattering the men. And knowing Squirrel Martin's mind as I do, I grabbed Dahlia Rose's arm and dragged her out'a there, running fast as we could out toward the backfield and the pitch dark, where Squirrel Martin had positioned himself. Squirrel Martin's little assault of well-aimed little measly .22 bullets took those idiots in wide-eyed surprise. They hadn't even reached into their secret Klan robe pockets for the whiskey bottles yet to summon up courage as they decided what they were going to do with us. And me thinking fast and running us out'a the firelight circle and into the dark so quick, we plain outfoxed them.

Before they could figure why their friends were screaming in pain, we got pretty far out in front of'm. We lived here all our lives and know every bump and stone on the mountain. The Kluxers, about twenty of'm altogether, were having a terrible time, slamming into low branches, tripping over all those exposed pine roots. One of'm ran into the old bee boxes and howled loud as a run over dog when he snapped his left leg bone clean in half.

And I couldn't imagine what Tolbert Greaves must have been thinking since we bushwhacked those men before a word was spoken. He couldn't even be sure I knew one of the Kluxers was him.

Squirrel Martin ran out'a the woods on an angle, carrying his rifle in his left hand and came up along the other side of Dahlia Rose. He helped pull her along. Together, we hauled her up the long rise and then down the apple tree hill that leads right to the cemetery field. Squirrel Martin and me never talked about it, we just knew. It was the only place to go. Before we even got there, Squirrel Martin and me knew that once we crossed that line into it, we would be perfectly safe.

So, when we reached the boundary line we stopped running. Squirrel Martin let go of Dahlia Rose and turned around to take a bead on any Kluxers that came hooting out'a the dark. I rubbed slow circular motions on Dahlia Rose's back with my palm to help her relax and feel better. With her thinking we've flipped our lids because the Kluxers were finally gaining and we're just standing there, Squirrel Martin smiled over at her. He said so quiet and proud of himself you could only just about hear him, "Dahlia Rose, you ain't to feel no fear."

In our family, we all knew Squirrel Martin's rare utterances mean something absolute, and you could trust it completely. She calmed down right away. Kluxers bearing down, she took a long breath, smiled at both of us mischievously and said with pretend seriousness, "Dirty bastards broke all my glass flower vases."

Then, holding hands, we strolled into the cemetery field talking about my sliced up feet. Once in there, one after another, we slowly turned around to see the clutch of big brutish Kluxers, their torches casting flickering shadows up into the tops of trees. Every one of'm was standing there not ten feet away looking straight at us, but not seeing a damn thing.

Too scared to walk into the spirit field directly, they looked like they were pushing up against an invisible window that completely encased us. Then, they decided big strong men like them shouldn't be afraid of much of inathing. They threw their legs forward to step into the graveyard and their legs stuck fast in the air. One poked his torch forward with all his strength and accomplished nothing but the torch pushing back violently and nailing him square in the face.

This is where I shoulda left well enough alone. However, how often does a spited woman find herself completely unseen by a gang of rednecks who ain't even found their courage yet because there's still been no time to yank the cork out'a the whiskey bottle? Letting my better judgment act all childish, I walked right up to the edge of the grass and howled my Hollywood beautiful ass off—scaring the Kluxers into apoplexy.

Dahlia Rose and Squirrel Martin hooted and wailed from where they were. Legend says, because Yankee soldiers massacred our womenfolk, men in uniform can never cross the line into the Johnson graveyard. Kluxer clothes are not quite a uniform but it was uniform enough. After what we did, scaring the piss out'a them already, the whole field sparkled up bright red. The lovely Civil War Johnson women were all floating around with their long hair trailing behind. The long lengths of exquisite white silk they were carrying flicked and snapped like heavenly bullwhips. Five feet away, these amazing visions were right flat in these terrified men's eyes, which had all puffed up bigger than a thumb after a rattlesnake bite.

So afraid, even the man with the broken leg was running fast. The Kluxers grabbed their fallen comrades and made tracks, already arguing whether they should tell anybody in town what happened. Whether they would be seen as heroes for their assault (though unsuccessful) on us. Or seen as imbeciles for being defeated by two gals and a retarded boy.

Unfortunately, before they reached any conclusions, they took their loss and humiliating brush with the supernatural out on the house.

Heading down the mountain with much different intent than when they came up, they flung most of their remaining torches through the broken windows of a structure that has housed the Johnson kin for two hundred years. Where it finally and spectacularly burned to the ground.

We did not stay long in the spirit field. Squirrel Martin was over excited and kept pulling us by the hands to the back of it. He wanted to take us somewhere. The woods were Squirrel's kingdom.

He knew every inch of it. We felt safe letting him lead us.

It was so dark in the woods Dahlia Rose and me felt like we were sleeping. With remarkable ease, Squirrel Martin led us over paths, around and through great stands of fir timber trees, up steep inclines. He guided us around great boulders, and along the sides of creeks that I just knew had bottomless peat bog sinkholes in every direction ready to suck us down. Squirrel Martin knew his way right around every conceivable obstacle and place of danger.

In woods so dark it made you blind.

"Ruby," Dahlia Rose said every few minutes, "is he takin' us inawhere?"

The first few times, I didn't respond to her question directly, but said things such as "Darlin', keep walkin' and save your breath." Then after she said it for the fifth time, I stopped short and waited until she noticed I wasn't walkin' behind her.

"Ruby!" she called out terrified into the dark. "Jumpin' Jesus, Ruby Lee?"

"Girl," I said from back there, "I have no idea where he's taking us. But have a little faith. This boy is more magic than I'll ever be."

We continued on for a time.

And just like that we looked up into the trees and see lights. Looking longer, we saw windows with light shining out from the inside. A few more steps and we saw a house with all the windows lit up about twenty feet off the ground.

If it wasn't floating up there, it would'a looked like a hundred other mountain cabins spread out in desolate places throughout the high country. The types of cabins containing the types of people who don't see another human being for years on end, and don't want to.

Dahlia Rose said serious as can be, "Ruby Lee, we have died and…gone…to…Heaven. What in the world?"

I agreed. Smiling out'a one of the lit up windows, up there was Squirrel Martin. Behind him inside the little house, you could see painted walls with framed pictures hanging on them. Old stuffed chairs and polished wood tables. Man alive, I even saw what I thought was an angel, a great big thing with all pretty shapes and strings and everything. Just as quick as he appeared in it, the window was empty again, and Squirrel Martin was standing right back next to us holding a lantern.

"Them other times you saved our ass weren't too bad, Squirrel

Martin… But this…" Dahlia Rose started, but she just could not git any more words out.

Of all'a his "I done it's," we three knew this one topped them all. An' he didn't even say it. In a voice like someone underwater afraid to open their mouth, Squirrel said, "Fiddlin' turkeys" instead. To us, not a clue why he said it. But to him, it explained everything.

For who knows how many years, Squirrel Martin had been building this tree house. I suspect since he was a young'n and he used to stay out in the woods for days at time. We'd know he was safe because Boolie'd come romping home for a bowl of dog mash. Then, romp right back out into the woods back to him.

Up the ladder we climbed.

By the look of the inside, the house itself had been raised up and built good for years. It was about the size of our big open family room at home, pretty good size. Scavenged for probably a hundred miles around, he had everything a person needs to live anywhere. A lovely old decorated wrought iron cook stove with swans all over it. Dahlia Rose and me were not gonna think about how he got it up there twenty feet. Big old fluffy stuffed wing chairs, four of'm, one in each corner. An eating table with six matching chairs. A little sideboard. Two bookcases, one with old books in it. Pretty oil lamps. In fact, a few too many. Squirrel Martin's tree house was blazing like a sleeping comet.

And right in the center of the ceiling, an enormous crystal chandelier hung down about three feet, and was maybe five feet across. It had hundreds of little hanging down slivers of crystal that shined like a kingdom of fairies and clinked softly as beating wings when breezes came whispering in the open window. Then, when I looked close at the window cut-outs, there beside them on the wall, he had full open-inside windows on hinges, including panes of glass like a door that I suspect he just closed shut when he wanted some privacy.

Me and Dahlia Rose didn't know where to begin asking questions, although we knew all the answers inaway. He musta been roaming and roaming everywhere in the mountains looking for old, abandoned mountain folks' shacks. Some of it looked like antiques maybe absconded by Yankees during the Civil War that they abandoned on their march back North. That really happened. The Yankee soldiers looted the riches of the South but got tired of lugging them and began leaving them on paths and dirt roads all over the mountains. Of course, hill people found them. Some, great treasures that they hailed back to the shack. All this stuff he found somewhere. All this stuff he had to carry, drag, maybe wheel on something he made, beg, pray to, and swear at to git it from wherever it was to here through our forest primeval.

I thought something was a little funny because the inside didn't seem as big as it did from the outside. Over in a corner behind what looked like a wall but was beautiful lengths of the purest white silk there ever was on this earth, behind this elegant curtain was another part of the house.

A little bedroom with an over-size feather mattress all made up with scarlet silk comforters and white silk pillows on a hand-carved mahogany bed frame that I swear Queen Victoria slept on. Beside it, a matching ladies' vanity millionaire-looking thing if I ever saw one was set up with all kinds of old mother-of-pearl combs, brushes, and hand mirrors with what looked like real pearls and red diamond gems all over them.

There were face creams, dainty bathing soaps, and a big bone china washbasin with Chinese looking patterns in golds, reds, and purples that said *Limoges* on the bottom. There was a sewing machine with a foreign name on it that hid in a nice little fancy golden oak disguise table.

"Man, Squirrel Martin," Dahlia Rose kept gasping, "if this don't beat the band." Then she looked over at me once and said, "Ruby Lee, I ain't never been to a museum, but this stuff gives me strong feelin's that they should all be in one. If this don't beat all."

Back in the main room catty-corner to two walls, I hadn't been hallucinating. There was an angel five feet tall and gold as gold can be. It was a harp. I had to touch it to see if it might be real gold. It was scrolled, gold painted wood.

Squirrel Martin even rustled up a meal of salt pork, collard greens, lima beans, and apples. There were stacks of beautiful plates with that same Oriental pattern and handfuls of eating knives, forks, spoons, all sizes and all shapes that were pure silver and weighed about two pounds each. Three thick crystal drinking glasses had a French word that began with T chiseled gentle into the bottom but I was too tired to care about the undersides of things anymore. We were all powerful thirsty. Hungry, too.

Then, the same thing musta hit us all. In all the world, the Johnson family on Redemption Mountain was down to three.

Almost none. If not for this here magical place, we'd be homeless. Then, dead and gone.

While we ate and drank water from $100 glasses, not understanding their value, we all just fell quiet as can be. No one spoke for a long time, until long trails of tears rolled down Dahlia Rose's face.

Then, tears rolled down mine. Saying nothing, just like us, tears rolled down Squirrel Martin's face in such a way I'll never forget. He ain't never cried before. Never once in his life. And he didn't know how to do it. Maybe his tear ducts was clogged. Maybe the boy had no tear water in him.

Squirrel Martin was dunking a tiny silver spoon in his drinking water, holding it up just over his eye, and letting it drain down the side of his face slow and sweet.

We all knew our lives as they had been were over.

Not long after we finished eating the salt pork, apples and lima beans, Dahlia Rose and me just stumbled into the bedroom part of the tree house, slipped off all our clothes, and fell into bed. All night, we could feel the tree sway in the wind. And never once did that bough break.

Something we grew to love, the wind every time it shook up some, it gently tinkled the hanging down pieces of crystal on the chandelier. It sounded like the spiritual place where bells come from, and these were the innocent infant ones who ain't been rung properly yet.

Both to pass time and because it was calling me, I took up the harp. I suspect it was so easy and natural for me to know what I was doing because fiddle came to me the same way. With the fiddle, at six years old, I picked it up. I made some ugly scratchy sounds with the fiddle bow, and then me and it just started dancing together. I was playing with grown up men when I was nine.

Harp so far was the same. I wasn't sure how to sit when I played it, whether I should put my legs to the side or squeeze it between them. I settled on leaning it back on my left shoulder and letting it sit between my knees. In a month I could play almost any song I knew on fiddle pretty well. But I enjoyed just making things up as I ran my fingers in cascades of waterfall circles like spinning gold.

After a time, hiding out in the wildness seemed to suit Squirrel Martin but wasn't doin' a thing for Dahlia Rose and me. Winter was back and snow had been falling for three days, with wind that near ripped trees up on the ridge out by the roots and blew them to kingdom come.

Every so often a big wind would git ahold of our tree and it'd go a-shakin' so bad all the walls would stretch and squeal and grind, and we'd shake all over like we were a boat hitting choppy water.

And harp or no harp to keep me occupied, we had no money and as winter started to blow cold, animals fit for eating got scarce.

It was time. I couldn't put off my dark journey much longer. At the beginning of 1941, I decided to walk over to the other side of the mountain. To towns where I have never been, through snow and freezing temperatures, probably trudging right past hiding bears, too, to look for some cash money work.

Up here in our lofty house, surrounded by all our beautiful, magical things Squirrel Martin brought here somehow, unless I did better this time with what Hardy once said—"take drastic and irreversible measures"—we were plain just gonna perish.

Once when we were down in town, before I made the trek, Dahlia Rose and I, we heard that after the fire; the USACE put all'a its flooding plans on hold here in Redemption County, and, although nothing had happen yet, they moved those plans over the mountain to the town of Red Hand in Bulls County.

The USACE proclaimed flat out the town of Red Hand over there had not long to live. The flood and the big hydro project was coming. The whole town had to move. I still couldn't fathom that. A whole town, buildings too, on the move. And those jobs they were going to provide the folks over here to log our property way back…were now over there.

Me not knowing what those jobs were going to be in Red Hand, they were hiring like crazy. Probably horrible work but they had an economy in Red Hand. And I needed some of it. Even if it meant I had to go scrounging to the USACE itself.

CHAPTER SIXTEEN

One morning after snow fell all night, I walked over the mountain, by myself, in snow so deep in places I had to tunnel through it. It took eight hours.

Red Hand has the soul of a passed out whore with a mile or so of drunk, horny white trash drooling over her. The moment I broke out'a the woods and walked down a snowy hill behind a closed-down schoolhouse, the feelings of foreboding were only outdone by the forebodings themselves. In that town for two minutes, I stumbled over a dead man buried in the snow.

Trudging down that hill after walking for fourteen straight hours, and so tired, I was trying to lift my feet out'a the snow as high as I could. I was thinking if I could stop dragging them maybe I'd keep my toes from freezing off entirely, when I walked right up on this man's dead and frozen chest. Felt like a rock at first. Then, in a lightning flash, I knew I was standing on a corpse even though I couldn't see inathing yet but a boot toe stickin' out.

Freeze a person into block ice, when another human being comes in close contact, you know what it is before your brain and eyes make any connections. You just feel it. I just felt it. I got off the poor fella and brushed away a little snow from where I figured his face and head should be. It was a black man, so frozen stiff his face was pure white and his eyeballs all cracked. For some reason, maybe because I was so damn tired and nervous, I started talking to him.

"Gracious Lord, ain't you the most sorrowful thing I ever seen."

Not far from where I was lay a bunch of big rusty metal oil barrels cut in half, length-wise top to bottom like we do up in the hills to make a barbecue. Five or six of'm. I kicked one with my heel until it broke loose from being frozen to the others. After scooping the snow out'a it, it slid real easy. For the life of me, I wanted to walk away from all this horrible mess and go find the USACE employment center building and git going. But there was nothing forgivable about ignoring a frozen man just so I could go git myself a job I was going to despise inaway.

"This ain't gonna be too hard, sir. I'm just gonna scoop you up is all. You don't have to do nothing but keep your arm from snapping off or something."

The dead man scooped up surprisingly well, and I was intending to use the half barrel like a sled. But once I had him on it, he lay stiff and frozen on top with everything sticking out every which way. None of him inside it at all. So, awkward like that, I sledded him across the field like I was delivering a long flat sign somewhere, in a town I hadn't been in for more than five minutes.

And delivering him where exactly?

"I hope you were a decent man in your life, sir. I cain't imagine how these town folk will react when a white woman they ain't never seen before comes sledding in with a frozen black man."

Although I was trying to stay unbothered by the fact he was dead and froze, I started talking to him even more. I gave him a name—Mr. John.

Sliding him down the middle of the main street like that, we passed, maybe fifteen or twenty people. My black man, Mr. John, was like a piece of plywood in a running pose plonked on top of the half barrel. Two people looked over at us, but, my God, not a one of'm stood there wide-eyed at the sight of us.

For a while, I was beginning to wonder if these folks pull this same "we ain't at all surprised" trick on all newcomers.

The U.S. Army Corps of Engineers Job Recruitment Building was easy to find; it was the only building I ever saw that was sitting on a huge construction hauling wagon. This whole town must have all stood around the foundation of this building, counted to three, and hefted it up all at the same time.

This town was on the move. For real. The whole thing was being moved a couple of miles up the far end of the valley. All that trouble we went through with the USACE those ten years back about flooding valleys and getting thrown off our land and me burning down the mountain, it killed me now they never did inathing. And they were only getting around to flooding Red Hand now.

Staring at the building up on a huge flat transport wagon, wheels on it and all, "Well if that don't beat all, my unfortunate friend," I said to frozen Mr. John.

I slid Mr. John over to the side of the building on wheels. "You set here now, Mr. John. I ain't sure at all what I am getting myself into here. But I may need you to help me git out'a here."

I climbed the stairs up to the flatbed. Once I was in the building, I climbed the stairs to the second floor, where the office was. It was not a big building, more like a small-size two-floor house on a slab which is what it probably was before it got appropriated. I had feelings of the building suddenly rolling away down some treacherous hillside with me right there in it.

In a little room with documents that looked like land deeds in tall piles all around a desk that stood up on stilts some, sat a mean-eyed man with ink stains all over his clothes. Ink was even on his face like white trash war paint. This scary fella looked up, saw me standing there, and said right out loud, "My stars. Honey, you are one fine piece."

"Thank you, sir," I said for some dumb reason. I was so nervous and felt so strange about this whole town so far, I'm not sure I even heard what the man said.

"You here to kiss me or something?" he said and smiled me a rack of yellow teeth.

"Actually, I'm here to see about getting a job."

"Gittin' a job!" he practically screamed. He stared at me like a rattler hovering over a mouse. Then he said in slow talk, "Y'all's…here…to…see…a-bout…git-tin…a…jooooob?" He answered himself like I had asked him to open his pants and let birds fly loose. "You kiddin' me?"

I considered that for a second. "No, sir, I'm not kiddin' you. I need work. You got any?"

"Do I got any? Course I got any." This man did not know what to do, think, or imagine. "Do I got any? Work?" he repeated. Then, he started talking at me in a blizzard of words. "Looka here. Men folk work for the USACE doin' men's work. Construction, digging, cutting, haulin' and such. You want any of that?"

"I don't know."

"Women cook the meals, wash up the corpse laundry, scrub out the coffins, and sometimes put dead folks back together enough so we can git 'em back in the ground somewheres else. Let me ask you right off, 'cause I cain't believe a fine piece like you's willin' to stick her fingers into the dead. Why ain't you dancing or whorin' or some such? With a face and figure like your'n, missy, you'd be wearing fox fur and drinkin' mint juleps in the better part of a week."

Then, he stood up and walked around to the front of his desk, unzipped his ink-stained pants and hauled his pecker out. "Job's right here," he said, smirking at me, but looking cautious at the same time.

My God, then we *were* rolling. The building gave a shudder with wood and nails squealing and grinding against each other all over. "That goddamn stupid fucker," he spat, "can you believe he hitched up the team without telling me?" He asked me that like I was suddenly his drinking buddy.

"Son of a bitch...wait right here," he commanded and took off down the stairs with his stiff ole dick still waggling around until he was halfway down.

I heard him screaming and swearing at some man name Bass about not warning him first before hitching up the team of draught horses. Then, there was complete and abrupt silence for about ten long seconds until he blurted out to the whole town, "What the good fucking happy Jesus is that!"

One second later, he was clumping up the stairs and came rushing into the office.

"Missy, that yours out there?" he demanded, and waited for a response.

I was at a loss. I didn't have inathing now except a powerful hankering to go home. So I didn't say inathing back to him.

"The froze nigger. He yours?"

Mine? I wanted to yell at him. *He ain't mine you dumb ass baboon. I found him!*

"No sir, the iceman, he ain't...mine," I said. "He was lying buried in snow when I got here just now. Brung him here because it didn't seem right to leave him froze there all alone."

"Bother you to handle the dead?" he asked.

"Don't rightly know. Doesn't bother me much to handle the frozen dead."

He scratched at some ink on his fingernails. "We got need for moving five hundred dead bodies up to a new high ground cemetery. You come walkin' down one of our storin' fields this morning. Fields like that we'll keep the stiffs buried in snowbanks till the ground warms up or they thaw and start to stink, bad. Then we'll plant 'em. Meantime, we got five hundred holes to dig in ground colder than a witches teat, and harder'n your froze friend's watermelon."

He was looking at me quizzically as he dug his hand into his crotch to give it a good scratch.

"Don't take that thing out agin," I said.

"What you say?"

"Please don't take that thing out agin. That ain't the type of job I'm after."

"It ain't, huh."

"No sir, it's not. I'd prefer to handle the dead than that. Is there a grave digging job here for me or what?"

They had me beginning my work, three-week stints then a week off just like Silas and his coal mining schedule, that very afternoon a couple of hours before sundown. I had no way of telling Dahlia Rose and Squirrel Martin I'd be away for so long. They could run out'a food or freeze to death. Neither of those were likely with Squirrel Martin there, even if they had to snack on field mice pattering over the snow looking for seeds.

The man I reported to for my work clothes an' other supplies was a fella wearing something that looked like a headless cat carcass on his head. He wasn't too smart so I suspect the Man in the Moon coulda walked in and asked for a shovel and he would'a handed one over, asking if he needs a pick, too.

"I was hired just now to…" What on earth should I tell the man? Ta sled around dead frozen black men? But I didn't have to say inathing.

He wandered into a backroom with his cat hat's tail swinging and came back with a big pile of clothes and such all folded up neat and ready to go. They give you two pair of thick yellow wool climb-in clothes that have a zipper that zips you in from the crotch to the neck. A big jacket coat. Work gloves, socks and a pair of big ole heavy work boots. This fella stacked all this stuff up and sauntered back into the backroom. He came out this time with a big envelope full of official papers and such. He slid one out and had me sign it. Then he slid another one out and held it toward me without looking at me.

It had all the information I was going to need to know where to go. What I was gonna be doing exactly. What was expected of me. Ten ways to git fired on the spot: showing up to work drunk three times. Playing around with the corpses. Murder. Things like that.

Not one of those rules was no whoring. In fact, it mentioned that *workingmen should be discreet with their needs regarding females.* I doubt a person within a hundred miles, other than government men, know what "discreet" means.

I didn't either until I read it a couple of times and put two and two together. In other words, Gents, you can treat a woman any way you want—harass her, molest her, fuck her unwilling in the middle of the street—just don't let one of us catch you.

Mr. Cat Carcass had enough of me, I guess. He shoved all my clothes over to the end of the counter and went back to reading the local paper, a thing called the *Red Hand Mouth.*

Lordy!

I think I know what they were a trying to convey giving the paper that name. But man alive, it brought a mess of images into a person's mind, especially in a town with frozen dead people buried all around in the snow like a scavenger hunt. Government officials who whip out their weenies first thing in a job interview. And employment men who wear dead domesticated animals draped over their heads and don't say a word.

The piece of paper said report to the lower barracks on a backstreet named Southern Pride Circle. Southern Pride Circle was a circular dirt road with four or five big old workhouses that slaves lived in not that long ago. In one of'm, I had a room to myself on account I was female. All'a the other men workers lived in dormitory rooms with cigarette, pipe, and cigar smoke still thick as fog after they'd all been out working for two hours.

My room had a window, a feather mattress flopped on the floor, a bedpan, a bucket, an ugly table with a washbasin on it. A pile of neatly folded gray sheets, a blanket, and a pillow was stacked in the middle of the mattress.

Folks sure take their neat stacking up of things serious in this town, I'd give them that.

Most of all, there was a lock on the door, and a key stuck in it on the inside. I took that key, put it on a strong string and wore it around my neck inside my clothes like a secret diamond necklace. I was thinking, *More than food or friendship or just plain blind luck, this key is the most important friend I'm ever gonna have here.*

And I knew in my bones at some point I was gonna be right to think that.

Wages were $6 a week for a six-day week, Sundays off, for three straight weeks. Then a week off. Then, the cycle started again.

I didn't do much that first afternoon but walk into a work area and stare at shovels and look away from men. "You gotta be kiddin' me, man! She real? Looky over there." From that moment on, I had more men looking me over than flies trying to fly up a cow's ass.

The whole working field just stopped digging in mid dig and about fifty men of every size, shape, smell, and brain deficiency were imagining themselves making me whimper and asking them to fuck me a whole lot harder. A fella looking a mite less crude than most of the others come stomping over in a green work suit to everybody else's dirty yellow one. He was carrying a spade.

"I heard about you," he said, "I sure heard about you." Even with me inside thick shapeless work clothes, he took two steps back and rolled over me a few times with his twinkling eyes.

"They sent me here to work," I said about as toneless as I could muster.

"I sure know that, darlin'. And I'm mighty glad they did, too."

I knew right well there was nothing I could do about these men. If I protested or asked them to act like civilized human beings, not hound dogs, I'd be fired right there, or roughed up.

After another minute of Mr. Googly Eyes imagining what my body looked like, I said like nothing was bothering me at all. "I know it's probably almost quitting time but I wanted to come out here inaway. Might as well learn what my job is so I can git goin' all the faster tomorrow morning."

"You got a name, girl?"

"Mah name's…Macy. Macy Weathers from over Redemption."

There was no way I wanted to be Ruby Johnson on this side of the mountain. With a crew of men as vile and ignorant as this, no telling how they might react to that name.

"Well, Miss Macy Weathers from over Redemption, I spose you

know how to handle a shovel just about as well as any man. My question is—how long will you be able to use it before you start cryin' and askin' me if you can go bake biscuits or somethin'."

"I'm planning to do jus' fine," I said in a soft voice full of demureness. But with a strong hidden message that told him flat out, *I been overcoming struggle all my life and I can work like a dog so don't you fret none over me. Where's my shovel and where's those holes you want dug?*

This fella looked deep into my eyes and surprised me by saying pleasantly, "Okay now Miss Macy Weathers from over Redemption, mah name's Pen Kilgore. Inathing or anybody give you trouble, you come to me." He said this real, real loud so every man within hearing distance was receiving the same message. He saying that was the first nice and comforting thing my ears heard in a long time.

"Thank you, Mr. Kilgore. I appreciate that," I said sincerely, but not handing over my need for protection to him entirely. That would give a mostly honest and occasional churchgoing man too many of the wrong ideas to wrestle. Three extra swigs of Jack Daniels and a second of thinking about his fat wife, Velma, good-intentioned men like this here Kilgore are looming you over rabid.

I slept surprisingly well that first night. My little room had some friendly feelings to it. And all night long I kept that key to my locked door in my fist. All night long.

Early next morning, some kind of bell gong started jangling at sunup. I slept in my yellow work clothes so all I did was git up and wash. I skipped breakfast; did not want to face a dining room full of crude beasts as my first official workday experience here.

When I got to the place where I was to work, it was truly puzzling. There was still snow and ice all over the ground enough to keep five hundred dead bodies frozen stiff as concrete buried in it all over. But the dirt in this new high ground cemetery, and it wasn't that high ground, was barely frosted and dug out as easy as a clay bed.

I had been expecting to be trying to chip away at underground icebergs.

We were all assigned digging partners for each three-week period, and mine was a seventy-year-old Virginian, former Baptist minister named Elson Wren.

Everyone, naturally, called him Preacher. Or Old Wren.

This man had a way about him. He had a heavenly heat surrounding him. Even some of the mangiest workers who probably kilt some corpses lying out there in the snow softened up like changed men when they talked to him. A'course, once they went their ways, those men's hearts went black again just as easy as they whitened up for a while.

My first three weeks there went on forever and ever. The days were all cold feet, aching shoulders and blistered hands. Every evening about 8:00 I brought my pathetic dinner of chicken or ham cooked on greasy, dirty spits over open fires up to my room. Ate it quick and went to bed in my clothes.

I didn't dare git undressed beyond lowering my drawers to do my business and washing myself up with Ivory soap and water afterwards. Three or four times, I lowered my work uniform all the way to my ankles behind the locked door and washed my whole body for a couple of minutes, with my eyes nailed to the keyhole.

I and Mister Elson, I called him that instead of Mister Wren, became friends the moment we shook hands saying hello. I suspect the foreman, Kilgore, matched us up for obvious reasons. We dug twenty-five grave holes that first week in the strange half-froze dirt, Mr. Elson and I.

"What's your real name, girl," he asked in his smooth old voice the first morning we were diggin' out a hole together.

It wasn't any use me trying to feel surprised he knew that. They paired me and him for better reasons than he wouldn't try to bother me. It must have been for reasons of destiny beyond the comprehension of any foreman.

So right out I answered him, "It's Ruby Johnson, sir."

Even for a man chock full of intuition himself, hearing my name popped his eyes out a little. Slowly, this sweet little smile started creating itself on his lips.

"Well, I declare," he said. "That a fact?"

I was hoping he was going to just say, "Nice to meet you, Ruby." He didn't.

"Should I be wishing I hadn't been truthful, just now, Mister Elson?"

"No, child, it's my pleasure to meet somebody I been hearing about and wondering about for years and years. I'm pleased to make your acquaintance. Ah surely am."

He stopped digging for a moment. "Miss Johnson, do you mind

if I ask you one thing?"

"No sir, I don't." He scrunched up his twinkling old blue eyes and grinned wide as a window. "You folks really fly around Redemption Mountain at night?"

I turned to look at him. He was a sweet, sweet man who must of lost the call'a Jesus somewhere along the line to be out here digging grave holes, him seventy years old, to throw frozen folks in. I smiled for the first time since I trudged down that snowy hill and found myself balancing on a frozen colored man like I was balancing on the scales of truth and destiny itself.

Besides Granddaddy, I haven't felt such affection for any old timer as I did right off for Mr. Elson. Besides Mama, Dahlia Rose, Tom Sawyer and Squirrel Martin, and maybe Hardy once or twice, I have never felt such affection for anybody in my whole livelong life.

He was still smiling, ready to nod his head and say, "That a fact?" to about inathing I was about to answer.

"No sir, we living Johnsons don't fly around the mountain at night or at any other time." He was really smiling at me now. "But all the dead Johnson women from over three hundred years surely do. Anytime they please."

"Is that a fact? Now that's somethin' I truly would love to see, real live ghost women flying around all breezy and see-through." He looked serious for a moment. "Are them ghosts see-through?"

"Mister Elson, they surely are. They surely are. Hair down long to their behinds, too. Dancing in the air like butterflies. Not even angry anymore at what happened to them."

The old man looked down into the hole at where his shovel was dug in. For a moment, a peaceful sort of heavenly warmth filled up the hole and poured over me like a hot wind in July. He looked real happy and burdenless. Maybe it was the strange heat tearing up my eyes, but for one split second he looked as see-through as my Johnson kinswomen.

"I sure like the sound of that, Ruby Johnson. I most certainly do like the sound of'm see-through kinswomen."

"Why is that, Mister Elson?" I couldn't help myself from asking. He didn't hesitate to answer, "Because down the road a short piece I'm hopin' to fly around all breezy and see-through myself. Don't think I'm long for this world. I want to go peaceful right off to where I go next. I ain't been too good to this life, and it ain't been too good to me. All I ask is for a couple of minutes after I die feelin' myself flappin' and flyin' around, finally feelin' peaceful in my soul."

I wanted to cry. Then he looked right at me with those big twinkling sky blue eyes and said soft and gentle, "Can you help me do that, Miss Ruby Johnson?"

CHAPTER SEVENTEEN

By the third day, the blisters on my hands popped and wouldn't stop bleeding. I'd been digging and gardening and grooming, hauling out tree stumps, and tending hundreds of acres of wild raspberries all my life. Never as much as had a slightly angry blister. A few days in Red Hand, my hands felt as crippled as my spirit had become.

If it wasn't for the old, tired preacher with the gift of spirit that abandoned him—maybe he couldn't stop himself from pumping Holy Spirit into his female congregation the old fashion way and they booted him out—I don't know how I would'a survived those first three weeks digging grave holes.

He called me "pretty thing". He'd say, "Pretty thing, what in tarnation got into a beauty like you to git her to give up her life to come here to do this mule's labor?" Or "Pretty thing, don't you even think about lookin' for a decent husband among this shabby, worthless rabble. These men ain't fit to sit in the same room as you."

It was because of this man that I had my only worthwhile few hours in that awful place. On my second Sunday there, I heard a gentle knock on my door. A real nice-sounding knock like the world had just gotten changed from hateful to kind. Slowly, I unlocked and opened it, peeking around to see who was there. Mr. Elson was wearing a bluish color suit that looked like every old man in the South tried it on at least once. He had some kind of horsehair coat long to the ground flung over his shoulders like a waterfall 'a brown steel wool.

"Pretty thing," he asked sweet and polite, "would y'all feel like taking a Sunday stroll with me?"

It was still coldish outside, probably high 40s that day. I'd been cooped up in that room every night nursing wounded hands, a strained back, and fear of the male population in this shitty dirty, ignorant world of shitty dirty ignorant men since the moment I arrived.

While I was deciding, Mr. Elson saw my fiddle on top of the banged-up piece of unexplainably useless furniture.

"My, my, my, and ain't we gonna have a fine time with that!"

I had brought my fiddle to Red Hand as a familiar and friendly roommate more than a musical instrument. Most of the time I had forgotten it was even there. I didn't like my fiddle being there in Red Hand because it didn't like the place any more than I did. And sweet music didn't belong there.

I put on my thick USACE work coat, buttoned it up to my chin, tucked my fiddle case under my arm, and followed Mr. Elson down the narrow steps and out into the dangerous world of a work camp on the weekend.

He led on a fair distance. We walked out'a the camp up the twisty dirt paths and badly paved roads to downtown Red Hand. It looked as miserable and painful as always. We walked right through it down the main street and took a turn into the town cemetery. As we walked along in the chilly air, our breaths blew gusts of steam out'a our mouths that froze in the air and fell cracking to the ground. Or it seemed so.

You could see signs that workers had begun the ugly ordeal of digging up the graves and moving their contents and the correct headstone to a staging area by the graveyard's back boundary line. This was the town graveyard located on the highest ground. Probably why they were just getting to it now. We had been working in the smaller graveyards on lower ground below the town. The staging area, looming dark under a grove of trees, was dirty, dusty, and disorganized. It was full of half-filled wagons with gray tarps hanging over sides, corpse rabble, and every type of gravestone you ever did see. They were stacked up, lying down, leaning on one another. I thought I saw something big and lumpy on the ground that coulda been a dead workhorse covered over with a stiff dirty gray tarp with the stains of death all over it. The staging area looked like something that was a cross between a terrifying Halloween and the backdoor to Hell.

About halfway walking through the cemetery, I nearly fainted. My God, you would'a thought I'd seen a ghost. In a way, I spose you could say I did. I started to see inscriptions on gravestones read the name *Greaves*. We were strolling into a big patch of Greaves, about twenty of'm. All the headstones looked real old, chipped, faded, and untended. I did not want to stop; they gave me a bad feeling. But I slowed down and looked close as I could at a bunch. All Greaves men. On many, I could not make out the dates. Those I could make something out on the cheap slate, I saw Gander Greaves 1833 – 1878. Clovis T. Greaves 1827 – 1861. Honeybee Greaves 1741 – 1808. Heck William Greaves 1841 – 1863. Bethel Niles Greaves 1820 – 1862. Abel Greaves 1831 – 1864. Mernock Aloysius Greaves 1802 – 1811. And, then I near froze when I saw the names on a patch of bleached-out, salt-white miserable looking head stones: Tolbert Greaves, Sr. 1799 – 1870. Tolbert Greaves Jr. 1841 – 1901. That musta meant the Tolbert Greaves haunting my life with threatening terror and ugly lust was the third one of'm. I was standing in an ugly feeling nest of dead Greaves. Lord.

Many had died in or during the Civil War. Five or Six of those, except for Honeybee and a bunch of 1700s jaspers, had *Civil War Veteran, Red Hand, Bulls County, North Carolina Home Guard* chiseled curvy somewhere on the gravestone. Surrounding a Confederate flag chiseled with various levels of stone craft.

Not one Greaves female dead and buried did I see, except for the possibility of Honeybee being female.

Strange, I kept feeling that something besides old Mr. Elson brought me here. A presence. The powerful hand of something not human knowing I had to see this. Not to terrify me more. But for these Greaves men to tell me to watch out. That they wanted no more Johnson women injured or kilt at their account. I was receiving this clear: watch out for their relation. They wanted me and mine to find peace.

As we walked out'a the graveyard's other end, I was wondering if Mr. Elson took that route knowing I needed to see for myself: the field of dead Greaves. It always surprised me when folks I didn't know knew all about the history between the Johnsons and the Greaves more than I did.

We walked along some back streets lined with ramshackle mill houses that all looked the same except for the outside colors, how much the structure had declined and what kinds of junk littered the front yards. People were living in them. I did not recall any actual mill being in the area for dime-a-dozen shacks to be here for mill-workers to live in. Far as I was concerned, Red Hand had nothing in it that made sense.

Up ahead waiting for us was a scrawny little church built to face nowhere in particular. It was cheerfully run down. Some of it painted dull yellow and some bright white high gloss.

Closer we got, I could see people milling around, with human heads on trays. I didn't know whether to fall down laughing or turn and run.

As we sidled up onto the stiff cold grass in the front, Christians were everywhere. Carrying trays all right. But with boiled hog heads and buckets full'a mashed sweet potatoes. They were disappearing around the side of the church in droves.

Out front, a big cardboard sign strung with yellow yarn between two catalpa trees displayed words in what looked like red house paint:

Potluck Sunday

at

The Eternal Light Negro Baptist Church

Bring Your Appetites – Donations, Food,
Respect for All Humanity & Some Playin' Instruments
To While Away Some of God's Precious Time.

Mr. Elson and I followed them. We walked around the corner to the back, following all the food bearers but bearing no food of our own. Broken off the top of the church as if by some huge, annoyed demon's hand, the steeple lay on its side in a patch of early spring white azaleas.

A tall, thin ancient black man with big, graceful hands was making his way over to us.

He held out his hands to Mr. Elson. Clearly knowing each other real well, they spoke a little, smiled a lot, and hugged each other while the temperature seemed to be rising. No fooling. I was feeling hot from the grace and respectful friendship that was passing between them.

Then, the old black man took my two hands in his. His eyes twinkled and then widened into two enormous black sparkling diamonds. Bright white light was shining off him. What I was seeing had the feel of something holy. For a few moments, the old black man's skinny frame became nearly see-through, with nothing in sharp focus except his long, delicate hands.

With those amazing hands, he was cradling my hands like mothers cradling their children. He smiled wider. Those black hands smoothly floated to either side of my face. Ninety? One hundred? Five hundred-year-old fingertips? When they touched me, I felt my insides become warm silk.

Taking his hands away, he whispered, still smiling like dawn running over the ground, "Miss Ruby, now you go ovah there yonder like a good girl and have you some potluck before you play your sweet music for us."

I knew who he was before Mr. Elson could tell me inathing about him. Though I didn't know his name, he was the very same old man who led all those old colored folks to our cemetery field to bury that mysterious colored family. Man, my life in Redemption after only a couple of weeks here in Red Hand seemed like centuries ago.

In a big tent, me and Mr. Elson sat with some folks and ate the food placed before us heartily. Chomping their hogs' heads and smacking on their sweet potatoes and rhubarb pie, fifty or sixty folks, mostly black, sitting around little round tables with white table clothes billowing in the breeze coming through the tent's opening.

Suddenly, all the folks turned their attention away from potluck and straight to me. Like they were expecting something wonderful to happen.

I looked around for the reverend and caught his eyes. He smiled something mystical and those black diamond eyes lifted me into the air. And I swear, I floated a foot off the ground, all thirty years of my unenlightened self, right up the steps of a raggedy old half demolished gazebo they raised the tent right over.

When I got up there, I was clutching my fiddle and bow.

The reverend called to me, simply, "Jus' do what's in you, little girl. An' do it fine."

I touched my bow to the fiddle strings. These folks needed

something to stir their warm hearts. While I was tuning up, I thought about the loss of Mama, Daddy, Granddaddy, Bobby Lee, Tom Sawyer, and Macy. I felt thankful for Dahlia Rose and Squirrel Martin. I wondered if Hardy Jessup was happy in his life. And I was so glad I had made the acquaintance of Mr. Elson. Then, I closed my eyes and played.

Then, suddenly, I was done playing. I had no idea how long or how short I played. When I lowered my bow, every one of the folks sitting there came up and hugged me. Each taking their sweet time and hugging me soft and gentle. Every single one of'm. After a time I felt so much of my hurt and pain and bad memories fading away. I'm not sure any Johnson woman ever had some other person not a Johnson do a healing on them. All sixty of those wonderful folks held me in their arms and rocked me a little. I felt—only word that came to me—redeemed.

Imagine feeling redeemed in such a horrible place as Red Hand. I guess you never know where your blessings and your inspiration is going to come from. Instead of church or listening to a reverend scream the name of Jesus, I was being redeemed in the most God-awful town in the South, by folks nobody but themselves would ever know.

When we were leaving, the old reverend thanked me for playing and for coming to see him in such a way I swear he was thanking me for still being alive. Not given up on life for all'a the tragedy and pain that comes to a person who ain't like everybody else, in a world where being different can cost you your life.

The morning I was packing up to walk home; I was in my little room bending over with my back to the door. They gave me a little carpetbag to tote my stuff back and forth. I was packing it with my dirty clothes, my $18, and some food wrapped in a hand towel to eat along the way. I was zipping the case up when someone grabbed me by the hips from behind. He started rubbing a stony crotch against my rear end. He got my hips grabbed tight, and still he could keep me bent over like I was exercising and touching my toes.

In that way our minds bring up instant memories of things that feel a little the same as what's happening in the here and now, I was imagining Silas with his coal dusty dick up me, making my breasts swing back and forth like crazy while he rutted me hard.

Right off, I knew who it was. Most of the threatening men here were mostly bluff. There may be some danger in 'em, but mostly they just like to look mean and deadly to impress their worker friends.

Just then I heard coming from the doorway, "Thank God, Macy Weathers, you ah still here," boomed out a gentle voice trying to put some intimidation into it. "You might'a gone, and I would'a missed sayin' my goodbyes."

The man behind me let go of my hips in a jiffy and backed himself up against the wall, preparing to either explain himself or fight for his natural-born right to treat women white, Indian, or colored as he pleases.

"Ahhh," said Mr. Elson, "I see you have made the acquaintance of Mr. Tolbert Greaves. Nice to see ya, Tolbert. I brung Macy here a box of chocolates for her long train ride home. I reckon she don't mind if I open it up and give you a couple. Want some?"

I shoulda known that among all this dead and probably still alive Greaves kin in Red Hand, seeing Tolbert Greaves was inevitable. It was him.

I straightened myself up and tried to inhale some dignity. I was trembling and I near wet myself. My eyes wanted real bad to tear up, but I fought them harder than they wanted to cry. I cleared my throat and rubbed smooth my clothes that had ridden up some.

"Mr. Elson," I said, trying not to have a speck of emotion in my voice other than a grave hole digger thanking her diggin' partner for an unexpected kindness. "Such a thoughtful notion. I do thank you…" The tears were winning the battle but had not begun to show themselves.

Tolbert Greaves was losing his erection. Both Mr. Elson and me could see it fading away in his pants. He was going to say something to Mr. Elson. Did not. Turned my way and was gonna say something to me, but also didn't.

Like a cornered porcupine, suddenly seeing a way out, he was gone. His clanking footsteps echoed down the stairs and then the front door to this shabby awful place slammed shut behind him.

We stood there looking at each other a while. I was about to thank him for sayin' that thing about a train ride, trying to deceive the bastard. And thank him for the gift. But he put his finger up to his lips and just twinkled his blue, blue beautiful old man's eyes.

"Nobody ever bought me chocolates before, Mr. Elson. Not my run off husband, my first boyfriend, Hardy Jessup, my pa, or anybody."

Again, he put his finger up to his lips and just twinkled those blue eyes, full of more beauty and hope and more pain and desolation than I could imagine.

Those eyes were twinkling like blue moonlight on a glass smooth pond. And then I knew. Good Lord, old Mr. Elson had commenced to dying. I could feel his spirit leaving.

Thirty minutes later, he was turning back toward downtown Red Hand. He had walked me to the edge of the woods where I was picking up the trailhead for my walk home over the mountain. We didn't talk. We both knew words were unnecessary. I could tell he was just as happy to be with me when he left this earth as I was for him to see me off as I took a journey, too.

He hugged me close, still not talking. Just smiling and radiating his heavenly light. He nodded his head slow. I turned and began walking up the hill to the trailhead. At the top, I couldn't resist. I needed to comfort him one more time. I called, "Mr. Elson, when I git back, I'd be honored to help you know what it's like to fly all airy…"

Cutting me off gently, still walking away, he quietly held up his arm in a soft wave goodbye.

Then, he just plumb disappeared in thin air.

CHAPTER EIGHTEEN

Squirrel Martin's tree house all lit up, floating in the dark woods twenty feet above the earth, was a wondrous sight. I don't know how he did it, but if I ever had fears of us being visible as a lone star showing terrible men the way to our door, those fears could go to rest. Squirrel Martin had done a beautiful job hiding the tree house right in plain sight. The only way you'd see it all lit in the dark was if you bashed your head on a low limb, standing right under it. Imagine that, first Johnson male ever to do so, Squirrel Martin could even cast spells.

"Hey, you Johnsons!" I yelled up. "I heard y'all's a den of spooks and are just dying to steal the souls of Presbyterians. You up there, you spooks?"

Dahlia Rose and Squirrel Martin's faces appeared in the same window. Squirrel Martin fooled around with the hinges and then swung it open. A blast of warm air from inside ran out into all the chilly mountain night air and steamed. I could smell venison and carrots cooking. Something smelled like fresh baked brownies warming.

"Jeez, girl, ain't you a sight for sore eyes," Dahlia Rose called down. "We didn't know exactly when but after you didn't come home for a while, we figured they had you on one of those three-week things. That we're ready for your homecomin' this good is just from deductive reasoning. What do you think of that?"

Whether she meant she had used a couple of big words properly or that they guessed correctly when I'd be home didn't matter. She impressed me with both. I cain't describe how it felt climbing up the ladder and stepping into that magical place. Squirrel Martin was beside himself and kept feeding me venison in a way that said he wanted me to know he shot and cooked the deer himself.

Dahlia Rose was beautiful, with glowing skin and hair a honey white that probably no other person in the world had.

After we ate, we talked a while about Red Hand, minus most of it to tell you the truth. I didn't want to alarm them too bad just yet.

Then, I excused myself and sat down at the amazing harp. I eased it back to rest gently on my shoulder like a slow dancing lover. I wrapped my thighs around it a little too close on purpose. I could feel it reaching into me before I began to play. I closed my eyes and plucked and played slow, feeling gorgeous vibrations roll into me with every stinging beautiful note.

The week rushed by. Soon I was heading back over the mountain.

Into a soul-changing experience I did not see coming. Or maybe I did, and this was the time.

I was halfway across the mountain when I just got dog tired and sat down under an old maple tree. Could not help myself. Suddenly, I felt ancient and human-life-exhausted, like a woman from the Old Testament who is still alive in our time.

All at once I was a woman crying every pain she ever had in her heart and soul. I felt lost and alone in the middle of the Appalachian Mountains on a lost deer path near nothing human or man-made or familiar at all. This is what preachers and holy men have been trying to git their congregations to feel through religion since the beginning of time. Face the deep fears of your soul.

If I ever thought I knew God or purgatory or the feeling of Heaven colliding right into Hell like two blind clouds, I didn't know inathing.

Out there alone, until I took the rest, the farther I walked the more I became resentful. Of having to go back to Red Hand. Of God. It wasn't enough that I have been up against walls all'a my life, getting shot at by men's dicks, men's crudeness, men's abandonment, men's violence, and men's bullets. It ain't enough that our family had to scrape and paw for everything it ever had. It ain't enough that the name Johnson in these parts produces a little puddle of pee at people's feet and terror in their heart. It ain't enough there are folks that would kill us dead in a heartbeat if we run into them. It ain't enough that I have to bear the pain every moment of my life for killing my baby daughter.

It ain't enough that my family was down to three. It ain't enough we lived over three miles in the woods from our old place. And we don't know or see a soul.

And it ain't enough that I had to pull myself over this mountain again to go do a disgusting job with disgusting people for the most disgusting reason of all.

Cause now we were so damn poor and needy; we'll be dead inside a month if I didn't.

Besides man's work if they'll let ya, or housecleaning, the only other thing a woman in these parts could do with any certainty of making steady money was whoring or teaching school.

I'd rather dig grave holes and thaw out the dead, thank you very much.

Yes, it was about midway along my route through the wild, unapologetic wilderness, with all its natural comings and goings of seasons, weather, lives of all sorts—I decided to camp for the night. And have me an epiphany like they had done in the Bible.

It didn't much matter to me where I settled down for the night. I was thinking the whole point of letting yourself have an epiphany is to expose yourself to whatever and everything that's possibly dangerous and see how it turns out for you. Put your damn life in the hands of something real, simple, and unpredictable. And wait and see.

That's what I did.

Wearing my grave digging coat, sitting by a little campfire I made that wouldn't stay lit, I put myself into the hands of nothing that was gonna tell me I'm safe and okay. Out there, I was a speck of womanhood. Nothing there with me but cold air and stars so bright above there was no need at all for moonlight.

I slept in some cold temperatures in my life. I enjoy sleeping with my bedroom window open for almost three hundred nights a year. But there isn't cold I ever knew like open mountain cold. I was shivering so bad; it was worse for me to think about Dahlia Rose lying all warm and soft in scarlet silk than it was to think of myself out there freezing to death.

Many times, I tried to drive my mind into not thinking at all, which is something I read once that funny people in faraway countries like India and Japan can do. Sit down and have no thoughts. When they're done being quiet and empty-headed for an hour or so, they pop open their eyes. Their mind is all refreshed. They're smarter somehow. And they feel joined at the hip with God. No preachers. No Praise Lordys.

No church steeples with a tortured, murdered man stuck on the spike, telling people that love and generosity reside within.

In two or three hours, I was near froze. It was in the middle of the night. If that was my epiphany, freezing to death and looking like that colored man I found in Red Hand, that was fine with me.

With all that trying to git everything outta my mind still all on my mind, I started listening to the surrounding sounds instead. Most common sound was wind. I started imagining the wind as one big soul as big as the whole world. All we have to do is breathe it once in a while instead of wrestling with our own tiny little individual souls. This huge soul, nothing to do with Christianity, is like a Savings & Loan. Everybody who wants to can put a little something in and borrow a little something out. Everybody uses it. Everybody owns it.

Next to wind blowing, in all directions I heard trees cracking and stretching. Some of it came from the trees moving with the wind. Some of it came from the trees just speaking their mind and expressing their feelings in the way trees do.

Third thing I heard was silence. At night, if you took away the wind and the trees out there, unless there was a bear breathing in your face, you'd hear nothing at all.

Nothing.

It wasn't likely I was going to sleep I was shivering so bad. However, that was the most fortunate deprivation I will probably ever experience and come away feeling all full of epiphany.

Lying there on a nameless deer path five mountain man miles from inathing, with wind and cold ripping at my body like that Tolbert Greaves wanted to do, scaring me something awful, for a moment I thought I saw two men walking toward me outta the dark night. They came within fifty feet and stopped. Close enough for me to see flames around one and ice all around the other. Both were my friends. One man was one of the colored men I saw as a little girl that was on fire, Mr. John. The other was the frozen colored man with the white face I found in the snow, Mr. James. Both of'm frozen and flaming, not especially threatening or scary.

At some point in people's lives, I reckon even people like those ignorant, mean men in Red Hand, there must be a moment they lay down gentle on whatever is their mountaintop, and let their souls speak to them. I remember me and Hardy used to talk about whether we would all have one extraordinary defining moment in our lives, in all the millions and millions of moments we lead. A moment so amazing and pure, a person doesn't care if she lives or dies anymore. A moment that's the most important and deepest thing you're ever gonna feel. All you have to do is recognize it when it comes sailing along. Cause it'll surely change your life.

And most likely three out'a four people never even notice it shining right there in front of'm like the one and only blink of an enormous, gorgeous magical firefly. And they miss it.

Out there just one small female soul in all creation, I was experiencing that moment. Or maybe a better way of saying it: that moment was having me.

And what was that moment? That experience? *I wasn't going to be afraid of the darknesses in human life anymore.*

I fell asleep somehow. In my shivering dreams, under a sky soft black as velvet with a billion pin holes shining through, suddenly I knew what my colored men, one flaming, one frozen, were there for. What they mean to me.

I was to lead my life right there between them. They were like guardian angels. Black guardian angels. Which suits me just fine. They would give me my sense of knowing who I am. Me now, a person who lives between the fire and the ice. In between the good and the bad. In between good fortune and tragedy. A person ready to stand up to the world and everything in it with no hurt, no resentment, no regret, no guilty conscience, no hate, no fear.

I knew my two black guardian angels will stand to either side of me and be my guides. I knew my life was going to do some serious changing, and it was going to be for the good. Maybe not right away. But soon.

When I woke that morning, I was lying naked under the tree. Right there in the snow my skin was touching the frozen ground. Somewhere during the night I felt that I should undress, be naked, be as vulnerable to the elements and experiences of life as possible. Couldn't git any closer to that than being naked on a frozen night, miles into deep mountain woods. Knowing nothing was ever going to be the way it was.

And that was the whole idea. Not being someone who dragged their past along their life's journey, but someone who is always clear of mind and heart and is always thinking forward.

CHAPTER NINETEEN

When I finally walked out'a the woods at the end of the mountain path and entered the dismal grip of Red Hand, after nearly freezing out there all night, they put me back in my little room again. In a strange way that made no sense at all, when I walked through the doorway, after only a week away, I was happy to be in it. The dingy sheets and blankets, cleaned at least, were piled neatly in the middle of the mattress as they were the last time. The water pitcher and bedpan were newer looking. And it appeared to me somebody even washed the window clean with enough effort that Red Hand looked like actual human people lived and breathed out there. Not ghosties that passed dimly through some thick hazy, dirty world with important pieces missing, like it looked before.

I was even considering tucking my clothes into the little stack of drawers built right into the wall instead of leaving them all packed. It's like this, isn't it? You walk into an evil place in a good mood and for a while you believe maybe all the evil's gone and folks are as peaceful and good-natured as you.

Over the next half hour I wrestled with a wishful innocence that I believe all women try to convince themselves of at one time or another. I was still feeling the deep and freeing cleansing effects of my epiphany. But much had changed here in only one week. Most important for my nighttimes, the key was missing from my door lock.

Most important for my daytimes, Mister Kilgore, the foreman who had treated me so well, up and left.

Wages were down to $5 a week.

And, as I suspected they would, they found old Mister Elson Wren in the snow dead after suffering a heart attack the day I left. Some kids playing Civil War found him. I had no idea there were kids near this place. I never saw any.

Three new women were in the camp working with rakes during daytime and with their bodies at night.

One other thing. Coloreds were working there now. The snow has all but melted in what looks like a hot early spring. All the frozen corpses are thawing out fast. I could smell the rank odor of decomposition a mile out in woods and had to cover my mouth and eyes with clean underwear from my carpetbag when I reached the path into the town up top of that hill.

Coloreds were there to handle the corpses in the worst shape. Ones that were underground for years and years before they got hauled out last fall. With the heat coming on so soon and so quick, all the bodies were gonna be about in the same reeking condition by the end of the week.

They were paying the coloreds $2.50 a week. Not givin' 'em inathing as far as clothes or food. Making them sleep anywhere they cain't see 'em or hear 'em. Only thing they give 'em is shovels and picks. They made the coloreds wash the handles after they use 'em, before putting them back with the whites' tools.

My first night back I ate food I brought with me from the tree house as my evening meal. The day before I left, the three of us spent the afternoon smoking up the house preparing four bony chickens Squirrel Martin must have five-fingered from a farmer. We had wild early spring lettuce and mountain beets.

I had to convince myself that even though the missing key was grinding on me; I had to sleep. "Man, girl," I said to myself, "ain't it pathetic when your only friends in this place are a dead old preacher who lost the call, and an empty keyhole that lost the key."

Probably not much use when I think about it; I pushed the mattress up against the door when I was ready to lie down. It wasn't gonna stop 'em an inch. If these hound dog men were gonna git me, at least I'd feel them barging in instead of waking up with my clothes sliced off, some cracker with a knife at my throat.

My digging partner this time was a young twenty-year-old man-boy named Norman Niles Pethrow from Danville, Virginia.

He was an independent one, this one was. He was young and wild with a beautiful face and a warm, ice-melting smile. First morning I strolled over the steaming grass to join him, he was already digging a hole. He was standing down in it about two feet.

When he saw me walking toward him, he stood up straight with the shovel still stuck in the ground, folded his arms and leaned on top of the handle. The sun was running over his face and he smiled that warm smile that, I swear, went right into my body like a plunge into hot water.

"So you're Macy Weathers," he said with an accent that sounded like it had a little Georgia in it. "My stars, if this isn't my lucky day."

Then, right away he continued, "I'm sorry, Miss Weathers. Ah didn't mean it to sound disrespectful. What I meant is I don't have to share my thoughts, my digging or my hole with one of those brute fellas over there. Hearing 'Hey boy, don't you ever shut your damn mouth' several times a day is disquieting."

"Is what?" I asked him.

"Disquieting, mam. Means—"

"I know what it means," I said, sneaking in a smile and looking at him right in the eyes. "Are you ever gonna shut your mouth here with me?"

Without hesitating a moment, "I expect not, Miss Weathers," he said. He was grinning up at me in that cocky but charming way only special young men in their early twenties can do. A young, handsome boy who has succeeded in everything he's done so far—sports, girls, popularity, the envy of the other boys—and expects to just keep right being successful, cocky and charming right to the day he dies.

The other digging shovel meant for me was in the hole with him. He smiled again and passed it—handle first. I near froze when he did that. In all my memory, lots of tools have passed between men's hands and mine. But I cain't recall a man, other than my brothers, ever, ever, picking up a shovel like a piece of fine cutlery and handing it to me polite like, handle first.

I felt like he was a young prince offering me his hand to transport me from the normal person place to his place. A place of magic and beauty where people are kind and everybody looks into each other's eyes when they speak. Not like men there that looked straight to your breasts. Or the women whose eyes immediately dig into the ground.

"Well, I declare, a gentleman," I said like a priss.

Truth is, he *was* a gentleman. Maybe the first genuine gentleman I ever met. Besides that, how he talked and how he carried himself was so distinguishing. His warmth and the air all around him was different.

Maybe he is a prince, I was thinking, as I took off my embarrassing USACE coat jacket, laid it over a handle on the wheelbarrow, and hopped down into the hole with him.

"Ah'm Norman Pethrow, mam. Ah'm pleased to make your acquaintance."

He held out his hand for me to shake. Just like that, a fear bigger than Redemption Mountain took hold of me. I knew in my bones, if I touched this young man's hand, who knows where my life was gonna head?

When I didn't take his hand right away, a puzzled look rolled over his face that he quickly changed into one that raised his eyebrows, narrowed and twinkled up his eyes, and tilted his head to the side. A look that was telling me, "Come on girl, you want to touch me just as much as I want to touch you."

For a reason I couldn't fathom even to myself, I looked at him long and deep for a few seconds, then reached down and scooped up a handful of dirt. I scrubbed my hands with it, letting the dirt slip out until all'a it had fallen back down into the grave hole.

"This is to git us off on equal footing, Mr. Pethrow," I said. I reached out my dirty hand and gripped his. "I'm Ruby Johnson of over there in Redemption. I'm pleased to make your acquaintance, too."

He went a little blank. Running what I said around in his head. Without thinking, I had used my actual name with him. But then he produced that gorgeous smile and said as we shook our hands up and down, "Miss Weathers, I do believe this is the most delightful hand of any gravedigger I ever shook." Then he turned back to his work and continued digging.

I spit on my hands, rubbed them together, and got to digging, too.

After I heaved out a few shovelfuls, I heard, "Do you really know the meaning of the word disquieting, Miss Weathers?"

"Mr. Pethrow," feeling happy as I chucked out a shovelful of small stones and snapped off roots, "the exact meaning, no. Never heard the word spoke in my life. But can I figure out what it means by thinking on it a little? Unless we make some better progress here, the foreman, whoever that is now, is gonna feel more than a little disquieted. And so will we when they fire our asses out'a here."

He laughed, and I could tell without looking at him, he was relieved that I could impress him.

Work for that week was enjoyable and productive. The weather was warm, and me and Norman Pethrow dug thirty-five grave holes, which he said was a Red Hand record. Nights were far less pleasurable. Socializing with the community for me was not ever gonna happen. I knew if I wandered down to the conglomeration (one of Norman's great big words) of wooden boards they use for a whiskey shack, I'd be up against the wall, legs pried apart in no time. But staying by myself in my little room night after night was not too inspiring either. I spent a lot of time thinking about Dahlia Rose. And Norman. I wondered if Dahlia Rose would like Norman? Or would she become quiet and mysterious like she did when she was around most all men? Maybe Dahlia Rose didn't like men? Maybe she liked women?

Man alive, I never thought of that possibility before. I always assumed she was like me, got the intimates only for men, but never found any worth a corpse's crap.

Norman: I thought about him all the time, even when we were working there together side by side in a grave hole, talking about who knows what and laughing and flirting. Sometimes when he wasn't looking, I'd turn around and look him over while he had his back to me, digging away. His body was fine. Young and sweet and hard as an unripe peach. Sometimes I'd just look at his behind, enjoying myself immensely.

He was doing the same thing when I wasn't looking. I could feel his eyes traveling over me like two soft wet fingertips wanting to touch and explore every part of my body. Feel it. Taste it. Rub himself on it. Drawing me close to him and watching my eyes close just before he kisses me. Unbuttoning my shirt and sliding his palms over my breasts, feeling my nipples poke into his flesh.

A few times I felt my body tingling, just knowing he was watching me, and finding me desirable. One night me and him were walking back to the foreman's office to put away the shovels and wheelbarrow. We were strolling, in no hurry because in this place there was nowhere desirable to hurry to, when I saw a man about fifty feet away leaning against a tree in the dark. He was smoking a cigarette. But had it cupped in his hand when he took a draw to keep the sizzling embers from lighting up his face.

I only noticed this one man out'a all the other men lurking around or going someplace because he was noticing us. Studying our every move. I could feel him there. The shadowy man gave me the same horrid sensation I felt when I was anywhere near Tolbert Greaves.

Near the end of our three weeks on the job, the whole place began fuming and ready to explode. After work, right there in the dark, the new foreman gathered us all together, even the coloreds who stood off under the poplars, and made a big announcement.

A beefy man that took over for Mr. Kilgore named Jack Haddock stood up on a wooden cabbage crate and started clapping and whistling like he was just thrilled by a performance of Justin Shawl and the Banjo Boys. Everybody looked over at him and stopped what they were doing, which was mostly nothing.

The beefy man made a megaphone with his hands and yelled into it, "Y'all listen up," he said real loud. "Hey…y'all out there…sidle on up here so you can hear what I'm gonna say… Come on y'all… Behave now and come on over here…"

Norman and I were standing off by ourselves in the shadows of a little pine grove far enough away from everybody else so everybody, including Mr. Beefy there, was just slinking around like dusk silhouettes.

"Y'all…come on now. Shut up and listen." Things were quieting down.

"It don't make no never mind to me but I know it will to y'all so I'll just spit it out. There ain't gonna be no fourth weeks off no more. Government says we're way behind. That don't make our boss man too happy. If he ain't happy then foremen ain't happy. Meaning, I ain't happy. Startin' right now, all youse is free to leave or stay. But if you leave, there ain't no comin' back. No comin' back at'all. If you stay, there ain't no weeks off. Ain't no days off. That's all I gotta say. Work picks right up the same as today tomorrow mornin'."

"Don't we git to ask questions?" someone yelled.

Beefy walked back up on his cabbage box. "I ain't in no mood to be toyed with. Facts is facts, and these facts is pretty simple to understand—even for the likes of you."

"That ain't fair," another man shouted. There was a general agreement to that statement expressed by whispers buzzing that carried on for a bit until Norman called out, "What about people who have kin waiting? Waiting for them and waiting for the money?"

Old Beefy was getting riled up now. "Listen," he said menacingly, "what happens outside of these confines to anyone of y'all don't concern me in the least. Not one damn bit. No sir, not one motherfuckin' bit. You got problems, take it up with the U.S. government. Until they tell me personally to give a good shit about what any y'all feel or have to say, shut the fuck up, go eat your night meal, and be here diggin' in the morning, or somewhere else walkin'. Now git. Before I whistle up some help who'll help make your decisions for you. Git!"

"You okay, Ruby?" Norman whispered to me.

After that man stopped talking, my mind was heaving with what implications this was gonna have on Dahlia Rose and Squirrel Martin. My mind was already piling all the reasons to leave on one side, and all the reasons to stay on the other.

"Ruby…" Norman whispered to me, "what are you feelin'?"

"I'm not feelin' inathing good, Norman. Man, I don't know what to do with this." It hit me just then. "Norman, you just called me Ruby."

"Well hello to you, Miss Genius. What else am I going to call you, Jezebel?"

"You don't care who I am?"

"Should I?"

Here's where our flirty friendship went somewhere else. I put my open hand on his chest soft and gentle. "Makin' hard choices like this is nothing new to me, Norman Pethrow. Sometimes I believe all that wakes me up in the morning anymore is to be slugged over the head with something as tough to decide about as this. Not sure what I'm going to do. What are you gonna do?"

"I got nowhere better than this here to go to right now in my life. If you stay in this pathetic nowhere, then I got somewhere worthwhile to stay for a while. That make any sense to you?"

I didn't answer him in words. But my feelings and thoughts were already seeing us tearing off our clothes and our bodies clawing at each other.

CHAPTER TWENTY

That night, I wasn't caring too much anymore about horrible men busting into my room intent on doing horrible things to me. I moved my mattress away from blocking the door and back into its corner.

Locked door or no locked door, I was gonna sleep graceful and strong.

On the Monday morning of the fifth consecutive week since I was home with Dahlia Rose and Squirrel Martin, old Beefy stopped Norman and I as we were fetching our tools. No hello. No good morning. He just waddled over and said ignorant as hell, "You two ain't diggin' today. Git in that wagon yonder."

Already hunkered in it were six colored men and one white. For as long as I'd been there, I never saw them mix the races. The coloreds were always down at the low places in the valley, digging out the rotted corpses and rotted coffins and loading them on wagons in piles like stacking up decayed logs.

The smell down there was so bad, the horses spooked anywhere near the place. So they only walked them in right when it was time to hitch 'em up and haul away the reeking dead.

"Mornin', gentlemen," Norman said to the coloreds. Then he looked over at the white man and said good morning to him, too. One colored man answered in a soft, unemotional tone, "Mornin' to you, too, sah."

"Damn it all to hell," cursed the white man, and just like that, he jumped down from the wagon. As he was walking toward the barracks to collect his measly belongings and leave, he told old Beefy the foreman to kiss his Georgia ass.

"Well, fellas," Norman said to the colored men, who had been dead silent and staring down at invisible and better worlds that must have resided on the floor of the wagon, "ain't he the hateful pip!"

That got a smile out'a most of'm.

Smiles didn't last long, at least not for us. The wagon pitched and creaked and slammed into every rock and root for the three-mile journey down a desolate country road. Every recently abandoned house felt like it had been vacated by humans and taken over a hundred years ago, instead of last month, by ghosts too stupid to know how to haunt a place proper.

We rounded a corner of tall pines. The stench that engulfed us was brain numbing. "Oh my God," I said to Norman, and caught his eyes.

The wagon continued down the rutted ugly road for another quarter mile before we came in view of the Old Red Hand Cemetery, with the smell of its centuries of deceased citizens getting more overpowering with every rock in the road.

"Here, take these," a colored man said. He handed Norman two thick woolen scarves saturated with something that smelled mighty close to gasoline. Along with his co-workers, the colored man wrapped a soaked scarf around his head many times so it layered over his face and covered his nose and mouth with a quarter inch of cloth up to just under the eyes.

Norman reached out to shake his hand. "Thank you, sir," he said. "This was mighty noble of you." The colored man shook Norman's hand for less than a second. But his eyes looked right into Norman and expressed everything.

To do this horrible work, we got heavy gloves covered in stains. The coloreds didn't git inathing to put over their bare hands. There wasn't one moment of handling the corpses that was any more or less gruesome than any other. We had thick black tarps to put the unfortunate souls into. Each had their own. There was supposed to be thick white chalk so we could write the names on the tarps, but we couldn't find any. Pieces of bodies came right off in your fingers. Petrified guts spilled out like long pieces of hard candy. It took eight hours for all eight of us to exhume ten bodies, with a hell of a lot of extra body parts lying around afterward we didn't know what to do with.

All that day I tried to play tricks on my mind. Imagining the corpses as timber. I tried imagining they were huge rolled up cigars that had waterlogged and rotted and it was our job to ready them up to be ground into mulch.

For a time, I tried to imagine I was paying homage to the Johnson women raped and murdered by Yankees during the Civil War. I had more success with that than with inathing else.

But I could not shut out'a my mind the six pieces of petrified bone and the small skull of an eight-year-old girl who died of consumption in 1853. I knew she wanted to tell me her story. She had probably been waiting all this time for someone with the magical gift to tell what happened to her since she was buried here. But I just didn't have the strength to ask her.

That week, we readied up sixty-five of Red Hand's lost souls and slung them up on wagons. We hauled them back up that road for three miles to high country and then tried to be respectful and git things right, put people in the hole and under the tombstone where they belonged.

On that last Saturday late afternoon, after we filled in the last hole and anchored the last gravestone into the ground at the head of it, we all crawled up into the wagon to git dropped off back up top. When we got up there, Norman was asleep with his head on a colored man's shoulder. And the colored man who gave us the turpentine-soaked scarves was asleep with his head resting on mine.

After we hopped down out'a that splintery wagon, the sight of that eight-year-old girl's little bones felt like it permanently seeped into my mind. I could see her little skull trying to communicate with me everywhere I looked. Norman said I was "probably experiencing some kind of temporary trauma from the magnitude of the impossible psychological conditions we had to endure for eleven hours a day, for seven straight days." I was not so sure about that. But I understood the meaning of every big word he said, straight off.

Death churned at me all night. My dreams were full of the eight-year-old girl and she spent every minute of the night trying to tell me how she died. But I just could not oblige her. I felt my place was with the living. I had spent enough time with the females of the dead.

I woke up in the morning to the bell jangler whipping his piece of iron around inside the round come-and-git-it bell, snapping the whole town out'a their sleep. I woke up trying to breathe.

I put on my work clothes. I walked straight out to the tool house to find Norman. A cigar stubby foreman came over to us pushing a wheelbarrow with two shovels and a pick rattling around in it. "You two go back up top and finish with the hole digging. Four more and that graveyard is done. Git goin' now."

Me and Norman pushed the wheelbarrow along the main street back toward the upper cemetery. Halfway, we heard a horse-drawn wagon clomping up ahead. It was about to swing around a corner with some decent looking old antebellum style houses lining it and a huge old oak tree covering most of the area with gently swaying leaf shadows. The air was sweet. We were way upwind from the lower cemeteries. Then, I heard whistling. Beautiful songbird calls. One after another, lovely musical birdsongs floated over to us just like some invisible nature person was serving them to us on a soft pillow.

"My stars, Norman, that's so beautiful." I stopped walking and listened.

More songs floated to us. I was trying to concentrate hard on hearing the whistling over the sloppy sounds of a horse and wagon that just reached the corner up ahead and were bending around it slow as a cold piece of lead heading our way.

We stepped off to the side of the street to let the wagon pass. Inside it, the same six colored men we spent the week before with, handling the corpses, were sitting in more or less the same positions and in the same places as we had left them last night. They looked like they were going back down to lower ground.

As the wagon jiggled by us, the songs of the birds were getting louder. Sweeter. More refined and clear.

One man sprawled in the wagon was sitting with his back up against the far inside wall with one leg stretched out, looking backwards at things as they passed. His mouth and lips were transforming into different shapes every few seconds and a different birdcall would fly out.

"Hey there, fellas," Norman called. "Good to see you again."

I had my eyes on the man producing such extraordinarily beautiful bird whistling. It was the man that gave us the scarves to cover our faces.

"Norman, I know that man."

"Sure you do darlin'; we spent all week with him poking into dead pieces of rednecks and their families."

I wasn't listening to what Norman said.

"I couldn't see his face wrapped under the turpentine rag. As a girl, I used to see him all the time. Folks used to call him Mockin'bird Man on account he was a powerful spirit charmer. Could charm inathing or anybody by whistling a tune into them. Used to kill white Kluxers every other day by giving 'em strokes and cancer. I heard once he knocked a nigger-hating preacher right outta his pulpit and he landed dead sitting on his ass with a heart attack. Not even whites liked that preacher. But, man, were they scared to death of old Mockin'bird Man.

"And my little brother Squirrel Martin spent most of his life traipsing all over creation with that man."

I called to Mockin'bird Man, "Sir, that is some beautiful music."

Before I could stop myself, I called again to the disappearing wagon, "Sir, thank you for so fine a gift as you brung us today! I remember you whistlin' me happy and doing good for my family many times when I was young. Many, many times!"

Maybe he could hear me.

I waved to him. So did Norman. The whistling man lowered his head and made a shy, pleasant face, looking right at me.

When we were finishing digging our last grave hole that week, the sun was setting and the bell jangler had already announced the evening meal had come and gone.

My back and hands were on fire. Norman kept climbing out'a the last few holes all afternoon to go pee in the woods he was drinking so much water.

I was trying to heft out a last few scoops of dirt to even off the bottom of the hole. Since it was the last grave hole that I might ever dig with Norman, I wanted it perfect. Every corner square. Every wall smooth. I made it about a foot and a half wider than necessary, seeking and re-seeking perfection with a square edge. If it wasn't perfect, I'd scrape into the walls another inch.

As it was getting on dusk, I wanted the shape just right to receive whoever was slated to rest in peace here in a town where peace never existed.

Down there waiting for Norman to come back to offer his hand to pull me out, out'a the fading light a ragged plaid blanket plopped down on the ground beside me. A long bottle of something followed and didn't break when it clinked against a stone. With a half-moon rising over the top of the mountains, petals of daisies and blood-red wild roses showered down on me and just kept showering.

I was being courted by a boy.

Young Norman Niles Pethrow, who chose to dig graves with undesirable human beings rather than join his brothers in overseeing the family cotton mill, was trying to love me.

Sitting down there with my back leaning up against the far dirt wall, I raised my arms up. Norman's flowers fell on me like a brief summer rain.

Then, Norman leaped down into the hole. I wanted him to ravage me. But he wanted to set up a romantic setting. He shook out the blanket and spread it out to cover as much of the dirt bottom as possible. By the light of the half-moon, he held up a bottle of wine, pulled out the cork with his teeth and grinned at me. He took a long sip and passed the bottle to me. But before I could take a drink, he kneeled down and pulled me down with him. I was sitting on my behind facing him. Gently he pushed me over on my back and unbuttoned my shirt. He pulled off my dirty wrangler pants, caked with the stains of hope, despair, indifference and death.

Spread open wide, my ankles were in each one of his hands.

Somewhere near dawn, we woke to a sky smeared pink. Our bodies were sore, bruised and covered in dirt. The wine bottle was empty. Wrapped in the blanket, we had slept in the smell of flower petals and deep earth. We made love throughout the night. In a grave hole. Norman released his seed inside me four times.

We had been in that town for almost three months. Then, that next morning, the work was done. They were closing down operations. The flood was scheduled to be let loose. After we got our pay, the USACE building went a-clanking and a-rolling on the big cart pulled by draught horses up the road. They opened the three dams. And turned the town into a backwoods version of Noah's flood.

They sank the people of Red Hand's history, their kin memories, their land, their sloppy old houses and everything else they knew and loved in a hundred feet of water.

Just like old Mr. Elson did the first time I walked back home over the mountain; Norman walked with me to the path opening. "You know," I said as we were walking up that long hill, "first time I come through here I found a frozen colored man in the snow." As I finished saying that I wanted to tell Norman about my horrible memory of seeing a colored man running around consumed by raging fire.

But I didn't. Some other time, I was thinking.

"You're coming then?"

After our long kiss, Norman said gentle, "By and by, girl. By and by."

CHAPTER TWENTY-ONE

Not an hour into the woods, I knew something was following me.

It was a beautiful early summer day but windy as can be. The treetops were swaying and crashing together, and the leaves were rustling like a billion small soft rattling bones. With all that nature's racket, I couldn't hear much of inathing else, let alone something straggling along just behind.

But I could feel it.

I found a good size walking stick with a big knot on the top, making it appear useful and lethal at the same time. Back there, me and Norman weaved up some leather strips and made a backpack-type sling for my carpetbag. Thumping against my rear end with every step, it kept reminding me of Red Hand, the corpses...Norman. But it kept my hands free, even if my rear was going to be solid black and blue when I got to Redemption.

For a long time after I knew something was out there, I just kept walking and walking. Five months ago, I ambled to a place I ain't never seen, thinking about the burdens of my life and the horrible mysteries ahead. Going back over the mountain home now, I was thinking on living, breathing and dying in a whole different way.

At some time in our lives we are all tested. Just us against an unknown, dark force. Until right then, I thought my test was Safire Dignity Johnson dying, kilt by me, four days old. Or trying to outfox the U.S. government and the U.S. Army Corps of Engineers to keep Johnsons in home and hearth. Or a whole goddamn lifetime of that town of Redemption trying to destroy us. Or all the kids moving out into the world. Or the mountain on fire I lit myself that took everything away. Or a trip to Hell named Red Hand to find Heaven again. Or losing Hardy. Now probably Norman.

But the test never comes in the way we imagine. Listening to feet kicking through the leaves just out'a sight, I expected to see Norman Niles Pethrow suddenly just standing there holding a bunch of red mountain roses. Or Squirrel Martin coming swinging down from some top branches and landing in a happy bouncing dance to walk me back home. Or all drunk and cruel, Silas come to take his revenge.

Or Lonny Dale back from the dead to profess true love.

Stepping out from behind a stately old maple on the path just ahead, Tolbert Greaves was suddenly just standing there pointing some kind of rifle at me. He had a cigarette dangling out'a his mouth like a stiff snake tongue, with his dirty, smirky grin screaming *I told you I wus gonna fuck you to death.*

"Well…well…" he said slow and scratchy. "Lookie here now, woncha. Here she is all stuck-up beautiful and womanly and all alone with nothing but me and my powerful needs to keep her company."

Greaves motioned toward me with the rifle. "Come on over here, beauty girl. Come over to me right quick."

I had no choice. I knew about other men like Greaves back in Red Hand. If I didn't do what he wanted, he'd give no second thoughts about shooting me. But he'd shoot me in the leg or arm, some place just to wound me enough to let him do his raping as violent and for as long as he wanted. He didn't care if I was gonna bleed to death. In his warped mind, he was gonna kill me inaway, probably while he was fucking me one last time.

Greaves motioned with his rifle again. Surprising him, I'm sure, I just walked right over in my usual walk and stood there in front of him, three inches in front of his face. I didn't mean to do it as brave as that. But as I was standing there, smelling his whiskey stink and the shit stains reeking out'a his clothes, thinking maybe by pressing right up into his face he'd back off some.

Greaves smiled evil and rammed his rifle butt into my stomach.

I fell to my knees, gasping, which is exactly where Greaves wanted me, with my face a couple of inches away from his crotch.

Greaves reached down rough and cupped his hand under my chin. With his other hand awkwardly holding on to the rifle, he unzipped himself and flopped out his dick. Then he pointed the rifle barrel down and jammed it right up against my vagina.

"You'd better git to suckin', girl. You'd better git to it right quick."

While I was terrified by this awful man, I was also feeling more calm and dreamy than a woman ought to feel when she's about to git violently molested and probably murdered. All the same, I couldn't stop my body from peeing itself. The pee started light at first and then came rushing outta me uncontrollable.

It ran down my legs, making a big warm stain on my dungarees and dripped outta my pants, creating a puddle that slowly bled into the ground.

Greaves was mighty stimulated by this. He got stiff.

"I declare. Ain't you a pisser," he said, screaming laughing at his fantastic joke. "Maybe when you're done suckin' me dry, I'll piss all over you some since you seem to like piss so much."

Then he got mean.

Greaves clenched his fist around my jaw and forced my mouth open. He jammed his disgusting penis right in. Breathing soft and steady, I just wasn't afraid of inathing, least of all this bastard. Who knows why?

With an evil, insane man jamming his dick into my mouth…after a lifetime of men drooling and masturbating over me. Saying disgusting things as I walked by. Rutting me into tears and soreness. Sending semen into my mouth, my vagina, and up my ass. Leaving me. Lying to me. And now about to rape and kill me…I was not gonna have any more of this Southern Christian gentleman cracker bullshit.

None at all.

With my Hollywood beautiful mouth, I sucked that dick for all I was worth for about a minute. I was gonna suck his cracker brain right out the damn thing.

Like he was masturbating with not a soul around for miles, he was groaning and whelping and letting fly a long line of "Oh my dinglin' Christs…" Then, throwing his head back, closed his eyes ready to come like I ain't even there.

Right when he released, I snatched that rifle outta his surprised hands so fast, only one of his eyes flopped open. The other was clenched shut with sperm shooting out'a him.

I swung the rifle around, pushed it up against his disgusting dick, and without blinking, I shot Greaves full in the crotch. The echo of the rifle shot took on a small life of its own and circled above us through and over the trees three or four times. I spit out a mouthful of slime and sweat and dirty saliva, with most of it landing on my boot. My jaw ached from how he forced my mouth to open more than it's meant to. I could smell my own urine.

For a few long seconds I almost forgot where I was. Who I was. What I had just done. I wanted to lie down and go to sleep. I wanted to sleep and sleep and sleep somewhere cool and high and safe. I wanted to be a hummingbird with beautiful silky wings, more like a fairy than a bird. I wanted to flutter and flutter up higher and higher until I was so high up and the air was so thin, my little million-mile-an-hour flapping wings sang. My heart would be racing. My mind would be breathing. I would cry but no tears would come. I would drift. All over the mountain. All over the county. All over North Carolina. All over the earth. Like an airy, unhurried cloud. Sadly going nowhere as it happily went everywhere.

For a long moment with his eyes bugged like his eyelids had stretched over the back of his head, he was silent and motionless.

Then, fear, terror, and pain hit him. The man screamed a sound of misery and agony that was louder than all the rustling leaves and bending limbs for a mile all around. And he kept on screaming. And screaming.

Greaves grabbed his crotch with both hands and melted to the ground, still screaming. Wriggling around like a broke back dog. Blood spewing out'a his pants, making a puddle a hell of a lot bigger than mine.

I was looking down at him.

"What now, Mr. Tolbert Greaves?" I emptied the rifle's bullet chamber as I talked and threw the handful of'm as hard as I could out into the long grass. Leaving only one.

"You want me to leave you here? Carry you some place to git your pecker put back on? Shoot you dead? Torture you up some? What?"

Greaves couldn't talk. His face was all contorted into a

grotesque mask like some devil heaping pain on himself and enjoying it.

I sat down right there on the dusty path.

I lifted the barrel and pointed it straight at his temple.

"What we gonna do here, Mr. Greaves?"

"Fuck you, you half nigger Johnson bitch," Greaves spat at me, blood coming out'a his mouth now. "You dumb ass Johnsons never knew it was my granddaddy and a shitload of my kin that kilt all your black heart women kin. It wasn't no Union soldiers. It was me and mine that took you and yours off this earth."

Somewhere deep inside, I already knew that. But just the same, it did my heart good to know the truth finally. And with the truth, when I got back home, I could walk into the cemetery field, call them up, and tell them they could be at peace at long last.

"Amen to you Mr. Tolbert Greaves. Consider this a personal message from all the women from my family that ever was, the earliest to me now, and those that still live ghostly where your men kin put them. Johnson women are unique creations of nature. There's nothing you can do to us now."

And I left him there for the birds and beasts of Redemption Mountain after I one-shot Greaves in the temple, dead.

***

Justifiable death does not always bring peace. Being vengeful does not always clear a painful heart. Far as I know, no Johnson had ever kilt anyone with a weapon or with force. All our killing was powerful spells and conjured up calamities. Walking away from where Tolbert Greaves lay in a bloody mud puddle with his mind blown free of his skull, I didn't feel a wall'a contentment come down and overpower me with relief. Or safety. Liberation. Or redemption. Nor did I feel a welling up of horror and guilt and shame at what I'd done.

I felt…nothing. Nothing at all. Not good, not bad. And being honest, just a small feeling of disappointment that taking somebody's life as ugly and hateful as that one was…was…like drinking a plain glass of water instead of sweet buttermilk. Or gasoline.

It was clear when I got back to Squirrel Martin's tree house that he and Dahlia Rose hadn't been there for a while. Birds had got in and ate up some bread and crapped around a little. Other than that, the place was still standing and still magical.

Except now, I was alone.

Dahlia Rose left a plumb lovely note she drew because she cain't read and write. It said that she just had to go find a life worth living on her own…somewheres out there in the wild blond yonder.

By the drawings sprinkled around the pages, I could see Squirrel Martin was going to lead her back through the woods to our mountainside, with our burned down house setting there still burned down. He was going to take her down the driveway road to the flat valley road. From there, Dahlia Rose was on her own. He would go no further than the last rut of our property before civilization, such as it was, began.

I spent a week by myself up in the floating branches, playing the harp, and washing five or six times a day in the little river that ran by about a quarter mile away. Sometimes I lay there in the water for hours. Letting the water run over me and into me and all around me, washing clean my whole life.

Washing clean every single moment and everything I ever done. Or was did to me.

Johnsons never have thought much of Jesus baptisms and preachers dunking folks under water in the name of being saved and suddenly making them better than everybody else.

Maybe I was baptizing myself.

Maybe I was just washing away my pain.

Maybe I was just bathing, smelling good and feeling good when I walked naked and free as Eve in the Bible up the riverbank and into the arms of the gently swaying willow trees every time I got out.

***

I was in there bathing when it come to me that my only option now was Mr. Jesse. In all the world, whether I stayed in this life or starved out'a it, I was in the hands of an old produce-brokering man that had always been fair to me. But might be dead as old Abe Lincoln for all I knew.

If he was dead, then I might as well just take me a stroll into the spirit field, say hello to all my flying kin, and say yes to staying there for the rest of time.

But after the two-mile walk down the driveway road and four more along the valley road, I came floating out'a heat waves and strolled soft as sunlight up to Mr. Jesse's office door. I lightly knocked on it. A hundred things passed over his face as soon as he looked up and saw me.

"Lordy, girl!" he said, excited and breathless. "Where in tarnation you been? Come on in here and take a seat." With his foot, he jolted a chair piled up with papers and booklets and knocked them all to the floor. "You just sit here nice and peaceful while I git us a couple of Dr. Peppers."

Practically falling over himself, the potbellied old man lumbered out the door and disappeared around the corner of his produce warehouse. When he came back, he was holding two Dr. Peppers and a big bag of pistachio nuts.

"Here you go," he said cheerfully, handing me a bottle of sweet cola drink and then holding out the big bag of nuts for me to dip my fist into.

For a minute, we just sat there. Saying nothing. Mr. Jesse was looking old. But he was in tip-top shape for a man carrying around a belly and smoking Viceroys all day with the filters ripped off.

Finally, he said mournful, "Ruby, I'm sure sorry to hear about your brother."

Maybe because I was tired, or that so much living and dying had passed my way, I immediately thought of Bobby Lee. Had he been kilt in some secret war I didn't know inathing about?

When I didn't say inathing back to him, a different mournful look covered his face. "Ruby Lee Johnson, you don't know…do you."

Land sakes, I didn't want to know more. About nothing. About inathing. Ever.

"Shot him twenty, twenty-five times. They say the fellas was out shooting at bats. Some of'm fellas where the ones that burned you out. Some of'm was just rifle shootin' men. One of'm, a store clerk, claims he's the only man of flesh and blood that ever fucked Ruby Johnson. Now he wanted the sister.

"Just as dusk was getting too dark to see any more bats a-twitterin', down she comes, her and Squirrel Martin. Those men cain't believe it. It's the younger Johnson sister in the sweet flesh. An' since your brother shot up a mess of'm that time, they hated him bad."

Mr. Jesse took a swig of Dr. Pepper and flicked off the shells of a few pistachios and crunched down on them. "Them boys figured what comes down must go back up. They lay a trap there in the dark, waiting for them two to come back from wherever they went. A short time later, when only that wordless boy appears out'a the dark, and your pretty sister ain't with him, the boys just ain't fit no more for game playin'. Them hid in a dark grove of trees; your brother is walking right by 'em not twenty feet away when rifles start shooting. Some of'm boys was still shootin' into him after your brother was already gone. Nobody ever did find out where your sister run off to. She just disappeared. That's it, Ruby Lee. Another one of you Johnsons just up and went plain gone, telling nobody nothin'. Gone," he finished.

I took that information in some.

"It was that old whistlin' colored man that found him. That next day about the same time, dusk. Guess he was planning on burying the boy up in your cemetery field. Not far up the driveway, your brother slung over the black man's back, those men return because one of'm left a little ammunition bag with his name scratched into it at the scene of the crime. To hedge their bets, they shoot that old man, too."

I sat there for a full half hour.

That horrible feeling of absolutely nothing in my heart and soul was vibrating throughout me like it did when I shot Tolbert Greaves.

Why is this? Cain't I feel nothin' anymore? All my life, I wore my feelings like see through clothes. Even those old USACE men knew what I was feeling and tried to use it against me.

Probably now, after so much heartache and trouble, most of the conscious me is asleep or run off somewhere. In a toneless, feelingless voice, I looked straight into Mr. Jesse's face and said, "We got us a raspberry deal or not, Mr. Jesse?"

To my surprise, he responded pleased as punch, "We do, girl. We surely do." He opened his desk drawer and after fishing through a mess of paper and envelopes and empty Viceroy packs, he came out with a big yellow envelope.

"Here," he told me, "read this here while I go take a leak and see if it's all you been hopin' for. I done all this long ago. It's bin waitin' for you."

With perspiration beading down between my breasts, and me remembering that I was past my lady's time by two or three weeks while I was reading, the contract said he wanted to buy half the damn raspberry acres outright. We would co-own them. And pay me more money than I could comprehend sitting right there.

To boot, he was going to build me a new house. Right on top of the old house.

After he came back, I was sitting there numb. Too numb to cry because my dearest brother had been murdered. My dearest sister was gone. My entire family disappeared.

But for the first time in my life, I wouldn't have to worry about nothin'.

Not a thing.

"Where do I sign this here, Mr. Jesse? And you still have some slugs of still whiskey around this place?"

They built my new house. I live in it happy as a clam. Digging new gardens. Pruning fruit trees. I convinced Mr. Jesse to build me a new barn, too. But the best thing...leaving him shaking his head exasperated by my newest request but tickled by it too—I had him build a new woodshed. And pulley the old, rusted Model T up and put it back on the roof. I could never mix up a batch of colors that turned into Squirrel Martin's holy murple color. So I painted the woodshed and ancient Ford setting on it bluebird egg blue. Color of innocence. Squirrel would like that.

I bought myself a good used truck that was decrepit enough to make me smile. And workable enough to keep that smile in place. When I drove down into town, nobody bothered me. People were actually polite. Being well off financially compared to them they had a reason to respect me they could relate to. Or not relate to since all pooled together their net worth was probably $1.98.

Six months later, Mr. Jesse drove up here with another fella who said he represented an investment group from Charlotte. With Mr. Jesse J. Brown smiling big as a bear, this man wearing an ironed up north blue suit and shiny black pointy shoes was telling us he wanted to give me even more money than I got already. He said he was going to give us $500 an acre and a 20% share of the company's profits. And his land surveying was a mite more accurate that the USACE's. Excluding the property around the house, the back and side woods, the spirit field, the Raspberry Acres, the driveway road and its surroundings all the way to our front door, there were 5,500 acres of Johnson ground, 1,500 acres of it over-abundantly fit for growing fruit of all kinds. And the 4,000 acres of forest land, he was going to negotiate with us for that, too.

"Miss Johnson, you have yourself 5,500 reasons to talk to me this morning," he said all polite and educated. "Mr. Brown has just finished showing me around the most lush and healthy and endless amount of raspberries and fruit growing land in the South—1,500 acres worth. A million raspberries in every one of'm. A fortune for somebody who wants to farm them properly and build a modern processing facility up here."

The investment fella took off his expensive city hat and fanned himself. He cleared his throat and shot a nervous look over to Mr. Jesse before he looked back at me.

"And a fortune for the two people who own it and who might want to sell it."

Mr. Jesse was drooling like a dog. The city fella was sweating like a pig. I swooshed my long hair around a little like tired red angel wings and ask two questions.

"You ain't ever gonna bother me up top here, are you?"

"Not if you don't want us to. No reason to inaway. The Raspberry Acres are a half mile below your place if I remember correctly. We'll even build you your own road up if you want."

"I don't want you to build me my *own* road up," I said polite enough. "I already got my own road up. Build your own road."

Mr. Jesse was about to have a cow.

The city fella said nervous and confident at the same time, "We can do that."

Mr. Jesse started to breathe a little again.

"How many people will it take to work this…modern processing facility?" I asked.

The city man thought for a second. "Hard to tell right off. *De*pends if the facility does more than just pick and package raspberries."

"Like what, for instance?" Mr. Jesse blurted out, until then, afraid to utter a word for fear of blowing the whole thing.

The city fella made a face and answered, "Like a canning operation. Also making pies, jams, jellies, desserts. That type of enterprise. A hundred workers maybe. A moderately ambitious national business."

"…Oh," Mr. Jesse and I said together and looked at each other, not really grasping this.

"I'll be damned," I said right out loud, "here I am providing an economy for Redemption folks after all. A hundred jobs and a hundred families, probably over five hundred folks all told. My o my."

"One last thing," I said to both men. "At least half the workers gotta be coloreds and Injuns."

They looked at me as if I just said all those raspberries have to be stuffed up someone's ass before we sell them.

"Now, Ruby..." began Mr. Jesse.

"That's all I got to say," I said and smiled pretty at both men. I offered the city man my hand, and gave him the eye that this is what it will take to seal the deal, "Mr. ...?"

"Lorde." He shook it, not exactly sure what he had just agreed to.

With those two haggling with each other, I walked away, six months pregnant, and smiling to myself, remembering what Reverend Pine Gregory kept a-sayin' to me so long ago right after I gave birth to Safire...about the Lord helping those who help themselves.

And I remembered Dahlia Rose as a child thinking Macy went off to be a New Orleans workingwoman because her shee-it had finally come in.

Mine just did. Overflowing with cash money and sweet red fruit.

In two weeks, I was the richest single woman in all North Carolina. Probably the richest witch woman in the world. Even without the twenty percent of profits mixed in, me and Mr. Jesse had near $2,000,000 to split and hide under our beds.

In three months, I gave birth to Gracie Pearl all by myself on the kitchen floor.

I raised my girl child to be inathing she wanted. Doctor, healer, gravedigger, movie star, whore, even a Hollywood beautiful local high mountain girl who'll never go to another place for all her life.

When she was a tiny one, I mixed my mother's milk up in her tiny mouth with a mountainside of burning memories and a simple loving squeeze of sweet, sweet raspberry juice.

And I never abandoned her 'cause life is hard, like my mama did me.

CHAPTER TWENTY-TWO

Ruby Lee Johnson (72 years old)
August 26, 1983

My Gracie Pearl's daughter Dulcinea Rose and I are sitting out under Boolie's old cottonwood eating breakfast, doing nothing more industrious than drinking coffee and slicing up fruit. The sun is shining. The fog is burning off and the mountain ridgelines are appearing one at a time across the valley. Phoebe birds are calling their mournful tunes.

Dulcie Rose is artfully chewing the end of a long stalk of grass into various types of braids. She's lying on her back, with her three feet of auburn red hair, close to the same color as mine was when I was a young woman, spread all around her head on the ground. Her graceful grass-stained bare feet are on my lap, one of'm tapping a rhythm to something only she can hear.

"Ruby?" she asks. I don't want anyone calling me Grandma. She's eating a peach between grass chews, with the juice sticky all over her hands. "Why don't those birds ever find each other? I have never in my life heard two of'm lost souls singing from the same tree."

Dulcie Rose is seventeen years old now and lovely as can be. Sometimes I look at my beautiful granddaughter and see more of Dahlia Rose in her face than I see of Gracie Pearl, or of me.

Right then we hear, "Hey there, Ruby, darling. Ain't this old thing Squirrel Martin's?"

After fifty years, Hardy Jessup just comes moseying up the driveway road. He's holding a little old fashion rusted-up bird-shootin' rifle he found just leaning there in plain sight near the bottom in a clump of lilac bushes.

For that second, I don't know whether to jump up and throw my arms around Hardy or take the rifle from him and because it's all that's left of my brother, hug that thing to death instead.

Before I can do either, Hardy walks over to Dulcie Rose and plunks down in the grass beside her. Dulcie Rose looks Hardy over, then turns to me. "This man my granddaddy?"

I look at the two of'm sitting there with sunlight and leaf shadows rustling all over them. I think of Norman. I think of Silas. I think of Lonny Dale. "No, he's not, honey. But he sure could'a been."

Turns out Hardy's been living in Nashville, Tennessee for all these years. Married a few times, managing a roadhouse where there was live country music raising the roof every night.

After telling us about his wife dying last year, the first thing he mentions is Tom Sawyer. "That boy done himself real well, Ruby Lee. He's written songs for some greats. Bill Monroe and Patsy Cline themselves. He drives a big ole white Cadillac and married himself into the Davis family that owns all the record labels in Nashville. Tom has a bunch of grown up kids and grandkids. Not sure how many. A bunch are good with fiddles, guitars and such."

Then Hardy looks glum. "All'a these years we thought you were dead. Tom told me one time that y'all died in a mountain fire that burned your place clean away. Then I never heard inathing more about it. I came home yesterday to sell the old place. Some kin were living in it all these years after Ma and all her sisters died. I got a letter from a lawyer telling me the kin's all moved out and that I should come see about settling my affairs before they auction it off. Just five hours ago, the bank gives me $25,000 for the house and the land. Cash money. I never had this much cash that belonged to me in my hand in my life."

Hardy looks tired. Seventy-three years living in this world has taken a toll. But he's still handsome. Still funny. Still charming in his up mountain way.

Dulcie Rose loves Hardy right off. And he loves her.

"What's this I hear about you being a rich old crazy lady nobody ever sees unless they dare come up here for one of your healings?"

"That what they say?"

"That's what they say…unless they're sayin' what a fine specimen of Hollywood beautiful woman you still are. Hidin' all that beauty up here. And what a shame it is, too, to waste it doing nothin' but playin' a big ole harp all day. Wanderin' around the mountain with a granddaughter gorgeous as you. And dippin' people into the Red Field every once in a while."

"The what?" I ask, confused.

"The Red Field. That's what folks down the valley call your spirit field out back yonder on account of the story about the women kilt in it bloody during the Civil War. And all the folks that been healed'a somethin' have seen up close all twenty-five lady ghosts flyin' around in dazzlin' red light."

"The Red Field…" I say out loud, liking the sound of it.

"The Red Field," Hardy repeats good naturedly, "place where that red-haired Hollywood beautiful eccentric old, millionaire…"

"I ain't a millionaire, Hardy." I am, but mountain folks are shy about money. We're embarrassed for folks that don't have it. And we're embarrassed if we have it. Generations of poverty will make you feel uneasy with the stuff. No matter what, you'll never feel like it's more than a hundred dollars. You'll never feel content. No, deep down I ain't a millionaire…

…*But I shot a white man dead once,* I'm tempted to say. *With not one regret or torment of conscience, I haven't thought about it since. I found a frozen black man I named Mr. James. And saw a black man on fire I named Mr. John. And I think about and talk to them all the time. My first boyfriend, your charmin', reckless twin brother got hanged for murdering a deputy sheriff who raped about twenty black girls and was getting away with it. I raised five brothers and sisters not much younger than me, alone, and I caused the death by fire of one old senile granddaddy. I saw an entire town on wheels git up and go. I dug up about five hundred grave holes and hauled away and reburied about a hundred corpses. I set an entire mountain on fire. I fought the U.S. government and won. All my brothers and sisters gone to the outside world or dead before I was thirty-one. I won the only fiddling prizes ever won by a female in Redemption County. That competition, once a year, is about the only reason I drive down to flat land anymore. I kilt my own child. I made love and conceived another child in a grave hole. I slept naked in the snow on a freezing night on the mountain and didn't die. I gave birth to my second child by myself on a kitchen floor. I lived in a tree house with a harp stole from the Atlanta Symphony by Yankees in 1864. I healed a brainless boy, a wordless girl, and more folks with cancer, arthritis, migraines, snakebite, and pleurisy than I can recall. Charging nowhere close to what I could have. Then, for free.*

I disappeared off the face of the earth for ten years. I sold what grows wild and free, our raspberry acres, and most of the Johnson land for more money than was ever in the county of Redemption at the same time. After three hundred years, I was there when my whole Johnson magical female family line ended at the Red Field.

And that damn flood never came here. Ruining our lives back then, the U.S. Corps of Army Engineers held it over our heads. Threatening us to give up our land to them. Or the flood would kill us all.

Right after I left Red Hand to come home, the flood slammed over that town, over there, not here. The furious water drowned a hundred folks just above the area where we had dug new graves. Hard-headed about taking orders from strangers, they moseyed up close but not close enough to safe high ground. Whoever let the water loose couldn't stop it. It destroyed the old town and most of the new one. Where's the justice in that? Those folks and the Army Corps of Engineers had a full year to make land tests and prepare for Armageddon. They must not have read the fine print on their Christian God's Divine Plan.

And my wounded brain baby brother just might have been the Christ child of Appalachia. Somehow getting himself plunked here among folks even more ignorant and hateful than Jesus had to bear with those cruel Romans and Israelites.

And, not doing my tired heart much good, Norman never turned up. I held out hope for a long time. He was the last man I ever loved. !941.

And my beautiful daughters Safire Dignity Johnson and Gracie Pearl, both dying before their mama. I never gave Safire a father's last name. If she was Silas' daughter, I didn't want to share her death with Silas' people. If she was Hardy's, I didn't want to make Hardy cry. In all my life, their leaving this earth too young and before me is the only thing that ever truly broke my heart. Broke it clear through. Every day, I feel the sharp glassy pieces of my crushed heart scratching, grinding and slicing against the soft inside'a my tender soul. Fearsome hurt like that will never go away. Just never. I feel it right now.

Maybe I would tell Hardy some of this. Maybe I'd just keep it to myself. Over a lifetime, people our age should be full of untold stories and experiences, some magical, some life-or-death, some tragic, some just every day. What's the sense in telling other people about it? They're yours. They are who you are. Telling people too much about yourself, I have always thought, is like showing your privates to a stranger. Why would you want to do that? From my way of thinking, a life of pain is just as worthwhile as a life of grace.

It's living life deep and real and courageous that matters.

And then there's the Red Field, as folks call it now. Only it isn't there anymore. Not as the Red Field. One hot July night back in 1978 or '79, under a huge smoldering orange moon, I went up there with my fiddle and sat on a grave in the fiery moonlight. I played made up laments for a while. The kin ghosts could tell something was wrong by how sad the tunes were. I called to them all to show themselves. And with the air above all alive with a-dazzling blood-red light, I told them I was sorry. I shoulda given them the truth about forty years earlier. I hadn't been ready to let 'em go, I said.

Then, I told them what I had learned about their murderers. It wasn't Yankees. It was Greaves. A hateful bunch, not worth cryin' over. But they were mountain folks. They were ours just the same. "Besides vengeance, ignorance, and superstition, why had they killed you? God knows why."

Free to pass over at last, it was hard to see them go. And harder still when the spirit field lost its magic and was nothing but just another old rundown family cemetery lost up in the thick woods of Redemption Mountain. Some of those fields have real gravestones with the names wore off from weather and time. Or little wooden crosses that lasted a year. Most have no marker or little cross at all. So many rich histories that no one will ever know.

Hardy continues, "...Place where that rich old crazy Hollywood beautiful Ruby Johnson saves peoples' souls."

"I don't save nobody's soul, neither, Hardy I-been-gone-for-fifty-years Jessup. I put what's broke back together again."

"My old heart's broke, Ruby. You feel like putting *it* back together?"

Dulcie Rose walks back to the big house, a grin on her sparkly pretty face, looking over her shoulder at Hardy and me.

She has the Johnson witchy magic more powerful and more confident than any of us. That beautiful child marches to her own damn drummer just as I had. She loves the mountains just as much as I do. But she wants to bring Johnson women into the twenty-first century. She wants to be a doctor. Through some of my doing, she'll represent us proudly at Emory University. Then, my greatest wish is she can find the deep pure core of herself and come back here. Minister to ailing folks just like I did. But as a hill doctor, part magic, part medicine.

And imagine, my granddaughter is the first Johnson in three hundred years to go past seventh grade. Squirrel Martin and the kids would'a said a healthy amen to that.

Then, for the first time since the afternoon of his twin brother's funeral, Hardy Jessup leans over and kisses me. And I let him.

THE END

ABOUT THE AUTHOR

Born in Boston, MA, in 1955, Jason Taylor Morgan is the author of five novels. He attended Bard College, majoring in Literature and Writing. In his early twenties, living in London and Paris, he was a freelance writer and editor, and college visiting lecturer at Harrow College of Art and Technology, London, England. Back to the U.S., he became a senior marketing and public relations agency executive in the technology industry and founder of strategic communication firm Morgan Communications Inc. He was a mental health specialist on a children's hospital psych unit for at-risk kids. Also, a master energy healer for emotional trauma and teacher of advanced spirituality and consciousness. And, a traveler on a five-year spiritual journey/road journey (42 states) throughout America. His novel O'ROURKE, THE MEDICINE MAN, is a fictional account of his travels. Jason has two magnificent adult red-haired daughters whom he adores and to whom he dedicates almost everything. Retired, he lives happily—writing, and now painting, a budding artist of acrylic abstracts—in the magical little city of Cloverdale in Sonoma County, Northern CA.

Printed in Great Britain
by Amazon

57687156R00121